THE BEAUTIFUL DEAD

KIM HUNT

Copyright © 2020 Kim Hunt
The right of Kim Hunt to be identified as the Author of the Work has been asserted by her in
accordance of the Copyright, Designs and Patents Act 1988.
First published in 2020 by Bloodhound Books
Apart from any use permitted under UK copyright law, this publication may only be
reproduced, stored, or transmitted, in any form, or by any means, with prior permission in
writing of the publisher or, in the case of reprographic production, in accordance with the
terms of licences issued by the Copyright Licensing Agency.
All characters in this publication are fictitious and any resemblance to real persons, living
or dead, is purely coincidental.
www.bloodhoundbooks.com

Print ISBN 978-1-913419-29-5

For my mum, Elaine and my late father, Graeme.

1

A lover once told Cal she could've been a parfumier's 'nose', such was the acuity of her sense of smell. But that was an indoor job: it would never happen. Still, anyone with a tenth of her olfactory sharpness could have caught the whiff of putrescent flesh. Cal hitched the shoulder strap of her equipment bag, changed direction, due north east. Facing the breeze, she followed the necrotic odour.

The twig and leaf duff crackled under her boots. Four seasons, in whitefella terms, six if you were D'harawal, and the nature of the ground appeared to barely change. Dry. It was autumn. High humidity. Time of the *Marrai'gang*, or spotted quoll. She'd be lucky to see one of those, even out bush.

The reek intensified. Stumbling across a wallaby or wombat that had met its demise wasn't unusual. She'd record such deaths as part of her annual inventory. Part of her ranger's remit. This month was her insect count, well, moths mainly. She reached the apex of the small ridge, leaned against the rough trunk of an angophora. The bluff dropped away to her left. To her right and slightly below her, a flat rock-shelf jutted from below an adjacent cliff-face. On its surface, like clothes left on a rock before the dive into a swimming-hole, she could make out ragged denim and plaid.

Gripping the trunk in her right hand she swung her body clockwise, stomping the heel of her right boot into a tiny ledge formed by an exposed tree root. Her left leg arced around to the ledge and momentum helped lift her to the platform.

Not a pile of discarded clothing. Like a grisly altar, the rock-shelf held the splayed remains of a human corpse. Engulfed by the putrid odour, she reeled back, drawing fresher air into her body.

Finding a dead animal always gave her a small sadness. This felt different, sinister. There'd been no reports of missing hikers. She would've been a first point of contact if there had.

She glanced over the body then looked away. Most of the face was gone; the skull gleamed through pieces of tattered scalp and hair. The chest cavity was similarly exposed. All the easily accessed flesh, blackened, collapsed, had been attacked by scavenging animals and insects. The denim covering the lower limbs seemed to have provided more of a challenge. One foot, both hands and most of the left forearm were gone.

Cal stepped back, dropped her kit from her shoulder and withdrew her camera. This was probably a crime scene. She needed to record and preserve it.

She was an hour's hike into the bush from where she'd parked. No cell coverage. She had a satellite phone for emergencies only due to the cost. This find qualified. She fixed her position on GPS and dialled Richmond Police.

She was well into the reserve even without the one-hour hike into the bush. It could be three to four hours before anyone could get there. And she'd have to meet them at the track, guide them in. She took a final look over the rock ledge, and made her way down through the sparse forest and rock fall.

Back at the truck, she did some minor first aid. A long gash from a broken branch stung her left cheek and blood had dripped onto her shirt. She could cope with a facial scar but the stain on her uniform would have to be dealt with. All her uniform shirts and trousers went to a tailor, unopened, and were altered to her requirements; shirt sleeves shortened, small cuff mid-bicep. Trousers, men's fit, narrowed below the knee, fitting closely to the biker or cowboy boots she wore. The wide-waist and narrow-hip cut fit her perfectly. Much as she liked the formality of the ranger's uniform cap, it was hot and messed her hair. It lived a forlorn existence on the parcel rack in the cab.

Put on a clean shirt now? Nah, wait till the cops are dealt with. She pulled the first aid box from below the passenger-side of the dashboard, dabbed the gash on her cheek with tea-tree oil, then ran some water through her hands and hair. The long, dark spikes ran in a partial mohawk along her crown, half flopping over her forehead. Short trimmed sides and longer, touching her collar at the back, her styling was anything but fashionable. But like Keith Richards, it was timelessly rock 'n' roll.

So much for the moth-count. She took notebooks from her rucksack and filled in data while she waited. When she'd done that she made a coffee on the small burner and did a tyre check. She pulled the bonnet catch and checked her oil-level and fluids, put down a tarp and checked the emergency water pipes strapped under the rear deck. She crawled further in towards the centre where the driveshaft tunnel ran and gave the dust-layered, purpose-built stash tube a shake. Solid as. Even though the job was law enforcement, firearms were not approved ranger equipment. She could lose her post if they found the Remington rifle. But she wasn't travelling the outback sans protection. Not outback, not anywhere. Learnt that lesson long ago. Whenever her rig was due for workshop maintenance she withdrew the rifle and underlay wrap and replaced it with tent poles and a waxed tent fly.

Around 1pm she saw the dust cloud drifting eastwards off the trail as a police cruiser approached ten kilometres distant. She watched through her binoculars then swigged from her canteen and brushed non-existent sand from her trousers, stomped her boots, stretched her neck from side-to-side.

Eight minutes later the police vehicle arrived, sliding in the dust and gravel behind her truck. Two plainclothes.

The passenger climbed from the cruiser. It was rare to run into another woman on the job. She was about five-eight, pale hair pulled up off her neck, looked like she ran and worked out. She offered her hand. 'DI Liz Scobie.' Firm, dry grip.

'Cal Nyx.' She smiled grimly.

The driver shut his door, stretched. Blandly handsome, about five-ten with a number-one haircut, try-hard tatts on his left forearm. He shook Cal's hand. 'DS Glen Avery.'

Scobie slung notebooks and cameras into a pack, nodded at Cal. 'Not a pleasant find.'

'Bit of a hike. You guys got plenty of water?'

Avery gathered equipment from the back of the vehicle. Aluminium cases and gear bags hit the ground.

'Lead the way.' Scobie gave Cal a small smile.

They set off.

When they reached the site, Cal ran through her movements. 'I climbed up here, took a couple of photos, came down the same way. Haven't been up there.' She lifted her chin towards the top of the bluff. 'Didn't move anywhere else around the scene.'

Avery dropped his gear.

Scobie scanned the site. 'Can't tell if it was accidental. Body's in a bad way. Treat it as a homicide until we know otherwise.'

Avery unzipped one of the gear bags.

Scobie directed. 'We'll do a walk-through then secure the

scene. Go from there. I'll call the coroner. We're gonna need pathology as well, state of the decomp.'

'Need them here before dark,' Avery said.

Scobie turned away and made the call on a sat-phone. Then she and Avery got to work. After their walk-through, while Avery taped off the scene, Scobie took out her notebook and asked Cal a series of questions. 'So, what were you doing out here? Obviously you're a ranger. Even so, bit off the beaten track.' Scobie kept her tone light.

'I do surveys. Insect counts. Part of our conservation assessments. I was checking moth traps,' Cal said.

Scobie wrote but kept her eyes on Cal. 'Where were your traps?'

'Down lower, about three metres inside the forest margin. I followed the smell.'

'Fair enough. How're the moths doing then?'

'Better than some.'

Scobie took Cal's contact details then returned to the site examination.

Cal sat on a rock in the shade though the heat wasn't diminished any there. Three times she'd made the hike now. She was exhausted. Her calves burned. She emptied one of her water canteens as the officers squatted and spoke near the body, taking photographs and making a close study of the scene. Though the environment was Cal's workplace, familiar and comfortable in many respects, it still seemed to her a lonely place to die. *What the hell was he doing out here?* she wondered. She assumed it was a bloke, though that was indeterminate at this stage. It was possible he was a hiker, but he wasn't really dressed for that. People got lost in the bush all the time. It was a harsh place if you didn't treat it with respect. Even then, things could go awry.

Cal poked at a cluster of dry wombat droppings with a stick. No smell, rapidly sealed and desiccated in the heat. Ants crawled across the sand, entering and exiting a tiny hole beside a scrubby acacia. She picked up a fallen branchlet of yellow gum, the leaves still green, probably broken off by a browsing possum in the tree canopy. Cal crushed and rolled the leaves in her palm, inhaled the aroma. The astringent eucalypt scent blasted through her sinuses like a hit. *Wakey wakey.* Rocks clattered nearby and she looked across the narrow plateau as a pair of small wallabies bounced down the ledge towards lower ground. Feeding time. They were heading for the herbs and grasses on the forest margins below. Cal was hungry too. She stood and stretched.

It was late afternoon by the time the police had done their initial examination. Scobie came over, her notebook held beside her thigh. 'Coroner's on his way. Glen can go down and meet him. We've got all your details. You're free to go. We may need to interview you again at some stage.'

'You have to get this body out. I'm happy to stay, give you a hand.'

Scobie smiled. Her teeth were bright and even.

Good childhood, Cal thought.

'That's decent of you. Four of us should manage, though. Pathologist is coming too.'

'Okay.' Cal reached down, lifted her rucksack. 'Will you let me know when you get an ID?'

'Of course. Be in touch.'

Cal and Avery went back to the road. Cal's extended workday was finally over. Avery had to wait for the coroner and pathologist. They'd get a few more hours of good light to work in. She didn't envy them the hike out with the body bag.

'You wanna top up your water before I go? I've got plenty.' She thumbed towards her ten-litre carrier.

'Cheers.' Avery filled several flasks.

Cal refilled one of her own canteens then drove slowly back along the rough trail, sipping until it was empty. When she hit the tarmac she sped up, heading back towards Kurrajong. At the first highway petrol stop she went inside and grabbed a cold drink and chocolate. That would keep her eyes open until home. Friday night. She wasn't up for much.

Some weekends she spent in the city. Her aunt Zinnia had a tiny bedsit in her Petersham backyard. She no longer drove herself so Cal could park her '64 Futura off-street when she stayed. Cal visited friends and clubs semi-regularly but she wasn't making the one-and-a-half-hour trip tonight. Her weekday home, on a rural block south west of Kurrajong, was in the neighbourhood of three national parks, six if you spread the catchment a little wider. There was no point putting in massive commuter miles when her work required her out bush. Sometimes she went interstate on special field trips and knowledge-sharing with colleagues. But the vast expanses of the reserves in this corner of the state could keep her busy for a lifetime.

Dee, a vet, had a smallholding, rehabilitating native animals hurt on roads or in forestry accidents. Cal paid her a nominal rent for an old shearer's quarters some distance from Dee's cottage. There was space under cover for an enclosed workshop where Cal could tinker on the Ford and she'd framed-up and insulated two small rooms for herself in the old wooden building.

Dee did mostly equine work around the lower mountains. At home she fitted in the animal rehab.

Cal had another project a hundred metres from her crib. She was converting a disused grain silo into a holiday cabin for Dee to rent out. She'd already built a staircase that curved in a gentle spiral around the walls up to a sleeping loft. Chances were, she wouldn't be toiling on that this weekend. All she could think of was a deep bath, a few beers and a movie.

She rarely slept late, even on her days off. With no fixed plans that Saturday morning, and away from the city's distractions, she had her feet up on the verandah. She sipped coffee and waved to

Dee feeding out with the quad bike and trailer. Banjo, the three-legged heeler-cross ran ahead announcing to the other animals that chow was on its way, his yapping reduced to a hoarse rasp from years of overuse.

The gruesome scene in the bush troubled her. The pathologist wouldn't have autopsied the body until this morning she reckoned, and an ID would take a while. She'd spent a lot of time in reserves and bushland, the backcountry. Came across all sorts of dumped rubbish: couches, engines, fridges, inanimate crap people were too tight or lazy to take to landfill. It angered her. Aside from being unsightly and a pain in the butt to get rid of, it meant leakage of all kinds of toxic shite into the surrounds. But the body was quite something else. A person, with a history. Someone who lived and breathed, who probably belonged to others. Just lost there, alone, dead. What if she hadn't found him when she did? What if he'd become a skeleton and lain there for years? Decades? She'd only discovered him because of the smell. That wouldn't have happened even a few weeks further on.

After a second coffee, she ambled around the back to the workshop and swung the heavy wooden doors open. It was a fine autumn day, no cloud. Maybe she could go for a cruise later. She pulled the dust cover and it slid across the waxed surface of the paintwork. Her XM wasn't in concours condition, it was original. The metallic blue paint was thin and getting patchy; there were a few small tears on the seats. It smelt of old car; steel oxides, burnt sump oil, shredded rubber from the rear tyres spattered in the wheel-well. She did her best to preserve it with care and polish. It didn't need to look perfect or have every piece restored. In fact, she took a belligerent pride in its authentic state. Though outwardly quite standard, under the hood she'd tossed out the original Super Pursuit engine and mounted a small-block Windsor V8. With lowered suspension, coil-over shocks and widened rims, the Futura had a hunkered-down profile. For an old beast it could move.

The car was already up on ramps from her previous session. She flicked on a paint-spattered stereo and gave Toots and The Maytals a nudge. Crouching down, she reclined back onto the wheeled crawler, and slid her body under the vehicle where she could spray fish-oil into the chassis members. Later she'd apply underseal to the outsides of the metal rails.

Something wet ran across her free forearm. Banjo's nose. 'Naughty rascal.' She scratched and tussled his head. 'Where's your ball?' Guaranteed to agitate him. He scampered, as best as a tripod could, among the sawdust and paint cans. 'Where is it?'

Banjo howled in frustration.

A pair of Blundstone work boots appeared. Above them a small, intense woman, with shaggy, mousy-blonde hair and wire-rimmed glasses. 'Thanks for winding him up. You were late in yesterday.'

Cal ran herself out from under the car.

Dee hurled an indestructible purple orb through the open doorway as Banjo's claws slipped on the concrete, seeking traction.

'Crazy day. Found a body in the bush.'

Dee's eyebrows rose. 'Human?'

Cal nodded, stood and stretched her spine backwards.

'Can't remember anyone going missing?' Dee frowned. 'Sounds dodgy.'

'I reckon.' Cal went to the bench and flipped the lid off the underseal with a screwdriver. A waft reminiscent of hot tar melting on summer roads. It would disappear in a few days as it dried. She pulled a small paintbrush from a nail on the wall.

'Come and have a beer later. You okay?'

'Yup. Thanks.' Cal forced a smile and returned to the underside.

∼

A little later, her phone rang on the bench. She slid out from under the Ford, flicked the music down. 'Hello?' Her eyes fell on the club, lying beside the belt-sander on the bench. Orangey-red hardwood root, hewn by hand. She'd made it from a thick piece of dried tree root. A gift from near Uluru.

'Hi Cal. Maur here.' Maur always named herself, even with caller ID. A nice formality, preferable to those who launched in while Cal guessed who the voice belonged to. 'I'm at the hospital, been here since seven. Addie's really deteriorated.'

'Oh Christ.'

'After we stopped those meds Wednesday. She's gone down rapidly. Thought I'd better let you know.' Maur had consulted with the senior medical staff the previous week. They'd decided to up the morphine and stop the other medications as Addie was never going to improve. Cal tried to think, tried to get her head into the hospital room. Addie had seemed pretty okay on Tuesday night when she'd last seen her, well, as okay as someone in such decline could be. Maur could be alarmist at times. Cal had her first date in a fortnight with Rach. She wanted to spend the night with her.

'She might pick up, Maur. She's had bad days before.' She wished she knew for sure. 'I dunno what to do.' Even as she said it, she knew how selfish it was.

'I don't think she'll last the night, Cal.'

'Okay mate. Thanks for letting me know.' She put the phone down on the bench, stared at the club. Addie had brought the tree root back from Uluru, given it to Cal. Two thirds of its length narrowed like a handle, right size for her hand. Both ends she'd carved into dangerous points. Dark knots dotted the grain, curved near the top, the original shape of the root. The business end of the club was two to three times the thickness of the handle. It didn't look symmetrical but it balanced perfectly in her hand. Always surprised her that a piece of wood could have such a reassuring weight.

Addie had been up at Uluru trying to find family. No joy. That was two, maybe three years ago. Not long after that she got the diagnosis.

Addie and Zin. Independently, they'd become like stand-in parents after the shooting. Zin was blood. She provided a home and safety in her precious, unconventional way. Meeting Addie was equally serendipitous. If not for her Cal may not have survived those early years. Addie's workshop had become Cal's bolthole. And Addie herself a huge presence who helped fill an equally large void.

Cal turned and leaned against the bench, stared through the doorway, blanked out.

~

The phone rang again. Unknown number.

'Cal? Liz Scobie, Richmond Command. We've made an ID.'

'That was quick.'

'We already had his dental records on file.'

'Oh. Is that usual?' Cal asked.

'No. Not unless we've requested them in advance, like when someone has gone missing.'

'So, you were looking for this guy?'

'He was a suspect for a homicide. We thought he'd gone interstate.'

'Wow. Okay. Still, what was he doing out there? Wasn't dressed for hiking.'

'Name's Phillip Leuwins.'

'Spelt with an E-U?' Cal held her breath.

'That's right.'

'Got a sister – Diana?'

'We spoke with her this morning.'

'This is crazy.' Diana Leuwins. Ran a vintage clothing shop. Drove a two-door Valiant. Could say she knew her very well.

Knew Phillip too. Pip. Twelve, fifteen years ago. Not that long after she got here. So what the fuck was he doing dead on a rock slab in the bush?

'Are you saying you knew him?' Scobie's tone had stiffened a little.

'It would be a strange coincidence if there were two brother and sister pairs with those names.'

'Indeed.'

'Think I need to get in touch with Di. Thanks for letting me know. Oh, did they find a cause of death?'

'Yes. I'm sorry I can't tell you more at this stage.' Scobie rang off.

Cal's thoughts ran back over the years. Di ran a second-hand clothing boutique in Newtown. Boutique. A tiny establishment you had to move around sideways. Bulging with second-hand gear. Musty. Occasionally Cal found a choice button-down shirt. She and Pip had worked as roadies one summer, a tour round rural New South Wales and Victoria. She did lights, he did the sound. They'd shared a room to save money. People probably thought they were a couple. Couldn't be more wrong. Hilarious. The leatherman and the diesel. They just looked heavy metal.

Liz Scobie called Glen Avery into her office. He leaned across the doorway, right hand grasping the jamb.

'Cal Nyx knew the vic. I think we need to keep an eye on her.'

Avery scratched his neck. 'She volunteer that? Seems odd if she's got something to hide.'

Scobie pulled several files from a stacked tray, shifted her coffee. 'Wouldn't be the first one to try and divert suspicion that way. Keep on your toes with her.'

'Will do.'

2

Saturday afternoon, still in the workshop, Cal had several calls to make. Neither one she relished. She raked her fingers through her hair. Rach first.

'Hi, doll.'

'Hey, bub. When should I expect you?' Rach's voice was always husky. Cal found it a real turn-on.

'You're gonna kill me.'

Silence on the other end.

'I've gotta go to La Perouse. Addie's bad. I've gotta go tonight.'

Silence.

Cal leaned back hard against the workbench, clenched the phone. 'I'm sorry, Rach. I'm hanging out to see you. You know that.'

Silence.

'Are you working Sunday night? Can we hook up then?' Cal dug the fingers of her left hand into her side.

'Mm hmm.' Stony.

'Thanks, hon. See you then.' She ended the call, put the phone on the bench. She closed her eyes, calmed her breathing, picked the phone up again, dialled Diana Leuwins.

'Di, it's Cal. Cal Nyx.' She paused. 'I'm so sorry about Pip.' A small wait.

'You know?' Di's voice quiet, hesitant.

'I found him, Di. It was me who found him. I need to see you.'

'Police just said it was a ranger. I didn't realise.' Her voice had no power in it.

'I need to talk to you, Di. You still in Darlo?'

No, of course not. Long time. Cal wrote down a Newtown address. 'I'll be in town tonight, someone in hospital. Can I drop round in the morning? You got someone with you?'

'Mum's coming up.' Her voice tired, distant, like it came from the bottom of a well.

'See you soon. Take care.' Cal felt helpless. How did you offer words of comfort to someone who's just lost a brother, especially under shady circumstances?

Cal went inside, showered, pulled on black jeans, Johnny Reb boots, a blue T-shirt and denim jacket.

She locked the door, went to the workshop and climbed in the Ford. It fired first spin of the starter. She felt smug, chuffed with her own handiwork. She'd replaced the points and redone the timing a week ago to avoid sluggish niggles when the winter cold set in. She reversed out and closed the shed doors while the engine warmed up. Tapped the throttle. A couple of gentle blips, then eased the car down the winding gravel driveway. A pair of Jerusalem donkeys, a jack and a jenny, lifted their shaggy heads as she passed a paddock on her left. She was fond of donkeys; they seemed less intimidating than their equine cousins, somehow more benign.

When she reached the end of the drive she flicked her eyes across her dash-mounted gauges, checked for traffic, then dumped the clutch and sent the Windsor V8 about one thousand revs above a gentle purr, heading for the city.

~

The coiled cat-o'-nine-tails Addie wore down the side of her boot was both a statement and an advertisement for her business; custom-made SM gear. Cal's first sighting of her was from Zin's backyard. When Cal was first shipped over after the shooting, she busied herself in the garage keeping Zin's old Ford in tip-top order. The same Ford XM that became Cal's current ride. She often worked with the doors open to clear the exhaust fumes. Whenever someone arrived for a pick-up or delivery in the yard opposite, Cal caught glimpses of this statuesque figure slicing lengths of faux-leather on a long wooden trestle under an awning. Addie.

On fine days Cal would sit under the solitary palm, looking out over La Perouse bay, or sometimes she'd just sit on the steps outside the ward, still close to Addie. On bad days she'd go further away, behind the chapel on the point. She'd lean back into the brick wall, crouched, trying to disappear, as the waves hit the cliffs below.

Maur was outside on the steps, smoking. Her medium height was jacked up with black platform boots, skin-tight denims and an ex-army jacket. It was always hard for Cal to reimagine her in her corporate weekday wear. They hugged.

'Just having a time-out. Been here since last night.'

Cal nodded grimly. 'When are you having a proper break?' she asked.

'I'm okay, mate. I'll do the changeover with you.' Maur took several deep tokes on her rollie and stubbed it out on the wall, dropping the remains behind a struggling azalea.

'I'm going in,' Cal said. Maur nodded, began rolling another smoke.

Addie's hair was thinning, lying flat, close to her head. A morphine drip pierced her stomach. Her skin had become pale during the long hospitalisation. Cal wondered if the process of dying was the same in the young and old. The skin stretched into a fragile veneer, pulled taut over her skull, her head seeming bigger, disproportionate, or was it her body shrinking? The look that had become too familiar to her. She called it the *death's head*.

She wet some tissues at the en-suite tap and wiped orange juice from the bedside table. Just a week ago she had sat outside on a step at the rear of the hospital while Addie dictated her will inside. Now Addie was beyond speech.

She sat beside her, holding her hand as she lay still, comatose. 'Not like you to be so quiet, mate,' Cal whispered.

Maureen had dealt with the lawyers for months. The Jehovah's Witness Church was trustee of Addie's inheritance, not a huge amount of money but anything would've given her some options. They wouldn't release funds so Addie could have a full-time carer and die at home. Addie's drug and mental health history meant she had little control over such things.

'She fits all their categories of worthlessness,' Maur had said. 'Crazy. Old. Dyke.' Maur fought and argued with them most of Addie's last days and every minute she did was one more she couldn't spend with Addie. The church continued to exert their power of veto. Cal felt she was the lucky one. She'd rested on the bed, hugging Addie just before she'd left a week ago, and confided, 'I love it when you call me Toots.'

'I'll remember that,' Addie had replied, closed her eyes. 'We'll do that Darwin road trip in the next life.' She'd never regained consciousness.

Maur took Cal's place at Addie's bedside. She began combing Addie's hair then nodded off in the chair beside the bed. Cal went outside for some fresh air. Beyond the cliffs the endless spread of La Perouse bay disappeared into a curve of blue horizon. She broke off the stem of an ice plant and wrote on the bricks of the wall; A-D-D-I-E. By the time she reached the last letter, the first had faded, dried in the heat. She wrote the name over and over, faster and faster on every brick, as if the very repetition could halt Addie's demise.

Dusk approached. The setting sun cast its final glow over the clifftops and palm trees. Maur came out and sat beside her, put her arm around Cal's shoulder. 'She's gone.' Tears streaked Maur's cheeks. Cal had never seen her cry.

'Oh fuck.' Cal buried her face in Maur's neck, put her arms around her, sobbed. They sat that way for a few moments.

'C'mon.' Maur rose. 'Addie's on her own.'

Addie looked like she had done minutes before; the waxy visage. With her eyes closed Cal couldn't have known if she was alive or not. Maur sat beside her, her head on the bed, one arm across Addie's body. Cal stood behind her, with an arm around her. They formed a solemn pair, lost in their own thoughts.

Maur pulled away, fossicked in her briefcase and produced some candles and incense. She lit them and placed them at either end of Addie's bed then straightened Addie's bedding. Cal was relieved the drifting fume from the burning sticks was coconut and not that patchouli shite. Neither of them spoke. Cal looked bereft, like a child who'd lost a parent and didn't understand. Addie had been a role model. She had few enough of them.

'I'd better make some calls, let people know. I'll tell the staff.' Maur broke away.

Cal sat beside the bed. She couldn't leave Addie on her own now.

A dead body did feel different to a live one. When the breathing and heart pumping ceased, something went. It seemed obvious, but she could understand where the idea of a soul came from. An energy, more than the sum of blood and air movement through flesh, had dissipated. Where did it go?

Maur returned after making her calls. Cal sat low in a chair at the end of Addie's bed and sipped from a water bottle. A nurse came in, carrying a clipboard and paperwork. 'Would either of you know what religion Adelia was?'

Cal looked to Maur. 'She made a lot of references to Jehovah's Witnesses,' Cal said, raising her eyebrows, waiting. 'But she hated them,' she added.

'She's a bloody old hippie.' Maur leaned against the en-suite wall, rolling a fag, her tobacco pouch clenched under her arm.

'What about all her Koori stuff, going back up to Alice Springs, the trip she was planning? Maybe she was atheist. Or pagan.' Cal turned back to the nurse. 'Why does it matter?'

The nurse clasped her hands together. 'We need to know for preparation of the body.' She changed the configuration of the clasp. 'Different religions have different requirements.' She smiled.

'Oh, right.' Cal learned something new. She stretched her arms, rolled her neck as she sat in the low chair. 'Have you checked all her records? It should be in there somewhere.' She straightened up and slowly stood.

'I haven't looked there yet, I just thought you guys might know.' They traipsed out to the desk, following the nurse. Maur was sidetracked by an outside doorway and another cigarette.

The nurse pulled on the heavy file drawer. She must've just started her shift, she looked more energetic than Cal felt. Her fingers ran back and forth, occasionally dipping in between folders, lifting one, returning it. 'Here it is.' She flourished a bulging file and dropped it onto the counter as Cal came closer. Cal realised Addie's records probably included all her psychiatric admissions, hence their bulk. She felt voyeuristic and decided not to read anything, blanking out and shifting her focus from the flicking pages.

'Aha!' The nurse was smiling, thumbing the pages.

'What?' Cal leaned over. There it was, on every separate entry, *Buddhist*. 'No, I don't believe it.' Cal threw herself back from the counter. 'Ohh Addie, you got us.'

Maur came in, the waft of nicotine surrounding her.

'She's a Buddhist, Maur,' Cal said, incredulous, but smiling. The nurse stood back, waiting.

Maur shook her head, took the corner of the folder and turned it to read. 'Bloody old hippie. Always gets the last laugh, eh.'

That night as Cal drove home through the scrubby dunes at the back of La Perouse, the sharpness of the cool, briny air woke her body from the lethargy she'd felt inside the ward. She liked the scenic route, even when she couldn't see it. The Ford sounded louder than usual in the thin autumnal air, the brash exhaust note more acute when the engine hadn't yet warmed up. The noise in the dark gave her comfort. Her grip on the steering wheel loosened as her face twisted in a moment of resistance before she began sobbing. Unable to see clearly she surrendered to the blurry emptiness that surrounded her. A cry moved up through the centre of her body like a lift in a mine shaft. She wailed into the blackness as she slumped in the seat.

The left front wheel hit a pothole and the car shook. She wiped her face with her arm and tightened her grip in acknowledgement. The duneland ended and she re-entered suburbia; street lights, curtained houses, taxis and shopfronts. Red light. *Stop.* She pulled up, dazed, like walking from a cinema into daylight. She became aware of something beside her, a Celica and a face, staring, too close.

She edged the XM forward, the other car moved forward, the driver leaning against the wheel with his head swivelled left, looking past his passenger.

Green. She slammed down hard on the throttle and dropped the clutch. The rear of the Ford bore down as the lightened front began to lift. She steadied the front end as she cut in front of the

Celica and threw the gearbox up another cog. The low seat hugged her body as the powerful engine drove forward.

She raced. They were gone but she kept the power on, toying with her fear. Up Anzac Parade and through the parklands. Her eyes watering from speed now, the Phoenix palms became her braking markers as the tail lights ahead appeared fuzzily red: 135km an hour, 140km an hour.

Five roads converged, brake lights, stop lights, everything slid into long red streaks without relative proportions or distances. She didn't want to stop, didn't want to be still. The gods heard, and switched on the emerald. Safely through and bouncing down through the back of Darlinghurst, she slowed a little, her sight was restored, then left onto Craigend Street and up towards the tunnel. No one was gonna spoil it. She threw the Ford to the right and mashed the throttle to the floorboards, passing a black Beemer to give her a clear run through.

Two rows of tunnel lights above her flashed off the bonnet, strobing shocks into her eyes. Still she held the throttle open, pushing the Ford as hard as it would go. The noise bouncing back off the walls obliterated everything. Traffic above and beside the tunnel ran into four lanes at the exit ahead of her. She broke out of the underground knowing one ill-conceived move from her or any other vehicle in the merging lanes could be terminal.

Red light. *Stop Cal. Stop!*

She lifted her foot off the accelerator, jammed it on the brakes, her right leg rigid. The car slithered to a halt, maintaining a near direct trajectory, just across the yellow lines. Pedestrians hesitated before stepping from the footpath. Cal held the wheel, arms straight, panting like she'd run from somewhere. She pulled several deep breaths into her lungs, held them. *Calm down, mate.* She watched the traffic light sequence, eased the car into first, drove sedately towards the Inner West.

She'd texted Zinnia from the hospital that she needed a

stopover, but warned she might be late. She idled past the front of her aunt's fence. No lights on, she noted with relief. She wasn't up for chat, even with Zin who was easy company. Cal drove around the back, parked in the garage and walked across the yard to the bedsit. She didn't turn the lights on, just lay back on the bed and stared out the window into the night.

∼

Cal woke early, the sun bleaching in through the windows where she'd left the curtains open. She went to the sink and splashed cold water on her face and through her hair, pulled her jeans and boots on before going across to Zin's back door. She gave a small knock and walked in.

Zin smiled up from her crossword, specs halfway down her nose, a cigarette waving from her languid left hand. She sat at a Formica-topped table against the wall, opposite the stove and sink.

'Come in, darling.' The kitchen was bright and sunny. The lemony-toned décor always felt welcoming to Cal.

She walked over, leaned down, kissed Zin on the cheek. Even on a lazy Sunday morning, the older woman's long grey hair was coiled, fluffed and scarfed into some kind of secret-lady-business coif that Cal would never understand but found intriguing.

'Rough. Losing your old friend,' Zin said gently.

Cal clenched her insides, determined to hold things together even though she was with Zin, someone she trusted so deeply. 'Can't prepare for it. Even when you know it's coming,' she said.

'Coffee's waiting.' Zin leaned back, looked up at Cal.

A large pot sat on the stove, Cal's Ford mug beside it. Zin would normally plough her way through the contents on her own.

'Cheers, Auntie.'

Zin looked thoughtfully at Cal.

Cal took a deep swallow from her mug. 'How's tricks?'

'Choir practice later. I'm being lazy until then.' Zin's alto was still fabulous despite fags, age and failing hearing. 'Eat something, darling. You can't start your day on an empty stomach.' Zin waved at the bread and preserves on the bench.

'I'll grab something later. Bit queasy.' Cal drained her mug. 'Gotta fly. Promise we'll do lunch or dinner next time.'

'Okay, pet.'

'Leave the bedding.' Zin was forever stripping and changing Cal's sheets. Seemed unnecessary.

'Okay, darling.'

She was already in the Inner West. Di's place in Newtown was barely ten minutes away.

The house was down a narrow dog-leg street, essentially one-way. Cal cruised the length and couldn't find a park. She retraced her route, took two lefts and found a spot in the far corner of a supermarket car park, hopefully beyond damage from shopping trolleys, reversing trucks and car doors.

She strolled across the asphalt wasteland, stepped over a low chain barrier and turned left into Di's street. She tried to compose herself, realised there was no way to prepare or defer and gave in to a low-level anxiety.

The house was a narrow two-storey terrace, faded pale pink with an overgrown avocado tree and a straggly leaning palm tree that diverted its upward trajectory where it met the balcony, resulting in a kinked trunk.

She knocked, waited, heard footsteps on bare floorboards.

Di opened the door. Despite being washed out and thinner, she still looked good despite the years and current circumstances. Slightly shorter than Cal, she wore her pale hair in a simple bob just above her shoulders. It was unfussy and kept the focus on her deep-set green eyes, strong nose and generous mouth. She gave a half smile. 'Hey Cal.'

They both hesitated then shared a quick hug.

'Come through. Mum's out back.'

The dark hallway led past a front room and stairway on the right then stepped down into a living area and kitchen where the original walls had been knocked out. She followed Di, noticed her strong, shapely calves, fine ankles, and felt a pang of old desire. Chastised herself for being inappropriate, but knew such wants were not governed by rules or etiquette.

French doors in the rear wall led to a bricked courtyard with raised planters. Di's mother, Gretchen got up from a round wooden table, greeted Cal warmly with a hug.

'So sorry, Mrs L. Awful time for you.' She could smell bergamot.

'Tea?' Di held the pot and began to pour as Cal nodded.

'Seems pretty odd, Di. What's been going on?' Cal asked.

Di pulled out a chair, sat with her hands in her lap. Gretchen pushed a milk jug towards Cal. Di looked at Cal. 'It's just as strange to us. Unbelievable. His disappearance after Stefan didn't make sense either.'

'Stefan?'

'His partner. They were together for several years.'

'And what happened?' Cal sipped her tea. Earl Grey. She used to think it tasted like flowery dishwater. Maybe it still did but her perception had altered.

'Stefan was shot. Murdered. A botched robbery, the police said. Pip went missing then.'

'Scared off?'

'The police suspected him. He lived there, did the gardens. I don't think they understood the nature of their relationship.'

'But they think Pip did it? Killed him?'

Di put her hands under her thighs, closed her eyes as she dropped her head. 'I think that was their view.'

'So, you put them right?'

'In the absence of anyone else, they believe whatever they like.'

Di glanced at Gretchen, looked at the sugar bowl. They were all silent for a moment.

'Wonder what they think now. Did they tell you anything, after the autopsy?' Cal said.

'Not yet. Still some pathology they're waiting on.' Gretchen got up and put dishes away from the rack on the bench.

Cal turned her cup back and forth on the saucer. 'When did you last see Pip?' She spoke slowly, carefully.

'Just before Easter. He came down, stayed overnight. Had some business in town.'

'We all ate together.' Gretchen spoke from beside the bench, her voice a little croaky when she said *together*.

'How was he?' Cal watched her face.

'Box of birds.'

'When I spoke to that detective, Scobie, she said they had a preliminary cause of death. Didn't they tell you anything? You're the family. Don't they have to tell you?' Cal's voice rose.

Gretchen leaned back on the bench. 'Tell her, Di.'

Cal looked from Di to Gretchen, back to Di. 'What? What do you know?'

Di began to sob. Cal reached out, put her hand over Di's. 'What is it?' she pleaded. Gretchen had come over, stood behind Di, placed her hands on her shoulders. Di broke down. She couldn't get the words out.

Gretchen spoke. 'His bones. The damage. They think it was a rifle bullet. It passed through his body. But the evidence…' She was crying now too.

'Jesus Christ. Who'd wanna shoot Pip? That's just crazy.'

3

Gretchen had left the room. Said she was going for a walk, needed some air. Cal could see the effect on the woman, her son's death. Though of a strong build, Gretchen looked physically diminished. Cal said, 'Where was Pip living, Di? This place with Stefan?'

'Up the Hawkesbury. A small block on Boarback Ridge, near Kaloola.'

'Part of my gaff. You mind if I take a look around?'

'I don't have a problem. The police went over the place. Don't know if there's anything to find.' Her voice drifted off.

'Just wanna have a sniff around. Satisfy myself. Did Stefan have family?'

'A sister, I think. In Victoria. They weren't in contact much, as far as I can gather. I guess the police would have got in touch.' Di wrote Pip and Stefan's address down for Cal.

The Hawkesbury. The great river. The region bordered the Blue Mountains foothills on its western edge. Cal lived in the southwest corner. She wasn't going to take the Ford up there. Most of the back roads were gravel and she wanted to move under the radar. Her ranger-liveried vehicle fitted the bill.

'I'll be in touch.' Cal hugged Di. 'Good to see you. Sorry it's like this.'

Di teared up, couldn't speak. She nodded, tried to smile, closed the door.

In the space of a week, one old friend had died in a hospice and another appeared to have died in questionable circumstances. She felt like one of those tennis balls on a spring, clobbered one way and then the other. She needed to gather her thoughts, get herself centred. She was already in Newtown. She had a favourite refuge in an old cemetery off the main road, spent a lot of time there, when she'd visited Addie in the past. There was a section around the church with high stone walls. Sheltered and sunny, she would often sit under one of the old trees and read or just close her eyes.

She left her car where it was and walked up King Street, stopping at a Thai takeaway to buy sticky rice wrapped in banana leaf. She crossed the road to grab a long black at a corner café before heading down Church Street.

Dodging blobs and smears of dog shit, she made the turn off the main street and walked down towards the park and cemetery. She felt an irrational loathing towards people on the footpaths, strangers. Her grief smothered her. It reminded her of the nineties, the avalanche of AIDS deaths. She kept her head down trying to control herself. She didn't want to walk, but didn't know what else to do. She turned into the cemetery, that well-known path, went towards a copse of trees on the left and sat in the shade, her legs pulled up to her chest, head on her knees, let the tears seep into the denim before self-consciousness shut everything back down.

Addie's gone. Jean, Taj, Viv, Tilly, Simon, Nate, all gone. Pip.

She'd never come to terms with any of it. *What did that mean anyway? One day it wouldn't matter? She'd just get used to the gaps?* Her portable ghosts accompanied her everywhere.

She got up, left the cemetery, walked a few metres down the road beyond the stone walls and into the park. Looked across the grass bank. From there, diagonally over the road, if she wanted to she could see the house. She came to the park a lot but she couldn't always look at the house, just blipped it out as she recorded the landscape. There was the spot where she and Addie sat and drank cups of tea. Addie had moved from her place in Surry Hills when she could no longer manage the steps. Cal remembered what they'd talked about, right there, less than a year ago after months of a kind of estrangement.

'I'm sorry. I couldn't cope,' Cal apologised for her withdrawal. The illness hadn't diminished Addie's generosity.

'Does it make you want to cram things in?' Cal had asked her when she'd stopped pretending Addie wasn't sick.

'No, it's not like that. Makes you prioritise things differently. Taking time with things that matter.' Addie had pulled daisies from the grass and begun making a chain, her fingers deft despite the arthritis. 'It's not about urgency and doing more, because you feel like time is pressing. Time is pressing, but you don't necessarily hurry. If anything, you slow down in a sense, you savour things.' Cal had joined in picking the flowers and handing them to Addie. 'Sometimes that doesn't mean rushing to be with people you love, it means wanting to be alone too.'

She watched the antics of a little dog, mostly white with a few black patches and spots. Not young, bit thick around the middle, touch of grey at the muzzle. One ear was gnarly and twisted and it had a blue kerchief at its throat. The dog was eager, but not manic. His carer was in a motorised wheelchair, throwing a ball with one of those long plastic chucker things. A mynah bird divebombed the dog from a gumtree and a barking chihuahua added its distraction, but the dog never lost focus on the ball.

It was one o'clock. Cal felt restless, pent-up, lethargic and stodgy, all at once. Maybe she should go to the gym, punch bags, and lift weights? It was a usual response, and she knew what she was doing. Trying to punish the pain away. It was good for anger, safe. But something lay beneath the rage. It required a more gentle approach. She left the park and braved the noise and stink of King Street, so well hidden and muffled while she was in the cemetery. Diesel, rotting garbage, cigarette smoke, voices yelling, buses. She made her way to the station, caught a train to Circular Quay and walked around to the Museum of Contemporary Art.

Not a huge fan of paintings, she spent some time at an installation. Patrick Jones' *Food Forest: a poem, after Blake's The Garden of Love*. A mesostic, where a vertical phrase like a spine, intersected the horizontal text. "Aerating the poem," Jones called it in his artist statement. "This air also assists the demilitarisation of the page (John Cage), moving it from an environment of organised violence, letters lining up like soldiers. Rows of monological food crops, it produces a slow-text and a slow reading of the poem follows, so as the clockless rhythm of the forest can be felt in the sounding body."

Cal read on. "The most destructive culture in history." Yeh, she was lucky to work where she did, she knew that. She still maintained a contact with the non-urban world, knew she was animal. That was part of the grief. Knowing what her lot were doing to the wild things. Forget our conjoined history at our peril.

It wasn't working. Her mood hadn't lifted. She really did need a distraction. Rach wouldn't finish work till seven. She didn't want to go back to the bedsit, didn't want to feel guilty that she'd shut the door and pull the curtains and couldn't speak to Zin.

At four she caught a train to Central Station and walked up Chalmers Street, turned into Rutland and then left into Little

Buckingham. A minute or so later she stood before a two-metre high solid wooden door. Painted matte black and studded like a medieval template, it barred entrance to a terrace house whose windows were lined with block-out reflective. She pressed the red button on the intercom, turned her face up to the camera and waited for the gate click to allow her into the next entrance.

Ninety minutes later she emerged and turned in a loose-limbed stroll up Little Buckingham to Cleveland Street. She turned left and headed to Fatima's. Ordered a mixed platter and ate at a small table in the side room, diving into the green beans, hummus and fresh falafel. After a Lebanese coffee she paid and walked along Cleveland to the Crown Hotel. She ordered a beer and watched league on one of the screens. Her viewing was disengaged. She hadn't followed the footy since the Tigers left Leichhardt and merged with the Magpies out west. She spent a couple of hours in the bar then walked back down to Central Station, caught a train to Newtown.

She walked to her car, changed into a sleeveless black T-shirt and clean jeans then drove to Marrickville. Parked the Ford in a well-lit area in front of a panel beater's in Victoria Road then walked back down Sydenham Road to the Marrickville Bowlo. Despite the lockout laws, halting alcohol sales after 1.30am in the entertainment precinct, there were still places to party. So much for the attempts by the councils and premier to turn the city into a cultural desert. The old Bowling Club catered to some of the citizenry who wanted more than casinos, poker machines and Netflix.

Inside, she grabbed a beer at the bar and moved around the edge of the dance floor. A messy-looking blonde, hanging off her bloke, slunk towards Cal with the intense familiarity, passed off as love-drug caring, which Cal abhorred. Nothing to be afraid of apparently. The blonde, brain paddling through a chemical fog and believing she was lucid and fabulous, inclined her body towards Cal. 'Smile, don't be unhappy,' she beamed, reaching out to stroke Cal's cheek.

Cal recoiled. *Hey, and don't you be unhappy when I slap your insipid face.*

Then she saw Sandi, emerging from the dance floor. 'Oh darl, save me from these morons,' Cal begged, hugging her. 'Hey, look at your hair.' She should've been used to the three-monthly style changes that maintained an ahead of the pack elitism.

Sandi grabbed at the tufts with one of her strong, elegant hands.

'Oh love, I went to Master's. It was so dark in there I couldn't see it till I got out. The queen who dyed it called it Cointreau. It's just a bloody euphemism for piss yellow.'

'I like it, darl, the colours. You look like a bantam.' Cal believed she was paying a compliment.

'What am I gonna do? It's so feral.' Sandi primped with her fingertips as though this might alter the hue. Cal shrugged. She was in unknown territory.

'How'd you get off your shift?' Sandi didn't usually finish until 2am, not a bad time to arrive for a dance party.

'Oh, one of the girls owed me. Who're you here with?' Sandi looked over Cal's shoulder.

'Rach. You don't know her.'

Sandi pursed her lips and nudged Cal. 'Ooooo, love...'

'Stop it. I wanna see the floor show. You coming in?' Cal went to move off.

'Just gonna touch up. I'll see you in there.' She pushed a tiny kiss Cal's way and sashayed toward the queues.

Cal watched the show, which was literally taking place at floor level. Cocooned larvae-like bodies wrapped in white, writhed along the surface as legs slowly cleared a path. The prostrate forms were like animated corpses in winding cloths. One, shaped in tapering black segments had red reflectors flashing through its eye slits.

As Cal leaned against the wall, watching the show, a woman walked past and grabbed her bicep, giving it a squeeze. Cal turned slowly in acknowledgement. Her eyes left the floor as she searched for the woman again. She watched her through the crowd until the show ended. When the woman moved away Cal followed her into the toilets.

The room was dimly lit and she could hear the mutterings and grunting of men. The woman was directly in front of her. Cal put her hand on the woman's neck and pushed her towards the one remaining cubicle. She shoved her against the back wall and held her with a pincer grip at her neck, then grabbed a fistful of her short hair to bring her around to face her. Forcing the woman's arms down behind her back, Cal pinned them there, letting the weight of her body fall against the other woman as she bit into her neck. The woman went limp. Cal licked the warm, bruised flesh and whispered into Rach's anxious silence: 'Next time you wanna test my guns, girl, at least ask me to flex first.'

After dropping Rach off around 4am, Cal headed home. Waiting at traffic lights on a backstreet in Redfern she watched a woman standing at the side of the road holding a giant-sized white teddy bear. Looked like she might topple over. A mufti police car switched on its lights and sped up Cleveland Street in the opposite direction. Cal slid the Ford into first, eased forward and suspected she might need more caffeine before Kurrajong. She planned to change into work clothes at home, grab the truck and head straight up to Boarback Ridge. Adrenaline would only take her so far. She stopped at a Caltex servo in Ashfield, grabbed a warm muffin and a double strength long-black. Hit the road. 4.30am was a great time to commute. Near-empty lanes all along the M4.

She arrived home just after 5.30, garaged the Ford, changed

into work gear, filled a thermos with coffee and took off to the Hawkesbury for a quick recce before work.

In the north-west area beyond the city, there were three national parks, five if you included Blue Mountains to the south west and Marramarra to the south east. Wollemi, Yengo and Dharug formed a fan left to right around the upper regions of the Hawkesbury. The Colo River fed into the Hawkesbury from the west. Stefan's property was on a sparsely inhabited ridge road north of the Colo region.

Cal had extensive topographical and survey maps of all the national parks she worked. Kaloola wasn't really a community as such. There were small villages in other parts of the region, places with a general store and garage with petrol pumps. Kaloola didn't have a shop and the inhabitants were separated by lengthy stretches of bushland. The idea of community was applicable only in the sense that everyone who was physically capable was a member of the volunteer bushfire brigade. People looked out for each other because they needed one another for survival.

She knew many of the other byways pretty well. One in particular, Juta Road, was the only sealed road north through the adjoining national parks. Boarback Ridge ran off Juta Road.

It was a clear autumn morning, no cloud, the sky a pale azure blue. She turned off the main road and headed east along the ridge. A few properties with fenced paddocks bordered the road at the beginning, houses with horse-floats and post and rail fencing. As she continued, the stretches of scrub and bush grew longer and thicker. She'd driven about seven kilometres and hadn't passed another house for some time. Stefan's should be coming up she reckoned, watching through the bushland to her right. She saw a clearing, the opening of the driveway punctuating the bush margin and she turned right into the property.

She left her ranger vehicle near the entrance, visible and hopefully not suspicious. The driveway was covered with a scattering of fallen leaves, and judging by the well-tended borders she imagined these would have been regularly swept had the home still been occupied. The house was set back on the left, a low, ranch-style seventies build. To the right, a large workshed. She tried to imagine Pip living there. Happily, if Di had been correct in her assessment of the relationship. She wondered what would happen to the property now. Would it be sold?

The workshed had windows all along the side. She peered in and saw a carpeted area at the far end like a chill-out space. A pool table stood in the middle with a bar behind it along the back wall. Framed Georgia O'Keefe prints hung above the bar. Two sofas formed an L-shaped nook at the far end with a pair of brown and white cowskin rugs in front of each one. A frame with pieces of yellow and black road signs jigsawed together hung on the back wall. Something about it was familiar.

She continued past the main buildings to the backyard, trying to get an overview and sense of the place. At the rear of the house a courtyard with a pergola adjoined the back wall. The grapevine was beginning to drop its leaves. Adjacent to the courtyard and behind the workshed was a slightly smaller building, a shadehouse. She pushed open the door and saw shelves crammed with buckets of orchids in bark-mix. The roof had steel cross members strung with hooks and hanging baskets with more of the drooping strap-like foliage. Some were flowering, garish pink and purple splotches on their butterfly shaped petals. Cal always found them rather strange, artificial-looking blooms. She closed the door and went to the back of the house. Tried the door which was protected by a louvred porch. She didn't expect it to be unlocked, and had no intention of going in. *Just sniffing around,* she reminded herself.

Beyond the courtyard, more planted borders gradually transitioned into the bushland behind. The rhododendrons and vireyas were looking a bit leathery. It hadn't rained in some time and no one was there to water the beds. She continued past the cultivated part of the garden and made her way into the bush. The ridge was effectively the highest point on that particular north-south range. As she made her way through the scrub and sapling trunks, she saw glimpses of the hinterland, the gum tree forest clothing the sides of the mountains, falling away on either side of the ridge, and the back-country, as far as she could see, stretching into the distance. As she gazed through the tree trunks and scrub, she saw occasional gaps beyond, like clearings where trees had been blown out in storms. Not unusual this high up, it was pretty exposed. She pushed on, just to confirm what she'd surmised. Within minutes, she broke through the undergrowth and emerged onto a swathe of cleared ground, a bulldozed track about seven metres wide. It ran right along the apex of the ridge and curved off beyond to the west. A fire-trail, an access track for bushfire control lines. Theoretically, the lack of vegetation could also help curtail the spread of forest fires. The intensity of some recent fires was so great the massive wall of flame simply jumped the breach.

She returned to the truck and pulled out the survey maps. There it was, a fire-trail running along the crest of an adjoining ridge, in the backcountry between Juta Road and Boarback Ridge. It didn't run all the way but it was only a few kilometres short of joining up at the Boarback Ridge end. Effectively, it began less than five hundred metres behind the property where Stefan and Pip had lived.

Phillip's body was found in bushland that adjoined the other end of the fire-trail near Juta Road. Was it purely coincidence that this track linked the two sites?

4

Cal's phone buzzed on the dash. Maur.

'You doing okay?' Maur said. Cal could hear a bus accelerating and wind rush in the background of the call.

'Just keeping busy. You?' Cal replied listlessly.

'Same. Hey, y'know we talked about giving Ad the full send-off. A Harley escort, homage to her days in the States. Any chance you can rustle up a pair? Know you don't ride now. Just a one-off. Something special.'

Cal watched an orange-winged black cockatoo flying across, above the road, the brilliance of its underwing totally distracting.

'Cal?'

'Far out. Yeh, sorry. Leave it with me. When's the funeral?'

'Friday. Service in The Cross. Cremation at La Pa.'

King's Cross. Of course. Addie had spent so much of her time there, trying to help the street kids.

Cal put the paper maps away and did an online map search to see what satellite images revealed. Her topo maps were detailed but didn't show recent changes or buildings. It was 8.30. She needed to get to work, but she was dying to follow up her discovery.

She left the property and drove back the way she'd come, more slowly, taking in the surrounds, noting the other properties along the way. They were mostly established-looking, not weekenders. The half-dozen homes she passed looked to be owned by folks with a bit of money, the post-and-rail fencing wasn't cheap, neither was keeping horses. Maybe they were retirees? Several properties showed children's play gear in their yards and there was a small school in Bradley, the nearest town.

On her left she passed a driveway that disappeared into the bush and no building was visible. Maybe something over the crest? She slowed, reversed back. About one hundred metres in, a single chain looped across the driveway, padlocked to a heavy galvanised bollard. Check it out another time. She really was running late now. She carried on, only a few kilometres from the Juta Road junction. She passed a property on the right she hadn't noticed on the trip in. It was on the inside curve of a corner. A bush-covered rise preceded the driveway. She wouldn't have seen it coming the other way. Through the trees she noticed a faded caravan on one side of the track and a shipping container on the other. The battered rear of a faded red Hilux with a canopy parked between. Someone with a holiday camp-out before building perhaps.

She paused at the junction, rubbing her hands over her face. Her head felt fuggy and sore, like someone had bounced a basketball on her skull. Her eyes were gritty and irritated. The thermos was empty.

She planted boot back along Juta Road, heading for Misty's Creek. She could resume her counts there and combine that with another recce of the site where Pip's body was found. She wanted to view it now with the knowledge a firebreak trail ran roughly between there and Stefan's place. And what did the police know? Had they noticed what she had? Did they have more news on Pip's cause of death? The bullet?

Five kilometres before her turn off to Misty's Creek she stopped at the general store. It had a pair of petrol pumps and served as a post office as well. A standalone, it was the only garage for forty kilometres in any direction. People who boated or drove relied on it. To one side was a workshop with a tyre-removal machine and hoist visible inside the doorway. She idled towards the workshop, not wanting to block access to the pumps. A pair of denim-clad legs stuck out from under a silver Mazda station wagon.

'Look out, fella, 'less you wanna lose 'em,' Cal called out her window. The legs pulled up into letter As and she eased the truck in front of the air pump.

She got out as the body emerged from beneath the Mazda. He stood and smiled crookedly at her, a length of wire in one hand. About five-eight, he had shaggy blond hair and pale skin. Kinda Kurt Cobain. Cal smiled back and went into the store.

She walked to a tall fridge in the rear and grabbed a pair of Red Bulls. She paced the two aisles and checked a low freezer section, looking for something she could get microwaved. No joy. She went to the counter. In a warmer oven there was some kind of hash brown-cheese-chutney concoction layered together and wrapped in cellophane. She grabbed one. A woman in a dust-coat stood at the counter, her brown hair pulled back in a loose ponytail, a heavy strand falling across her face. Her cheeks and lips were red without make-up.

'How ya goin'?' Cal placed the items on the counter.

The woman didn't smile. 'Could be worse. You need petrol?'

'Nah. All good thanks.' Cal proffered her card as the woman totted up on the till.

Back outside, a red Hilux had pulled up in the entrance of the workshop. A burly bloke in a faded plaid shirt was talking with the Kurt Cobain lookalike. He looked towards Cal's vehicle. She climbed in, nodded in his direction as she closed the door.

~

A few clicks down the road she turned left and followed the road that led along one reach of the meandering watercourse. Five kilometres in and the road became gravel. She closed her air vents and wound the window up, scoffing the warm food and one of the energy drinks as she drove. For thirty-five minutes she followed the lonely track to where she'd worked four days ago. When she reached the spot she parked and filled her water canteen. She checked her compass and GPS were in the haversack. GPS was a boon but she still used the old-school gear as well in the event of battery failure. It kept her sharp, having to work out her own coordinates. Thankfully the air temperature was in the low twenties and the humidity had dropped as well. Still, it was going to be hot work checking out the ridge. She skulled the second Red Bull and set off to where she'd found Pip's body.

She thought of happier times. She'd returned to Sydney after a road trip to Melbourne. Pip baked mud cake and they had some for breakfast. Later he showed off the vegetable garden and roses he grew; red and yellow and white floribundas. Who wouldn't be impressed?

'We had everything, Bill and I. It was perfect.' Bill was his longtime partner, gone in the early AIDS years. Pip never really got over that. He was on the electric polisher, wearing tiny faded shorts and old Reebok runners, full body tatts exposed. He knelt beside her bike and worked his way around it, burnishing the aluminium casings.

'They've never looked so good, darl. I'll never do them by hand again,' she said.

'You've got to take better care of it, Cal, it doesn't take much.' He was stretched almost horizontal getting under the low front of the engine.

'C'mon. I've just ridden from Melbourne. Anyway, it's just

cosmetics.' He ignored her as she went around the bike checking for loose nuts after the long ride, making sure nothing was about to leave the frame in a hurry.

They laid out on their backs looking up at their Harleys, discussing them like new lovers before scrubbing up and hitting a couple of clubs.

They both had bikes then, but Cal stopped riding when a friend was killed. Viv, a more cautious rider than her, was wiped out by an inattentive car driver. Cal could be reckless, took out her frustration on the road. When Viv died she had a moment of clarity. It didn't matter how careful she was, when things went pear-shaped on two wheels, it could be terminal. She swapped her two wheels for four.

Fifty minutes later she arrived at the rock shelf. Police scene tape fluttered from the trees though Forensics had well and truly finished. She leaned on a tree trunk and drank deeply from her canteen. The energy drinks were keeping her wired but the underlying lack of sleep made her limbs feel heavy and sluggish. She wanted to explore the area above and beyond where Pip had 'fallen'. She'd noted the coordinates where the firebreak ended and planned to find that now. *C'mon mate, let's get this done*, she prompted.

∼

At seven thirty Scobie gathered the troops in the incident room. She leaned back on her hands against a battered wooden desk.

'I'm putting together a team. Obviously this Leuwins death is not an accident. He was our main suspect for the Stefan Toblensk killing and now he's been murdered. That doesn't rule him out for the Toblensk killing but the matter has become more complicated. We're looking for someone else.' She folded her arms across her chest. 'I don't believe in coincidence. I want a re-evaluation of the Toblensk murder. I want a team at Boarback Ridge.

Forensics went over the area at Misty's Creek and we have very little. We believe he was shot with a rifle, maybe a .308 bullet. No bullet or casing as yet to help us. But Stefan Toblensk was shot with a .308. That bullet was recovered from a wall at the Boarback Road property. No casing found at the scene. We're still looking for the rifle that fired it. So, what was Phillip Leuwins doing out there?

'Drugs, skip?' Frank Birch offered, lank fringe hanging over one eye. He stretched, yawned, went back to his breakfast sandwich.

'Always a possibility. Isolated spot. High unemployment out there. Maybe Leuwins stumbled on something. Nothing came up in our original inquiries. Speak with Finlay at the drug squad. Get some overheads of the area.' She turned away from Birch. 'Glen, I want you and Tony to go over the Boarback site this time. Fresh eyes. When you're done there, I want reinterviews with locals.'

'Frank and Janice, you're checking into all associates and family of both men. Glen's brought in files from the first sweep. Go through them all. Dig deeper. Okay everyone. Chop-chop.'

∼

The rock shelf was one of numerous outcrops. When Cal reached the area above, she was on a long plateau, spiked with occasional spindly saplings. There was little humus above the sandstone to support vigorous growth. She followed the plateau, which ran in an east-west direction, until it fell away to the south. Above it, another layer of rock ran back into the hinterland. She climbed up and rested. Depleted and aching, she knew she couldn't safely go much further. She pulled out her compass, slowed her breathing. She could smell early mugga blossom, red ironbark, on the breeze. She must be near the apex of the main ridge. One hundred metres to the northeast should take her to the termination of the firebreak. She stood, stretched and resumed her search. At least she didn't have to fight through vines and wet undergrowth. It was easy going in that regard, gum bark and twigs the only obstacles underfoot and clear walking between the sparse trees.

Her sense of direction was near faultless. She could see the bright expanse of bare land directly ahead of her, the bulldozed swathe of firebreak. She was literally at its terminus and it curved off across the ridge like a yellow highway. About twelve kilometres away, its other end passed behind the Boarback Ridge property where Stefan and Pip had lived.

She breathed heavily, turned around on the spot, taking in the surrounds. Her fatigue diminished as she congratulated herself, satisfied that her theory had been spot on. She was certain her discovery was significant. She half hoped to find evidence on the ground that Pip and someone else had been there. But there would be no telltale signs. The constant fall of leaf litter and bark, the scuffing and movement of animals would disturb any indications on the ground. Even if an item had been dropped somewhere near, the likelihood of finding it would be akin to winning Lotto. Still, she remained buoyant.

She made her way back down the rock ledges, past the taped off site and onto the flat land. Skirting around the scrub at the forest margins, she checked her traps. Two butterflies, one Common Silver and an Eastern Ringed. She recorded the findings and began her trek back to the truck. Another clear autumn day, a cloudless, pale blue sky.

What the hell was Pip into? Why would someone want him dead? Di might be more up for talking now. And Addie's funeral's coming up. So much going on. *Time to take some leave, Cal. That's what it's for.*

When she arrived back at her truck, a police cruiser was parked behind it. A pair of officers stood outside the vehicle. One was smoking. The other had the boot open.

'Thought you fellas were done,' she said, unlocking her truck. She threw her rucksack on the passenger seat, went to the back of the vehicle, filled her canteen and swallowed half the contents.

'Popular spot.' The smoker screwed his ciggy under his boot.

'My workplace.' Cal got in the cab. 'Catch ya.' She turned her truck around and drove off slowly, trying not to raise too much dust. Dreamer.

Bone tired, she needed to go home. Check two more traps on her way and she wouldn't feel so guilty. *You can do it, Cal, one at a time.* Pace yourself. Should be doing some track maintenance as well but that won't be happening.

She approached the last one-way bridge before the gravel ended and the tarmac began. Yawned so hard her jaw clicked. She slowed down and checked the other side for traffic. As she did so her eyes dropped below the bridge abutment. A vehicle looked to be bogged in the muddy track that ran alongside the creek. The driver was packing sticks under the rear wheels for traction. He put his head up. That fella from the store workshop. She slowed down, crossed the bridge then veered right to the side track. She stopped and engaged four-wheel drive before edging down to the other vehicle.

'Give you a tow, mate.' She went to the rear, got her heavy-webbed strap. Handed it to him.

He looked sheepish. 'Too much of a hurry. I never get bogged. Cops everywhere.' He leaned under the rear, hooked the strap around his axle. He stood up. 'No rego. Don't wanna fine.'

Cal glanced down at the licence plate. The police had number plate recognition cameras in their cars and fixed cameras on main roads. 'Nah. Pretty exy,' Cal agreed. 'I'll pull you onto that rise. Bit drier there, eh.'

'Sweet.' He got behind the wheel, waited for Cal.

She eased the station wagon out of the muck and hauled it onto dry grass up close to the road. The Kurt Cobain lookalike got out, offered his hand. 'Nolly. Appreciate your help.'

'Cal. No worries. Cops'll be a while. They're exploring back where that body was found. If ya wanna get your wagon home safe.'

Nolly looked away. 'Yeh. Sorry business.'

'You local? You know 'im?' Cal said.

He nodded, got in his car. 'Nice bloke. Everyone knows everyone round here.' He started the car. 'Better go. Thanks again.'

Off the gravel she opened her window and planted her foot. No trap checks. Straight home to bed.

∼

She woke flummoxed by the daylight. Checked her watch: 4pm. Went to the sink, splashed water on her face. Went outside, tousled Banjo, always the visitor on her porch if she was home and Dee was out. Busy fella. He followed her back inside.

'Coffee, mate. None for you. Not good for pooches.' She put the pot on the gas ring, got her phone, plugged in the charger, rang her boss. 'How's my leave looking, Fisho? Got a funeral this week and some family stuff to sort.' She heard him clicking keys. Looked out the window at the donkeys having a head-butting game.

'Ah, twelve weeks, five days. Admin will be over the moon if you bite some of that off.'

'Two weeks, okay? Starting now?'

'Davey can take over your trap counts. The maintenance will keep. Enjoy.'

The coffee pot spat and gurgled. She poured a full mug and went to the porch. Sat on the wicker chair, rested one foot lightly on Banjo's flank. Not a flinch. *Leave, Jesus. Glad I'm busy*. Cal was neither familiar nor comfortable with spare time.

She rang Di. 'Any news?'

'Just confirmation. It was a rifle bullet, large calibre.'

'Any indication where the investigation is heading now? If Pip was a suspect, surely this changes things?'

'I don't know, Cal. They're not letting on. Early days I guess.'

'I'm taking some leave. Got Ad's funeral. I'll be back in town. Can we talk some more, Di? I wanna help.'

She had a shower and applied moisturiser to her face with the finesse of someone puttying a window. She dressed, packed an overnight bag and sent Zin a text. Banjo wagged excitedly as she closed the door and headed for the shed. 'Sorry, mate.' She couldn't look at him. How did dogs perfect that woebegone look?

She fired up the Ford and headed for the city.

~

It was early evening when Cal got to her aunt's. Zin didn't align food types with specific mealtimes. Part of her charm. Cal lowered two bread slices in the toaster.

Zin had several jars of preserves on the benchtop. 'Try it. Tell me what you think.'

Cal opened a jar, sniffed. Limes in there somewhere. Divine spicy fragrance. 'Interesting.' She raised her eyebrows. 'You been behaving yourself?'

Zin lowered her glasses down her nose, stared at Cal, remained speechless.

Cal's toast popped. She put on coconut spread, spooned on the marmalade, took a bite. Chewed thoughtfully. 'You've excelled yourself, Auntie.'

Zin wasn't one for blushing. 'I didn't have a proper recipe. I had some grapefruit, then I looked up a recipe and the quantity wasn't spot on, so I added some oranges and lemons to get that right. Had a couple of limes, so I added them as well. I looked at the amount of sugar in that recipe, I thought, *Oh, that'll be too sweet,* so I added less. It set really firm so I added more water. Didn't know how long to cook it. My friend came round. He never looks in my pantry. I'd hidden the marmalade in there because he's a great cook. I was ashamed of my marmalade.'

Cal shook her head, munched, licked her fingers.

Zin continued. 'He looked in the pantry, wanted to try it. He wanted some, but I was embarrassed to give him a taste, to give him any. Next time I saw him he said, "That was the best marmalade I've ever tasted. Can I have the recipe?"'

'Not surprised. It's a winner. Don't s'pose you wrote it down?'

Zin pulled a face, shook her head. 'I like it different every time.'

Cal wanted to tear her hair out.

5

Scobie strode into the incident room at 6.30pm on Monday. She fizzed with energy.

'Okay people, what have we got?' There was no instant response. 'C'mon. I know you're all tired. Faster we share this the sooner you all get a break. Glen?'

He had sweat stains under his arms, his cuffs were smudged with grime. *Bloke who shouldn't wear white,* Scobie mused.

'Tone and I did another recce at Boarback. Nothing new there. Finlay said there's been underground hydro bunkers further down the mountains, so it's always a possibility. Not easy to spot though. We've begun our search of properties along the ridge road, done halfway along one side. Few possibilities tomorrow. Also, got those overheads. No above ground crops. But, something interesting.' He looked to Tony Cobbin.

Tony stood beside filing cabinets behind Avery. A nuggety, dark character, solid build, receding hairline. He swigged from a takeaway coffee. 'There's a trail, skip. A firebreak running along the ridge. It passes behind the Toblensk property and runs across an adjacent ridge westwards. Terminates close to where

Leuwins's body was found. Eight to ten kilometres, I reckon. Would be an almighty coincidence if it wasn't relevant.'

Janice Ottering stretched her legs under her desk, turned back to Cobbin. 'You reckon that's the route Leuwins took, rather than by road?'

'He was shot in the back. He fell down onto that ledge. It's entirely possible.'

Scobie drank from a water bottle, rubbed her hands across the small of her back. 'Certainly needs consideration.'

'Any joy, Frank? Janice?'

Frank Birch was a crumpled-looking man. His skin and pale thinning hair were yellowed by cigarettes. His face, craggy and pocked, formed a grimace as he cleared his throat with a rasp like metal on concrete. *Jesus Christ man, when are you going to give them up?* Scobie looked towards the ceiling. He was her most experienced detective.

He read, flipping pages in his notebook. 'Few of the locals have form. Terry Scarborough, twenty-two. Son of Trent Scarborough, ex-rugby leaguie, Paramatta Eels legend. Mother's family had money. They breed a few horses. Entitled and nasty. Got off two indecent assault charges already. He also has an interest in a club down the mountains, Bronto's. Wouldn't be surprised if he was involved in something shifty there.'

Ottering spoke. 'Phillip Leuwins had club involvement with his sound systems business.'

'That's right. Might be a connection,' Scobie added.

'Okay,' Birch resumed, 'Nolly Pratt, nineteen. Mostly vehicle offences and trying to sell stolen property. He didn't do the thefts. Stupid. Bit impressionable. Hangs around sometimes with Craig Dolan. He's older, thirty-seven, done time inside for GBH. Thug.'

'No one else?' Scobie raised her eyebrows. Birch shook his head.

'Okay. Thanks, Frank. Keep on it. Janice, what have you got?' Janice Ottering sat up, reached her hands back to her tiny ponytail and tightened the elastic. The clump of hair pointed behind her like a small cylindrical brush.

'Stefan Toblensk had a sister, Sylvia, in Victoria. Still haven't tracked her down. She's on the road. Police spoke to her when Stefan was killed. Next of kin. No other relatives. He was basically retired and led a quiet life. No one has a bad word for him. He was liked in the community. Pitched in, supported projects. Had become a bit of a homebody with the rheumatoid arthritis. Phillip Leuwins was his partner and carer, well, it wasn't at that stage yet, but basically he was young and fit.'

'Anything there? Was Leuwins having affairs or anything? If he was, what, fifteen years younger?' This from Cobbin.

'Trying to follow that up. And Leuwins did work in the club scene. He came to the city regularly. Nothing firm there yet.' Ottering gave a small shrug.

'We're still looking for a motive. Two men who lived together are dead. Who benefits from that?' Scobie spread her arms. 'Nothing was stolen from the property as far as we know. Have we found Leuwins's vehicle? If he didn't leave the property in his pick-up, then where is it?' She paused, crossed her arms. 'If it wasn't Phillip Leuwins killing his partner and doing a runner, then what was it? Or did that scenario happen but something else was going on as well? Was it a botched robbery? I want all the original evidence gone over.'

'Hate crime, boss? Two gay men dead now.' This from Cobbin again.

'Exactly. We need to dig into backgrounds, unearth all those secrets people keep. Something's been going on out there. We need to find it.'

'I assume there'll be a funeral now for Phillip Leuwins. Might be an idea to have someone there, just spotting. Can you follow that up please, Glen?'

Avery nodded.

'Okay everyone. We need a big push tomorrow. Get some sleep tonight. Everyone here for eight o'clock please. Thinking caps on.'

~

Tuesday morning Di answered the door. She still appeared pale and somewhat slumped. Cal hugged her with one arm, carried a small bakery box in the other hand.

'Mum's in Melbourne for a few days. Like a cuppa?' She led Cal down the hallway, then gestured for her to sit at the table. 'Tea? Coffee?'

'Tea's good.' Cal looked out through the glass doors to the courtyard. Little red heart lights glowed from the branches of a Japanese maple.

Di flicked on the kettle, got a pot and cups from a cupboard, went to the table. 'Okay, what's in the box?'

Cal pushed it towards her, lifted her eyebrows.

Di pulled the sticky tab, raised the paper wrapping, smiled. Portuguese custard tarts. Small, crisp pastry cups, glistening golden with their soft filling. 'Four?' she said.

'They're tiny.' Cal smiled, pleased with herself.

She put her hand out, covered Di's. 'You been okay?'

Di nodded, her sadness so apparent in every weighted movement.

'I've got some time off. I wanna help if I can. Been a while since I hung out with Pip. You'll have to bring me up to speed.'

Di got up, filled the teapot, brought it to the table. She swivelled the pot back and forth as she spoke. 'He helped around the place. Stefan was basically retired. The rheumatoid arthritis made things difficult. He loved his orchids.'

Cal nodded, remembered the shadehouse.

'So Pip took on all that around the garden. Stef had a good

pension. He had his art collection and the old Jag. Pip looked after that for him.' She pulled the bakery box from its wrapper. Cal could smell the vanilla. Di passed a plate, smiled and offered the box. Cal took one. Di poured tea.

'Was Pip working?'

'He consulted and set up new sound systems, for clubs, pubs. Didn't DJ or work them himself anymore. He had a number of hire rigs, so he'd just deliver those, pick them up after the gig.' She bit into one of the tarts, closed her eyes. 'Oh my god, these are good.'

Cal smiled. 'So, the lock-outs must've affected business.' Cal thought of all the live music venues, no longer able to sell liquor after 1.30am.

'Don't think so. Those clubs and bars that closed were so established, decades old.'

Cal nodded, remembered the haunts of her early days in the city, the slum areas now long since gentrified.

'If anything, the dispersal of underground parties and alternate venues beyond the Cross and Darlo was good for Pip's business.'

'Did they have friends out there?' Cal asked. 'It's kinda isolated. Who did they socialise with?'

'Oh, you'd be surprised. A lot of older queens live beyond the city. Up the Blue Mountains, all over really. They all took turns hosting dinner parties. They socialised with other people too. You know.'

Cal nodded. 'Anyone in particular?'

Di refilled the tea cups. Cal was relieved the tea had had time to draw.

Di looked at her with hound-dog eyes. 'Gotta have another.'

'Go for it.' Cal pushed the box towards her.

'Funny. A few of the local blokes hung around a bit. I remember Pip telling me. He thought they were fascinated by these two poofs. Pip and Stefan passed. They weren't like *Priscilla, Queen of the Desert* were they? And Stef had his old car, and they were both "blokey" in their own way.'

'You think they broke a few myths among the locals.'

'Well, that's often the way, isn't it, once people got to know them. You know, Stefan had his workshop, he could lend tools and equipment. They'd have drinks there on a Friday night.'

'Did Pip ever mention any names?'

'Yeh. Actually, one had a funny name. Nobby? Noddy?'

Cal pulled a face. 'Nolly?' she offered.

'Yeh. That's it. How'd you know?'

Cal sat back, tapped her spoon on the table. 'Met him yesterday. Anyone else?'

'Someone this Nolly hung around with. Just local guys, I guess. Can't think of any names. Sorry.'

'Ex partners? Something crooked was going on somewhere.'

Di just shook her head, shrugged in apology.

Cal felt hesitant but had to ask. 'Police tell you any more about the cause of death?'

She saw Di draw herself in, tighten up. Her voice was quiet. 'It was damage to bone that showed the bullet trajectory. Even though the decomposition meant much of the evidence was gone.' She began to tear up, pressed her lips together. 'The bullet entered at his right shoulder, from behind. The trajectory was downwards, so they think the shot was fired at some distance. A good shot.'

Cal put her hand across the table, touched Di's hand.

'Addie's funeral this week. I've taken some leave. Gonna poke around a bit more. You be okay?'

Di swallowed, nodded, smiled weakly. She squeezed Cal's hand.

∽

Cal left Di's around nine, walked to the car, got in, made a call. 'Tommy, you old crock.' She wound her window down.

'They not locked you away yet?'

'Still chasing bugs, mate. Hey, is Nicko still inside?'

'On remand. No date yet.'

'Who's lookin' after his scoot'?'

'I am, as you very well know.'

Cal flicked her thumb across the seam running down the thigh of her jeans. 'Need a favour. Escort for an old friend. Her funeral. Just one day.'

'Cheeky. I'll ask 'im.'

'Need it for Friday.' She winced.

'Okay. Be in touch.'

She looked through her windscreen, across the half-empty parking lot. A guy emerged from a side-lane riding an old delivery bike. It had a tiny front wheel with a long carrier above it. The carrier held two Australia Post mail boxes stashed with things, not mail, and he wasn't in an Aus Post uniform. He rode diagonally across the laneway, rising off the seat to push harder up the slope towards her. He had long frizzy hair, like a fallen afro and he was singing out loud. He didn't have headphones on, and he sang this one line really hard, 'When you were my man!' like he was angry at someone.

Cal smiled. She loved the Inner West.

Her phone rang. Rach. She let it ring out.

~

Janice Ottering drove the squad car. She had all the windows down.

'Someone been smoking in here?' She grimaced.

'Don't look at me.' Birch clicked his seatbelt.

Second thoughts, it's just what's coming out of his pores, Ottering thought. 'You had brekkie?'

'Don't eat breakfast.' Birch tried to thumb an address into the GPS.

'Let me.' Ottering flicked her digits over the pad. 'Any of these roosters work?' she asked.

'Pratt does a bit of casual spannering at the Misty's garage apparently. Scarborough's an employee of his parent's holdings, some kind of stud consultant.' Birch flipped through his notebook. 'Phfffttt.'

'Got it in for him?'

'You'll understand when you meet him. Anyway, clubs, drugs. You know the score.' Birch looked out the window, eyed the number plate on a Toyota pick-up.

'What about Dolan?' Ottering turned onto the main road and floored it.

'Used to be a forestry hand, tree-felling, machinery.'

'Used to? Now what?'

'Had an accident. Got a compo payout. Runs some hire equipment, diggers and trucks.'

'Who's first then?' Ottering adjusted her mirror.

'Let's try the brat. Terry Scarborough.' Birch bit the press down thing on the top of his pen. It snapped off. He dropped his window, spat it out.

Ottering looked sideways at Birch. Laughed. 'Jesus, Frank. You really should reconsider the breakfast routine. The club or home?'

'Doubt he'll be at the club this hour. Try the home. I want to suss the place anyway.'

~

Cal spent the afternoon visiting various hardware stores, gathering pieces for a surprise project. Zin's upcoming birthday. Cal planned to hand-build new planter boxes and bench seats for Zin's courtyard.

Later as evening fell in Newtown, Cal left the car, walked down a service lane beside the mini-mall and came out on King Street. She stood in a doorway near the station, rang Zin.

'I'm grabbing some Thai. You like anything?'

'Might be nice. I was naughty. Had some more toast and marmalade.'

'You're outta control, Auntie.'

'Some rice-paper rolls would be lovely. I'm binge watching *Breaking Bad* again.'

'Don't get any ideas. See you soon.'

When she arrived at Zin's she quietly unloaded the timber and hardware and hid the pieces at the back of the garage under a canvas tarp. Her phone rang. Maur.

'Any joy with the bikes?' Maur said.

'I'm onto it. Looks promising.' She locked the car, carried the takeaway and her overnight bag in one hand, crossed the yard.

Maur continued. 'You know who's doing the funeral? White Ladies. Ha. She'd arranged it in her will. So camp.'

'Perfect.' Cal walked up the two steps onto Zin's back porch, knocked lightly, went in, still with the phone to her ear. She unloaded Zin's rice-paper rolls, blew her a kiss and left.

'Can't get over it,' Maur chortled. 'Old diesel being sent off by ladies in white.'

'It's spot on. She had manners and charm. Everything else going okay?' She unlocked her bedsit door.

'Yeh, sweet. Executor will have a nightmare job. Never mind. See you Friday then.'

Cal put her gear on the small table and stretched out on her bed, hands behind her head. She stared at the ceiling.

Her stir-fry went cold in the bag.

∼

She woke next morning lying on top of the bedcovers, still in her clothes. *Classy, mate. Pull yourself together.*

Ten to seven. She fired up a coffee, heated through last night's dinner and ate it as she considered her next move. Pip's killer could have come from anywhere; the local community, work contacts, a jealous lover. Was Pip seeing someone else? Money, sex or hate? Maybe it was a random thrill kill or botched robbery. She chewed a piece of broccoli. Outside, a grey cat appeared on top of the fence and made its way along the rail. *Look out, birds.*

The police seemed to have passed over the robbery-gone-wrong scenario. Why? Was nothing taken? Was the place not messed up?

Her phone rang. Tommy.

'Bro. How's it?'

'Got your ride. When d'ya wanna pick it up?'

'You bloody legend. Later today or tomorrow. Okay?'

'I'm home. Catch ya then.'

She felt a jag of electricity run through her body. *Fuck, I'm gonna be riding again. Hope I don't stuff up.*

Back to her present problem. *C'mon, Cal. Where you gonna start? Clubs? Not my current area of expertise. Need some help... Idaho!*

She quickly showered and dressed, shouldered her messenger bag and headed to Monetti's in Newtown.

Cal scored a park on King Street just doors down from Monetti's. That magical time just after the clearways ended. She passed the outside tables. *Why would anyone want to eat there breathing the fumes from ten thousand exhausts?* She took a seat inside at a small table near the back door.

She didn't bother looking at the menu but paged through a magazine. Several minutes later Gigi Idaho posed beside her table.

'Pumpkin! Where've you been?' He bent for an air kiss. Still lookin' buff. Donning more than just his underwear these days. Cal figured it was probably related to health and safety laws. She blinked, remembering him demonstrating his Prince Albert piercing during brunch several years ago.

'Hey, honey. Need a little catch-up. You get a break soon?'

'Of course, pumpkin.' His lisp went great with his muscles. 'What are you having?'

'Waffles and a long black.' She beamed at him.

'Right away. Chat when you're done.' He winked and sashayed behind the counter. *Nice buns.* Patrick the cook turned and waved a spatula. *Good to see the old team,* she thought.

The coffee and waffles arrived. The latter, a stack of crisp, golden triangles dripping with mixed berries and maple syrup, the carmine coloured drizzle pooling on her plate. *Yup, I just ate my leftovers at home and yesss, I'm gonna enjoy this too.*

When Cal was done she fought not to lift the plate and lick it. She drank the last of her coffee. Gigi put his head round the counter and nodded towards the back door. She waited outside, enjoying the morning sunshine and the warmth from the sandstone wall at her back. Gigi came and sat on an upturned milk crate. He unfolded a pack of cigarettes from his shirt sleeve, fifties style. *Well, he's a Yank, he's allowed.* His biceps were like those on a footballer. *Still workin' out too.*

'What can I do you for, pumpkin?' He blew a narrow stream of smoke overhead.

'You still with Pete?'

Gigi nodded. 'Still bangin' our heads together.'

'He's still a show agent?'

'Mmm hmm.' He drew deeply.

'Do any work out of town?'

'Only occasionally. Once a year kinda stuff. What're you after?'

'Trying to get a fix on who's managing all the shows and DJs in our clubs now. Are they our people or outsiders? You remember Pip Leuwins?'

'Course I do. And I heard about his death.' He nodded across the street. 'Di used to run her shop there.' Cal looked at the frontage of a specialist coffee roaster. 'Not totally drug-fucked, hon.' He stood, smiling.

'Trying to find out who his contacts were. He was running a few sound systems in the clubs. You reckon Pete might know? Or be able to point me in the right direction?'

'I can ask. Pete knows everyone. He'll be home tonight.'

She hugged him. 'Thanks, hon.'

She went inside and paid. Left through the front door.

~

The Scarborough property was off the Juta Road. On the river flats, west of the Misty's Creek region, its lush paddocks and post and rail fencing pronounced wealth. A long drive planted with formal, standard cherry blossom trees, led to a massive Georgian-style mansion. Ottering thought it looked ridiculous in the eucalypt bush surrounds. Beside the house to the left, a bank of stables, to the right, a four-bay garage. She parked in front of the garage. Birch pouted at the sight of the silver BMW and black Range Rover. The other two bays were empty.

'Let's do it.' Ottering climbed out.

'Dying for a fag.' Birch fumbled in his pocket.

'Afterwards, Frank. C'mon.' Ottering pushed a bell-press at the door, waited. Pressed again.

From behind them a woman's voice. 'Good morning. Can I help?'

They turned. Gayle Scarborough was a woman in her mid-forties. She wore light make-up and riding gear that showed off her trim figure. Her frosted hair was coiffed and framed her pixie-featured face. She smiled at the pair.

Ottering pulled her badge. 'DS Ottering and DS Birch.' She nodded at her sidekick. 'Richmond CID. We're making inquiries after the Leuwins murder.'

Gayle Scarborough's smile fell. 'Oh. Yes, awful business. Terrible. Out here of all places.'

'We'd like to speak with Terry, your son. He lives here, doesn't he?'

'Yes. He has a studio behind the house.' Her face became pale, stricken. 'Why do you need to speak with him?' She crossed her arms, holding herself.

'Just routine, Mrs Scarborough.' Ottering smiled. 'He has an interest in a club. Brontos.'

Gayle Scarborough nodded.

'Mr Leuwins may have had a connection there. We're just gathering information.'

'Is he home?' Birch rasped, attempted a smile.

'No. No, he wasn't home last night.'

'What does he drive?' Birch raised his eyebrows.

'A gold Nissan, GTR.'

Tosser. Birch hid a sneer. What he'd give to blast around in one of those on track day.

'Expecting him today?' Ottering smiled.

'I'm sorry.' She shrugged. 'Terry comes and goes. We're like ships in the night.'

Ottering passed her a card. 'Please ask him to call if you see him.'

'Of course.'

'Thanks for your time.' They returned to the squad car.

'Stop when you get to the road. I need a puff.' Birch had his lighter poised.

Ottering cruised along to a bend in the road, pulled over for Birch's craving. 'Frustrating.' Ottering drank gently from her water bottle.

Birch kicked the toe of his shoe through the gravel, puffed his cig, looked across to the sandstone cliff face above the distant creek.

'Who's next?' Ottering asked.

'Up the hills. Pratt then Dolan.'

6

Wednesay morning muster in the incident room. Scobie addressed Glen Avery.

'Did you follow up on the ranger, Cal Nyx?'

Avery nodded. 'Interesting. Came here in '95, a minor. Some odd absences in her history so I checked with our NZ brethren. Get this. She killed her stepfather.'

Avery already had everyone's attention. Scobie stopped mid-chew. 'Christ. Had a feeling about her.'

'Shot him with his own gun. He murdered her mother and her sister. She was next apparently. Caught him moving her sister's body. Got off on self-defence. She was fourteen. An aunt, Zinnia Nyx, became legal guardian. Moved her over here after the trial. Lives in Petersham.'

'Fuck me.' Cobbin stood mid-stretch at the printer.

'Anything since then?' Scobie resumed work on her croissant.

Avery shook his head. 'Clean as.'

'Dig deeper, Glen. Everyone has something to hide.'

'On it.' He nodded.

Later, on Boarback Ridge, Cobbin scanned the paperwork. Craig Dolan's history read like a career short list for a country male not interested in farming and not drawn to city life: forestry, roadworks, feral animal culling, earthmoving.

'Who owns this?' Avery slowed the squad car on the sandy verge.

Cobbin read from the printout. 'Earthmoves Contracting. It's Craig Dolan. I had forensic accounting do a search. Dunno why he needs to hide behind a company name. Got buggar all.'

'All helps with the tax write-offs.'

'Not exactly a mining magnate.'

They climbed over the chain and walked along the track, laid with heavy base course. A hundred and fifty metres along they rounded a corner to a wide yard.

An enormous truck and trailer unit carrying a massive digger stood on one side of an equipment shed. Various smaller backhoe diggers and trenchers stood under an open bay. A truck with a Bobcat on the tray stood idle beside an office.

'Not a lot going on. No wonder the chain was up.' Cobbin headed for the office.

Avery quickly scanned inside the open garage door. A yellow road roller machine had side covers raised and its engine exposed. Greasy drums lined a wall. Pieces of derelict equipment filled the back recesses of the shed. He followed Cobbin.

A red Hilux pick-up with a fibreglass canopy was parked beside the office. A man stood in the doorway. About five foot ten, he had the heavy build borne of decades doing manual labour. His face, dark from a life spent outdoors, attempted a relaxed look. Receding hairline, slicked back, his neck, short and wide like a tighthead prop. Rolled up sleeves revealed thick forearms, the musculature of the left one distorted by a long scar running from inside to outside up the length to the elbow. Belt cinched under a small paunch, his trousers wore grimy rust and oil stains down the thighs. He held his hands at his side with fingers spread. 'Do for you, gents?'

Cobbin pulled his badge, Avery followed. 'Morning. Just doing some inquiries regarding the deaths of Phillip Leuwins and Stefan Toblensk,' Cobbin began.

Dolan raised his chin, looked down his nose. His broad lips compressed. 'Unfortunate business,' he said.

'You knew them?' Cobbin continued.

'We all did. Small community. All help each other out.'

'Friendly? Knew them socially?'

Dolan drew back. 'Whaddya sayin'?'

'As I said–'

'You sayin' I'm queer?'

'Mr Dolan,' Avery joined in, 'we're simply trying to establish what happened to these men.'

'Come in here implying something cos I was good enough to–'

'When was the last time you saw Phillip Leuwins?'

''Spect me to keep a diary? How would I know?'

'Try.' Cobbin's tone hardened.

'Dunno. Could've been any time.'

'Where were you on April 12th?' Avery remained quiet as Cobbin asked the questions.

'Can't remember off the top of my head.' Dolan turned, went inside the office. He turned a filthy, dog-eared ledger on the desktop, paged backwards. The pages were mostly empty, bar an occasional scrawled entry.

'Was a Friday. Didn't have a job on that day. Not sure where I was.' He straightened up, stared directly into Cobbin's eyes.

'We need to know where you were. You often joined Stefan Toblensk for Friday drinks.'

'So?'

'He was killed on a Friday. Surely you're aware of that. The last sighting of Phillip Leuwins was that same Friday. Did you spend time with them that night?'

'Well, if it was a Friday, probably did. Haven't you read my statement? Don't remember seeing Phillip that night.'

'So, you don't clearly recall if you were there, but you don't think you saw Phillip Leuwins. Is that what you're saying?' Avery scribbled notes as Cobbin spoke, but he kept his eyes on Dolan's face.

Dolan stretched his right arm and held the door jamb, like he was blocking entry to his office. 'Trying to help. My memory's not good. Had a few beers that night.'

Avery changed tack. 'You own a rifle, Mr Dolan?' He saw a tiny tightening of the muscles around Dolan's eyes before he composed himself.

'Yeh, course I do.'

'Mind if we borrow it for ballistics testing? Standard procedure.'

Dolan hesitated. 'Been stolen.' He looked over their heads.

'Reported that?'

'Haven't got round to it yet.'

'You don't live here, do you, Mr Dolan?' Cobbin again.

'This is my workplace.'

'Lot of expensive equipment, sitting idle. Work dried up?'

Dolan remained quiet.

'You live at 227 Boarback Road. Is that correct?'

Dolan nodded.

'Mind if we have a look around your property?'

'Bit busy today. 'Nother day perhaps.'

'Today would be good,' Avery added.

'Sorry.' Dolan shook his head. 'Gotta job to do.'

Cobbin shot Avery a look. 'Be in touch then. Thanks for your time, Mr Dolan.' Cobbin handed him a card. 'Think of anything, give us a call.'

Dolan watched them leave, tossed the card at an overflowing bin beside the desk.

～

On the flats below Boarback Ridge, Ottering powered along the road and headed for Misty's garage. 'Gagging for caffeine.'

'Don't hold your breath. You're a long way from your lattes.' Birch's head was down, pencilling notes.

When they arrived at the garage a white Landcruiser was filling up at the pumps. Parked to the left of the workshop door, a silver Mazda wagon. Ottering cruised over to the other side of the building and stopped beside a battered picnic table that had been shunted and repaired numerous times. She and Birch got out. 'Need a drink before we start. You want anything?'

Birch shook his head and waved his ciggy pack at her. He leaned back against the table and lit up, eyeing the entrance to the workshop. He caught a glimpse of a lean, shaggy-haired youth. Nolly Pratt.

Ottering opened the screen door and headed for the refrigerators at the rear of the store. She grabbed an iced coffee and returned to the counter.

'Anything else?' the dour woman asked.

'That's it, thanks.' Ottering shook her head, swiped her card. She went outside, stood and drank half the contents, waited for Birch. The pair walked over to the workshop. Nolly Pratt had a Mitsubishi pick-up on the hoist. He worked at a brake line with a small spanner.

Birch began by flipping out his ID. 'DS Birch,' he thumbed at his colleague, 'DS Ottering. Looking for Nolly Pratt.'

Pratt turned, smiled, dropped his arms to his sides. 'That's me.' He looked expectant.

'You knew Phillip Leuwins and Stefan Toblensk?'

Pratt's smile dropped. 'Everyone knew them. Bloody awful what's happened.'

'You visited their home? Were friendly with them?'

'Sure. Stef used to put on Friday beers. Really nice bloke. Into old cars. I helped him out.' He swung his hand beside his thigh. Ottering watched his eyes.

'Any idea what happened up there? Anyone who'd have an issue with them?'

Pratt changed the weight on his feet, blinked several times.

'No. No. Really nice guys. Doesn't make any sense.' He was looking over Birch's shoulder towards outside.

Ottering spoke. 'When was the last time you saw them?'

'Jeez. That night. The night Stef died. Told all this to the cops before.' He stepped out beyond the hoist, rubbed a hand down his overalls.

'Where were you when you saw them?' Birch wrote in his notebook.

'At their place. Drinks. That Friday. Phillip wasn't there.'

'Who else was there with you?' Ottering asked.

'Just me and Craig and Stef.'

'Craig Dolan?' Birch said.

'Yeh.'

'What time did you leave there?' Birch again.

'Bit pissed.' Pratt looked sheepish. 'Half ten? Eleven maybe.'

'What about Phillip Leuwins. When did you last see him then?' Ottering said.

'Not too sure. Maybe earlier that week? He gets his gas here. See everyone pretty regular.'

'More specific?'

Pratt shrugged. 'Sorry. Not sure.'

'You own a rifle, Mr Pratt?' Ottering asked.

Pratt put his head to one side. 'Nah. Bit scared of them.'

'Really?' Birch raised his eyebrows.

Pratt nodded. 'Don't like the noise.'

Birch closed his notebook. 'Thanks for your time.'

Ottering's phone rang as she reached the car. She paused while Birch took the opportunity for another cigarette.

Avery calling. 'Speak to me.' Ottering gazed across the yard. A blue Nissan Patrol hauling a speedboat passed by. She reached into the cab for her iced coffee and drained it.

Avery said, 'Tone and I have just spoken to Dolan. He was there when we did the property run. Save you a job.'

'Any joy?'

'Evasive prick. Fill you in at muster.'

∼

It was another perfect autumn day, crisp, clear and windless. The sun cast its warmth through a pale sky. *Nice day for a bike ride*, Cal thought. *Don't wanna leave my car out at Tommy's. I'll get the train out, ride back, lock the bike up at Zin's.*

She drove back to Zin's and parked the car in the yard next to her room, leaving the garage free.

She gave a quick tap on the back door. Inside, Zin was working at the kitchen table, potting tiny cactus into equally tiny terracotta pots. She looked calm, beatific almost, as she adjusted an infinitesimal specimen with a pair of tweezers.

'Bringing back the bike, Auntie. Don't freak when you hear the noise.' She raised her eyebrows and gave an exaggerated smile.

'I'll be expecting a spin around the block.'

'Think I can manage that.'

No need to change my boots. She grabbed her helmet and jacket from the back of the car and left through the rear gate. Petersham station was a short walk. Stretching her legs to catch the sun, she sprawled on a bench, closed her eyes and waited for the train to West Ryde.

Avery started the car. Cobbin put on his seatbelt, looked through the windscreen, turned to Avery. 'Think we might pay a visit to 229 Boarback. Might hear something suspicious. Might end up in the property next door.'

'Gotcha.' Avery accelerated along the winding, ridge road, heading north, ignoring the other properties on their list. Less than ten kilometres later they reached 229 Boarback Ridge, adjacent to the property at 227 belonging to Craig Dolan.

Avery parked beside the entrance and headed down the driveway to 229. Cobbin followed. The small cottage had a threadbare area that might have once been lawn. But the porous sandstone and lack of topsoil ensured it reverted to scrabbly gravel. A tricycle and rusting swing-set were the only adornments.

Avery knocked at the front door, waited. Cobbin looked down the side drive that went to the rear of the house. No answer. They walked to the rear. Faded washing hung on a rotary clothesline. It was quiet and still.

'You hear that?' Cobbin winked at Avery.

'Try next door?' Avery raised his eyebrows. Cobbin nodded.

They returned to the front entrance and walked into Dolan's property. To the left among the trees, a circular bund of earth surrounded a small dam or pond. Cobbin walked up and stood on the rim. A black hose entered the dank water and ran up the bund to a covered pump. Another pipe ran from this to a water tank lower down the slope. Beyond this a caravan and aluminium awning stood on the edge of a cleared area that looked north-east across the hinterland. It had a stunning view across the endless sweep of bushland, extending to the horizon. Avery checked around the caravan while Cobbin walked the rest of the area. On the other side of the driveway a faded blue shipping container stood on a flattened section of ground behind a cabin.

Down the slope beyond, cleared trees formed a broad, semi-circular amphitheatre several hundred metres long.

He paced to the western end where a hand-painted target on a piece of ply had been nailed to a tree trunk. The rear of the trunk was completely blown out and shattered. He walked back to the other end of the clearing.

On a tree stump cut low to the ground, the worn imprint of a tripod. Behind the stump, the impressions in the dirt where two boot toes rested as a shooter lay on their stomach. The ground was littered with brass shell cases.

Cobbin took a pen from his pocket, lifted a .308 casing from the ground and put it in a plastic evidence bag.

∽

Fifteen minutes later Cal's train arrived. She took a window seat and tried to relax. Public transport was an odd and rare experience for her. As a child she'd walked or ridden a bike everywhere. She could ride a motorbike from the age of twelve, and drive a car soon after.

On a train, someone else was driving, in control. She tried to enjoy the view but felt voyeuristic looking into suburban backyards and dreary high-rise apartments. The alternating industrial sprawl provided no relief. She closed her eyes, felt vulnerable, so she unfocussed her eyes and stared into the blurred vision stream through the window.

When she arrived at the station she got her bearings and headed for the exit. In the middle of the day, the station wasn't busy. Her phone buzzed in her pocket. Rach. She let it ring out.

She always felt odd carrying a bike helmet. It was something you either wore or stashed. Carrying one implied maybe your ride had broken down, or perhaps you intended to steal a bike. Or you'd stolen the helmet. *Get over it, Cal.*

It felt strange, the not working caper. Not unpleasant. Just weird, unformulated.

She removed her jacket and shirt, walked in a T-shirt for twenty minutes. Stood at the bottom of a gently sloping driveway that led up to the double garage under Tommy's house. Trees grew in an informal hedge across the front of the property, flanking either side of the driveway. Closely mown lawns covered the slopes with a pair of flower borders nearer to the house. They were tidy and newly planted with primulas and antirrhinums. She tried to match the suburban vision with her old biker mate.

The right-hand garage door was raised. Inside, the white, custom Softail Harley gleamed, its light, elegant front end, stretched before the solidity of the V-twin engine. Tommy was at the workbench, stripping the brake master cylinder from one of his own bikes. A short, bear-like man, as wide as he was tall, his head was shaved and he wore a thick, black beard.

'Bro. Shouldn't be on the tools, nice day like this.'

He turned, smiling.

She hugged him with one arm, still holding her helmet. 'She's a beauty.' Cal gazed at the machine. 'Be perfect for Friday.'

'Time for a cuppa?' Tommy wiped his hands.

'Sure.'

'Show you my new ride before you go.' He led her up a set of internal stairs. 'Shaz is at work. Sends her best.' He pointed her towards a pair of bar stools at the bench. He flicked the kettle on, loaded ground coffee into a plunger.

Out the window was a suburban view but softened by the number of trees in the yards and on the verges. Three rainbow lorikeets flew across the top of the street planting and disappeared beyond the side of the house.

They exchanged news and took their coffees downstairs.

'So, Nicko's fine with me riding his scoot?'

'Trusts you.'

'Let's see your ride, then.' Cal finished her drink, put the mug on a bench.

Tommy crossed into the other garage bay, pulled a cover sheet from a long, sleek form. Cal whistled. The entire machine was painted a gunmetal grey, including the matched seat covering. All the other pieces were either stainless steel or billet alloy. Rather than looking monotonous, the different tones and textures in the same colour provided a slick, uniform elegance.

'Beautiful, bro. You do all the machining?' She bent down and touched the brackets holding the callipers to the front wheel.

'Four hours to match that pair.' His tone wasn't show-off, just proud.

'When's she ready to go?'

'Coupla weeks.'

'We should do a run.'

'You're on.'

She helped him replace the cover. Put her jacket on. 'Better get moving. Really appreciate this.'

He waved it away.

She put her helmet and gloves on, threw her leg over the seat, fired the bike up. It all felt so familiar, but it was someone else's machine. *No mistakes, Cal, go easy.* She smiled and nodded at Tommy, eased the gearshift into first and rode down the driveway. It felt lighter and more sure-footed than her last bike which gave her confidence. She headed for the motorway and rolled the throttle open, kept her speed legal but allowed herself a 'yii-haa' as she relaxed into the seat and enjoyed the view, an open stretch of road.

7

Scobie walked into the incident room at 6pm.

'So, people, what have we got?' She rubbed her hands together. 'Interviews. Glen?'

'Managed to speak with Dolan at his workplace. Defensive and unhelpful. Says his rifle was stolen recently. Cagey prick. Probably chopped into little pieces somewhere. Had a sniff around his other property. Tony got a shell casing for ballistics.'

Scobie folded her arms. 'What use is that? You had no right to be there. Christ, Glen.'

'If it's fired from the same rifle as the Leuwins casing at least we have a fix on the weapon.'

'No bloody good for court, though. And we're unlikely to find a casing in the bush.'

'Could go up with metal detectors, once we get specific on trajectory and distance,' Avery said quietly.

Scobie refrained from rolling her eyes. Held her tongue momentarily. 'In theory, yes. Trace is nigh on impossible to find in that dry debris. Assuming we could even get a reasonable fix on the shooter's likely position. The body fell onto that outcrop. To pin down an angle from where he may have fallen, so many variables. We'd need a huge team scouring...' She raised her hands, open-palmed. 'Nigh on impossible.'

Frank Birch spoke. 'We've tracked down the sister. Sylvia Toblensk.'

'Never married?' Scobie said.

'Seems not. Last address was in Daylesford, Victoria. But she's not living there. Place is rented out to an artist, Ella Mazur.' Birch read from his notes. 'Says Sylvia lives on the road these days. Her bank account is live. Regular withdrawals. Rent goes in there.'

'She needs to be informed. Developments around her brother's death.'

'Mazur was none the wiser. Gave us the renting agent's details. They have an email address.'

'Okay. Keep on it. I'm hoping this sister can throw some further light on Stefan's associates,' Scobie replied.

'Anything more? Janice?'

'Still trying to track down Terry Scarborough. No joy at home or the club. Gonna pass by the club again tonight,' Ottering began. 'Spoke to Nolly Pratt at Misty's garage. Came across very pleasant and helpful.'

'Not convinced,' Birch added.

Ottering continued. 'Agreed. We've got very little. Says he doesn't own a rifle. Doesn't like them.'

'Pffttt,' Birch scoffed.

Scobie scratched at her upper arm, frustrated. Knew she could probably do with a run after work. 'We need to apply some pressure. They were there the night Toblensk and Leuwins died. Hard to believe they know nothing and saw nothing. Any other names come up? Any neighbours remember seeing strange vehicles?'

Ottering shook her head. 'Making our way through them again. So far, nada.'

'Same. Nothing from the original statements.' Cobbin sighed.

'We're questioning them all again. Maybe some uniforms could help, boss?'

Scobie ignored him. 'I still think Dolan and Pratt are involved somehow. Until we get another suspect, I want leverage applied to them. No one mentioned their names?'

'Tight community. No one's gonna dob.' Avery again.

'Frank?' Scobie looked pleadingly at her senior detective.

'Money maybe? Bit of disparity out there. Landed gentry like Scarborough's type, then you've got the underemployed like Pratt and Dolan.'

Cobbin joined in. 'That equipment must've cost a fortune. All sitting idle. What's he living off?'

'There were rumours Toblensk had money. Place looked modest to me though. Bit of art on the walls.' Avery shrugged.

'Janice?' Scobie raised her eyebrows.

'See what we get when we speak with Scarborough, hopefully tonight.'

'Sex. Money. Revenge.' Birch crossed and uncrossed his ankles as he leaned on the table edge. 'Nothing's come to the surface yet.'

'Have we followed up the legals? Beneficiaries of their wills?' Scobie asked.

'Tomorrow or Friday.' Birch again. 'Glacial.'

'I want someone on Cal Nyx. Glen? You and Tony, tomorrow. Janice and Frank, carry on with the reinterviews. We need to push harder. If you speak with Scarborough tonight and get anything, call me.'

∼

Wednesday night in the car park at Brontos, Ottering yawned, checked the rear-view mirror and side mirrors, scanned the car park.

'Nudge me if I nod off.'

'None o' that. You keep your peepers peeled.' Birch crushed his coffee cup, tossed it in a bag at his feet.

The car park was half full.

'How we doing?' He felt for his cigarettes.

'Ten thirty. If he's gonna show it shouldn't be long. It's a Wednesday night for fuck's sake. Not like he has to wait till 2am cos it's cool.' Ottering got cranky when she was tired.

'Just gonna have a quick puff.' Birch climbed out. A gust of chilly air filled the cab. No problems with Ottering and doziness now. He pulled his old donkey jacket close and flipped the collar, lit his ciggy, stomped his feet, wandered over to a concrete encircled planting, littered with broken branches where drunks had reversed. *Poor bloody shrubs,* he thought. He kept his head down but glanced towards the rear doors of the back bar where patrons huddled in the roofed-off smokers' section. Fairy lights hung along the rafters, music drifted from the outdoor speakers mounted on posts. Clouds of grey haze drifted out from under the roof and dispersed into the autumn chill.

He could smell burgers, fried onions. His stomach growled. He drew deeply on his ciggy, scuffed the toe of his shoe across the gravel, stubbed out his smoke and dug his hands into his pockets as the bark of a racing exhaust announced the arrival of a gold Nissan GTR. It swerved in a massive arc, spewing gravel as the driver slid it to a stop in the empty *Manager, No Parking* spot. Insipid, paint-by-numbers muzak emanated from every corner of the vehicle.

Ottering had lowered the passenger side window. Birch leaned down. 'We're on.'

Terry Scarborough climbed out of his car and stood beside it, straightening his flashy gear. It looked like he'd spent half an annual wage at Prada. Ottering shook her head.

On the other side of the car, a slender leg tipped with a five-inch heel stabbed the asphalt. A long-haired waif wearing a glittering, skintight serviette, un-kinked her spine and rose from the minimal comfort of the racing seat. She looked barely adolescent.

Ottering noticed Scarborough didn't come and open the door for his date. Classy.

Just as he went to go inside, Birch swung in front of him, his badge out. 'Quick word, Mr Scarborough.' The girl pulled up behind him, swaying.

'The young lady can go inside.' Birch held the door. Scarborough stepped back, nodded the girl through.

Ottering pulled her badge, stood on the other side of Scarborough. 'We can chat here or go inside to your office if you'd prefer?' she said, forcing a smile, unable to forget the sexual assault charges he'd dodged.

'What's the problem?' Scarborough blinked. He pushed the middle of his torso forward, like he was Harvey Keitel in *Taxi Driver*. Ottering noticed. *Tosser.*

'Hoping you could help us with our inquiries. Two murders near Boarback and Misty's recently. Sure you've heard of them.' Birch pasted a flat smile on.

'How can I help with that?' Scarborough shook his head but remained neutral.

'Phillip Leuwins hired sound systems out to clubs, including yours, I believe. We're just following his movements, putting together a few leads. Deal with you directly, did he?' Birch leaned back, raised his eyebrows.

'I have a financial stake in the club. Day-to-day running is Jonty's scene. You wanna speak with him? I don't have a problem. Come through.' Scarborough pulled the door. 'Third on the right,' he said as he let them pass. *Defers to coppers then*, Ottering noted.

Birch looked in through the window to the kitchen as he went by. *Should've had dinner*, he thought.

The next door had a star on it and Scarborough's moniker. The following bore *Manager* in gold script. Birch waited for Scarborough to knock and introduce them. He led them into a dark, wood-panelled office. Two buttoned leather couches stood against opposite walls, a heavy desk between. It was not what Ottering expected.

A young man with an attractive face and premature balding stood up behind the desk. He wore a waistcoat and dark trousers. His shirtsleeves were rolled back revealing colourful work on his forearms. He put his hand out. 'Jonty Kapernick. How can I help?'

Birch and Ottering stepped forward, badges out.

'Be next door if you need me.' Scarborough closed the door behind him.

'Just making a few inquiries after the Leuwins murder. You leased a sound system from him?' Ottering took the lead this time.

'Please have a seat. Can I get you a coffee? Something else?' He gestured towards the nearest couch.

'We're good thanks.' Both remained standing.

'Of course.' He put both hands flat on the desk. 'Still can't believe it. Nice chap. Good supplier. Always came straight away if there was a problem. Actually, there rarely was a problem. He looked after his gear. DJs didn't have any issues. We'll miss him y'know.' He rubbed his hand across a small area of the desk surface.

'So, you didn't see much of him then?'

'No. I could pull his contract if you like?'

'That's okay for now.' Ottering shook her head.

'He set up here maybe five years ago. Came once a fortnight to check the gear, cabling and stuff. Totally routine. He'd come during the day, before opening. If the DJs had issues they'd leave a note with me. Can't get them here in daylight.' He laughed. 'But like I said. His gear was top notch and he looked after it.'

'Who did he deal with when he came, for the maintenance?' This from Birch.

'Me, if I was here. Otherwise one of the bar or kitchen staff. He was a regular. Just here to do his job. Everyone knew him.'

'Anyone here might've had an issue with him?' Ottering again.

'No. Not at all. I can't imagine. He was a really nice guy. Sounds cheesy, but he was.'

'Did he spend more time with any one particular member of your staff?' Birch said.

'Not that I recall. He was like part of the furniture. I don't mean that in an awful way. He just floated in, did his thing and left.' Kapernick put his hands palms up and shrugged.

'Okay. Thanks for your time, Mr Kapernick. You mind if we pop back and speak with your staff when they're not so busy?' Ottering asked.

'Of course. Not a problem. Sorry I couldn't be of more help.'

Birch went to the door, held it for Ottering, nodded at Kapernick as he left.

Ottering passed Scarborough who seemed to be fiddling with a fire alarm switch on the nearside wall.

Scarborough straightened and stood, arms folded as they left. 'Have a nice night, officers,' he said.

What a fucking juvenile, Ottering thought as she headed for the car park.

∼

Tempted though she was to just point it down a long highway, Cal rode home and parked the bike in the garage at Zin's place.

As she stashed her riding gear she realised again she was in unfamiliar territory, holiday mode. *It's a Wednesday night. I can party if I want. Ha. Might just do that.*

Inside the bedsit, she flicked a text to Dee on the farm to let her know she was on leave and might be a bit scarce.

She took a quick shower, changed into clean black jeans, T-shirt and cowboy boots. In deference to the autumn cool, she wore a sleeveless black waistcoat. She drove to Chippendale and parked in a backstreet, beyond the overhanging branches of a

Moreton Bay fig tree. The flying foxes would poop everywhere anyway, but it might give her paintwork some respite. The air was sharp and cool as she wove left and right down the back alleys to the club. It was 10.30, a civilised arrival time for early in the week.

She smiled at the burly security woman outside Pinks. At least two metres tall, solid and dark with her hair pulled tightly in a knot, her bulk looked the result of hard work rather than steroids. Cal wouldn't have balked at being frisked.

She strolled slowly to the far end of the main bar, passing the dance floor on her left. To her right, small tables and patrons filled the space between the main thoroughfare and the far wall. At the end of the bar a doorway led out back to the poolrooms and a staircase to an upper bar.

She climbed the stairs to the smaller, quieter bar and took a stool near the door end where she could survey the whole room. She raised her eyes at the barwoman and ordered a Peroni.

Her right foot tapped out the rhythm of a Skrillex track as she took a long pull from the frosty bottle. The bar was surprisingly busy, not crowded, but close to full. The patrons were a little older than those downstairs, mostly women, a few tables of queens. Her gaze ran in zigzags across the room then around the horseshoe of the bar as she took another long pull on the beer.

She noticed a familiar form at the bar, recognised the stance before she saw the profile, the upright neck and straight back, held in a flat plane like a dancer's. Liz Scobie. Her hair was pulled up off her neck, slung into a quick French plait.

Well, well, well. She with someone? Cal watched for a few moments. There were others sitting at the bar but Scobie wasn't engaging with them. An empty martini glass sat on the bar in front of her.

Cal made her way across the room and sidled next to Scobie. 'Please tell me you're not here on business.'

Scobie looked her way, smiled. 'Always on the job, I'm afraid.' Her gaze slipped over Cal's upper arms and then away.

'Let me buy you a drink,' Cal said.

'That would be totally inappropriate.' Scobie looked straight ahead to the bar mirror.

'In that case, name your poison.' Cal turned and raised her eyes at the barwoman.

Scobie turned her eyes back to Cal. 'A gin martini. Dry. Three olives.'

'And another one.' Cal waved her bottle at the barwoman, then looked back across the room, but flicked her eyes beside her, checking Scobie out. Swimmer's shoulders, broad and flat. She imagined placing the palm of her hand between the shoulder blades, slipping her arm around Scobie's waist, pulling her back... *Get a grip, Cal.* 'Undercover then?' Cal took a small swig from her bottle.

Scobie twisted the stem of her empty glass. 'C'mon,' she scoffed, lightly. Her martini arrived.

Cal raised her bottle again. 'Chin, chin.'

Scobie sipped the drink, closed her eyes a second, swallowed. *The drink suits her,* Cal thought. *Old school. Elegant.* 'So... I can relax. Not under surveillance.' Cal grinned.

Scobie turned to her, leaning one elbow on the bar. 'I don't imagine you're ever quite relaxed.' A half-smile, and something else, a chink in the flinty gaze.

'You waiting for someone?' Cal drained her beer.

Scobie twirled her olives through the clear liquor. She pinned the toothpick between two fingers, raised the glass and took another sip, held the liquid across her tongue then swallowed. 'Not anymore.'

8

Thursday morning, Birch and Ottering drove back to the Toblensk property on Boarback Ridge.

'Know much about art?' Ottering hefted the camera case to her shoulder.

'Clueless.' Birch lit up.

'I'll take some pics, write down some names. Check it out back at the station. You need to look over anything again? The garage?' Ottering fiddled with the camera battery cover.

'Yeh, wouldn't hurt.' *Bossy cow*, he thought. Despite being very much her senior, he let Ottering direct him sometimes. His silence kept the peace.

Ottering started in the main living area where there were several large paintings on the walls. Modern, abstract, that was the limit of her judgement. One was a large, scribbly pen and ink of a man's head. The overlaid lines were disturbing. She took shots of the pieces in their entirety and close-ups of the signatures. On the sideboard some odds and sods, to her eye anyway, small sculptural ceramics. She clicked away, looked for markings on the bases.

In a display cupboard with glass doors, she photographed

what she took to be someone's best china, something their mum might have left them. On one shelf, a sculpture, like a piece of coral sticking out of a sardine can. She carefully replaced anything she moved. When she was done she went to the main bedroom.

The room was clean and spartan, as though the lack of other visual distraction brought all focus to the artworks. Simple ceiling-to-floor curtains, plain, elegant bedside tables and lamps, built-in wardrobe. She set up the tripod.

Above the bed hung a long, narrow painting and opposite, a series of three paintings, side by side, unframed, obviously by the same artist and somehow related. A triptych, she realised, but knew nothing more of their provenance. The colours were faded ochres and yellows. White handprints here and there. Maybe an Aboriginal artist. *Or a rip-off of one*, she thought.

The flash wouldn't flare. She replaced the battery and tried again, finished her pictures and left the house.

Birch poked about in the garage-cum-games room. He leaned against the bar and thought about the Friday night Toblensk was killed. Phillip Leuwins probably died that night, too, although the fix on that time of death was impossible with the state of the decomp.

Forensics had swabbed all the bottles and utensils from that night. What happened here?

~

In Petersham, Cobbin and Avery were parked opposite the northern end of the back lane where Cal stayed. If she left going out the southern exit they could catch up quickly as she had to make a right turn into the one-way street at the terminus.

Avery hated stakeouts. The waiting tried his patience. His body, like a winding of rubber in the core of a golf ball, was hard to constrain for long periods. But leaving the car for a stretch wasn't an option in case they had to take off in pursuit.

Cobbin was more relaxed. He spent the idle minutes imagining tying new flies for his next fishing trip. Tasmania's central plateau. Brown trout. Clear waters and dappled overhangs. He almost nodded off.

~

At the Toblensk property, Ottering locked the door and lugged the gear to the patrol car as Birch emerged from behind the garage, puffing on a ciggy. He stubbed it out and stashed the butt in the rubbish bag in the footwell. 'Let's get a move on. Still got to rattle Pratt's cage.'

'Any joy in there?' Ottering slung the gear in the boot.

'Just figuring what could've happened that night.' Birch's voice was strained, perplexed. 'Forensics only found three lots of DNA on the bottles and glasses that night. Toblensk, Pratt and Dolan. Nothing of Leuwins. What could've provoked two deaths?' Birch leaned on the car roof. 'Pratt and Dolan had been here before, socially. Drugs don't seem to be an issue. Toblensk and Leuwins were clean. They weren't crims. What the hell were Pratt and Dolan after? Money you reckon? I just don't see an argument ending the way it did.'

'Reckon someone made a pass at someone?' Ottering straightened and loosened her shoulders with small rotations.

'Maybe. Nothing else is jumping out. You think Toblensk made a pass at one of them?' Birch held his door open.

'Dunno. Seems like he was a sophisticated bloke. Would have thought he'd be practised and careful. I don't see a gay man taking risks like that.'

'Same. It's a real odd one.'

Birch's phone rang. Scobie. 'Boss?'

'Finally spoke to Sylvia Toblensk. Currently in Benalla,

working with some young artists there. She was helpful, apologetic that she was so hard to get hold of. Upset, of course, about the new developments re her brother. The upshot is this: Stefan was having an affair with someone. She spoke with him about six weeks ago. She wanted to impress on me that it wasn't a secret thing. Phillip Leuwins and Stefan had an arrangement. They both had affairs. But I think it needs pursuing. She didn't have a name. Just that it was someone local.'

'Got it.' Birch nodded. 'Thanks for letting us know.'

'See you at muster.' Scobie ended the call.

Birch passed on the information to Ottering as she closed her door and started the car.

Ottering whistled and shook her head, smiling. 'I like it.' She floored the accelerator.

～

Cal had forgotten to set her alarm. She woke at eleven thirty.

'Shit.' She rubbed her hands back and forth across the top of her head, as if that would clear the fogginess. Scobie. *What happened? Did I get drunk? Beers at the bar, a bit of banter. Did I put the hard word on her? You bloody muppet, Cal.*

Her phone pinged with a text. Maur.

All set for tomorrow? Service starts at 11. See you outside 10.30. X

She flicked back a response and went to the shower, braced against the chilly spray.

The cold shower quickly brought Cal around. She dressed, swept back her quiff, sat on the edge of the bed. Leave. Holidays. *Not used to time on my hands. Gotta sort the bike for tomorrow. That won't take all day. Tomorrow. Addie's funeral. Jesus, what a week it's been. Addie and Pip.*

I'm supposed to be helping Di. She had been sidetracked by

Addie's sudden passing and funeral. *Get back to it after Thursday. Give it all my attention.*

Her phone buzzed. A text from Rach.

What's going on????

Cal rubbed her knuckles across her scalp. She touched the green icon. Rach answered after several rings but said nothing.

'I'm sorry.'

Rach didn't respond. Outside, a siren followed by another passed on the main road.

'So messy at the moment. Bit of time out, ay.'

'Fuck you.' Rach clicked off.

Cal tossed the phone on the bed, stood, rubbed her hands up and down her cheeks and forehead.

'Fuck it.' She grabbed her jacket and helmet and left.

~

'Wednesdays and Thursdays he's not at the garage. Address here is up on the ridge.' Birch read from his notebook. '1175 Juta Road North.'

Ottering continued along the flats past the Misty's store and began the climb up through the bush. The whiff of nicotine made her headachy inside the cab. She opened her window. The insect and bird noise was loud, not noisy like midsummer with the cicada racket, but she was very aware of an abundance of life around her.

'Should be about half a K beyond the Boarback turnoff. On the left.'

Ottering nodded, kept the gas on as she neared the top of the incline.

'Can't remember much along there. An old campground or

something?' She looked to the right as she stopped at the fork, then pressed on northwest on Juta Road.

'Yup. Deserted-looking place. Woulda been better sited down near the water, but I guess then there's always the problem with flooding.'

Ahead on the left Ottering saw the faded sign on a pole, *Height's Holiday Park.*

'Think they would've removed that.' An uninviting entrance of wretched-looking shrubs, rusting chain-link and gap-toothed fencing greeted them. Inside the dusty entrance, a half dozen mobile units on concrete blocks were fanned around a balding dustbowl of ex-lawn with an ablutions building in the middle.

'Four A,' Birch said, pointing to a washed-out beige mobile with mustard-coloured stripes on its siding. The silver Mazda wagon was parked to one side and beyond that a washing line hung with faded towels and shirts.

Outside a nearby unit, a pair of toddlers played, one pushing the other in a plastic buggy, both squealing with joy.

Ottering and Birch walked to the door. A sloping timber ramp had been built up to the doorway. Birch rapped on the screen. The side windows were open and they could hear a radio playing country music.

'Nolly. Nolly get the door,' a scratchy voice called inside.

Minutes later Nolly Pratt opened the door, looked expectantly at the pair.

'Mr Pratt. Mind if we ask you a few more questions?' Birch said.

Pratt hesitated a moment. 'No problem.' He looked over his shoulder. 'Can we do it out back? Mum's in here.'

'Of course. Lead the way.' Birch stood back as Pratt walked to the rear of the unit.

A swing chair with a striped awning faced away from the back of the house, a long view west across the hinterland. A pinewood trestle table with an umbrella stand and bench seats beyond that. Paving and cacti in pots. Pratt gestured towards the bench seats. 'This okay?' he asked.

'It's fine.' Ottering smiled. Birch stood.

'Just that Mum's not well.' He shrugged. 'MS.'

'Sorry to hear that,' Ottering said.

Birch launched in. 'On Friday 12th, Phillip Leuwins wasn't at his home. Did you know he wouldn't be there?'

Pratt looked flummoxed, his brow deeply creased at the bridge of his nose, as though he didn't understand the question.

Birch waited for a response. Ottering clicked her pen.

'Simple question, Mr Pratt.' Birch again.

'No. He was usually there.' The frown eased.

'Stefan Toblensk was expecting you? He'd invited you that night?' Birch continued.

'Yes.'

'When did he invite you?'

The frown returned. 'Don't remember exactly. Sometime that week.' Pratt's thumbnail scratched at the woodgrain on the bench.

'Can't tell us when that was?'

'Maybe he invited Craig, and Craig told me.' Pratt raised his eyebrows.

'So we should check that with Mr Dolan then?'

Pratt looked a little squeamish. 'I guess.' His boots scratched across the gravel under the table. 'What's the problem? Like, we had a kinda standing invite for Friday beers.'

'Well, something particular happened that Friday, Mr Pratt. We need to find out why. And you were there. When did you first meet Mr Toblensk?'

Pratt sighed. 'Guess when he moved here. Everyone buys gas at Misty's.'

'When did you start seeing him socially?'

Pratt shifted on the seat, drew back slightly. 'Friday beers, you mean?'

'Is that the only time you saw him socially?'

Pratt was silent. His lips compressed.

'Know many gay men, Mr Pratt? Must've been a bit of a novelty out here.'

'What's that got to do with anything?'

'Just questions, Mr Pratt.'

Nolly Pratt stood up. 'Don't have to answer this shit.' He walked to the rear door of the trailer, yanked it open and disappeared inside.

∽

The team gathered in the incident room at 5.30. Scobie kicked off. 'Blow up those signatures on the artworks. If you can't work them out, get them to an expert.'

'Just take the lot to a decent gallery.' Cobbin bit at a splinter in his thumb. 'The Museum of Contemporary Art and Art Gallery of NSW are both near Circular Quay. Someone there should know what they're looking at.'

'Right.' Scobie pressed her palms into the desktop at her side.

'Phillip Leuwins's pick-up has been found. It was in a parking area at Gringly's Reserve. Burnt out. Still waiting on more. Techs had it towed this afternoon so we won't have anything before morning.' Scobie looked at Cobbin. 'Bring up the map, Tony. It seems on first inspection it was torched in the last twenty-four hours or so. Not weeks ago, when he went missing.'

'Have we got CCTV of any roads in the area?' Avery asked.

'Roads and Maritime have some cameras on the overpasses.' Ottering tapped at her laptop. 'If we pick up a vehicle at the Corbans Road interchange, and it's not sighted again at Westleigh overpass, the only exit between is Gringly Reserve Road.' She looked up. 'It's not conclusive, but it's something.'

Cobbin brought up a map on the main screen at the front of

the room. 'There's a petrol station just off Reserve Road. They'll have CCTV too.'

'Check it.' Scobie nodded.

Birch spoke for the first time. 'Gringly's Reserve. Isn't that a beat?' The old cop used the term for a gay men's outdoor cruising area.

9

There was a moment of quiet as everyone acknowledged what Birch had said.

Cobbin nodded. Avery stared.

'Nice one, Frank,' Ottering said.

'You two on it as priority.' Scobie indicated Birch and Ottering. 'Trawl the CCTV. Start now.' She rose from where she'd been leaning on the desk, moved her head from side to side, rubbed a kink that refused to shift at the back of her neck. 'Any joy with Cal Nyx?' Scobie raised her eyebrows at Cobbin.

'Negative.'

'How long do you want us to tail her?' Avery asked.

Ottering joined in. 'You really think she has something to do with this?'

'She knew Leuwins. Everyone is a suspect until we have the killer. You know how this goes.'

'Stay on her then?'

'For the time being.'

'We're likely to miss something anyway if we can't be on her 24/7.' Avery made an adenoidal snort.

'Full-time. For the next twenty-four hours.' Scobie gently

rubbed her hands together. 'Thank you, people. Let's keep on. Call me with anything significant.'

～

Nolly Pratt closed the aluminium door.

'Who was that? Police?' his mother said.

'Nothing to worry about. Just questions about the murders.' Pratt unfolded the wheelchair, eased it through to the living area where his mother lay on the couch.

'Thought they'd already spoken to you at work?' She tried to push herself up with her arms.

'Always have to interview more than once. New things come up, they have more questions.'

'You keep your nose clean, boyo.'

Pratt manoeuvred the chair in the tight space, leaned down for his mother to lock her hands behind his neck. He lifted and swung her into the chair.'

'Thanks, lad,' she panted.

He smiled, put his hand on her shoulder then wheeled her out, down the ramp to the wagon. He opened the passenger side door and adjusted the swivel seat, lifted her across, swung her legs into the footwell, helped her with the seatbelt.

'Plenty of time, boy. No rush. You catch your breath.' She fossicked in her handbag, checking her cards.

～

Neither Cobbin nor Avery were expecting to be following a bike. They wouldn't have recognised her under her helmet, but Cobbin saw her wheel the machine out before closing the garage. He ran the plates through the system as Avery nosed out from the kerb.

'Christ.'

Avery flicked the indicator and made a turn. 'What?'

'Bike belongs to Nicko da Silva.' Avery lifted his chin in acknowledgement of the familiar name. Cobbin tapped at keys. 'Currently on remand at Silverwater.' He lifted his head. 'Wonder if he knows she's riding his bike.'

Avery kept his distance, following her through the Inner West, Newtown, Chippendale, until she turned east into Cleveland Street, along until Chalmers where she headed towards Central before peeling off right into Strawberry Hills.

～

Mid-morning at the Richmond Police incident room, Ottering knuckled Scobie's door. 'Got something on the Gringly's burnout, boss.'

Scobie followed Ottering back to her desk.

Ottering rolled the footage from the Westleigh overpass cameras, paused on a frame. The rounded rump of a Nissan GTR.

'That's Scarborough's ride?' Scobie leaned low, peering at the screen.

'The very same.'

'After the interview?'

'Yup. 2.37am this morning.'

'Okay. You and Birch, back on it. Might be time to bring him in.'

～

Cal rode directly to Surry Hills, parked the bike close to Abbott's Café and went inside. She ordered a long black and pain au chocolat. Hangover food. On a stool in the window she chewed the sweet pastry and kept an eye on the bike.

Her phone rang. Gigi.

'Sugar.'

'Hey Pumpkin. Gotta be quick. Pete says Bronto's is managed by a guy called Jonty. Decent sort. Nothing to report there. Bit of goss on the club owner though. Terry Scarborough. Likes a bit of fruit.'

Cal pulled a bemused look. 'Sex with gay men?'

'Totes. Oh. Gotta fly, hon.'

Huh. She shook her head as she watched a thin waiter in a wraparound apron clearing plates from an outside table. So, Scarborough liked a bit of trade. And Phillip Leuwins was a regular worker there.

She finished her pastry and drained her coffee. She thought of Liz Scobie the night before, the trace of vetiver cologne as she'd stood near her. *Jesus, Cal.* She shook her head. She left the café, locked her helmet to the bike and walked up towards Buckingham Street. The bike would be safe in view of the café.

~

Avery worked his feet in the foot-well, moving his toes through arcs to keep blood flowing through his ankle joints. God, how he hated stakeouts. He tensed and released his thigh muscles and calves, like he was on a long-haul flight and trying to avoid deep-vein thrombosis.

'She's leaving on foot.' Cobbin beside him.

'I'll follow. Can't sit here anymore. You drive or wait here.'

'I'll come too. Can't be going far if she's leaving the bike.'

Cal strode up Little Buckingham Street, crossed Bedford, kept walking for another half block. The police pair watched as she stopped outside a terrace house on the southern side of the lane. She spoke into an intercom beside a two-metre high wall. The second-floor windows, visible above the wall, were blacked out with mirror film.

'Brothel,' Avery said.

'What were your movements Wednesday night until Thursday morning, Mr Scarborough?' Birch began.

Terry Scarborough stretched his legs out under the table. 'Was at the club then stayed with Cilla.'

'We'll need her contact details. Now, please.'

Ottering jotted them down then left the room.

'What's the problem? You came to the club Wednesday night, talked to me and my staff. This is verging on harassment.'

'Do you normally conduct business meetings at a known gay beat, Mr Scarborough?'

He stared at the detective in silence.

'Shall I repeat the question?' Birch waited.

Scarborough inched back slightly on his seat. 'Bit unclear. What are you asking?'

'Your vehicle was sighted on CCTV on the road to Gringly's Reserve. Phillip Leuwins's vehicle was torched there last night. That vehicle held potential crime scene evidence. Tampering with evidence is a very serious offence, Mr Scarborough.'

'I'm sorry. My vehicle was sighted on a road. Are you joking? Any other vehicles seen on that road?'

Birch ignored him. 'I'll return to my previous question, Mr Scarborough. What were you doing at a gay beat in the middle of the night?' Ottering returned to the room, gave Birch a nod.

Scarborough stood up. 'Okay. I think we're done here. Charge me or I'm leaving. Now.'

'Sit down Mr Scarborough. We're bringing Cilla Breslin in for questioning. You can sit tight until then. Meantime, you're free to call your lawyer, should you wish to.'

Thursday afternoon was cool, the approach of winter's sting

carried in the air that rushed up Cal's jacket sleeves and through the helmet vents.

Nearly home, she turned into Holmwood Street following an SUV. The driver suddenly stopped and began reversing in a three-point turn. *Fuck's sake.* Cal braked and waited, now exposed in the middle of two intersecting roads and oncoming traffic.

Once Mr SUV was done, she continued down Holmwood, turned into the back lane and parked outside the fence. As she opened the garage door a movement further down the laneway caught her eye. A man stood against a brick wall adjoining the footpath. He was bizarrely propped, with skewed feet some distance out from the wall, his body above angling in to where the side of his head and cheek plastered against the brickwork. He wore black shorts, a black cap and black trainers, with a white shirt tossed over his shoulder.

Cal watched him moving along the wall, swaying and stumbling. Perhaps he was injured. Did he need help? He continued, veering into and away from the side of the wall, his head sustaining each impact as he slid and bumped along towards the corner. Where the wall ended, he almost fell into the gap of the crossing footpath. As he staggered and straightened, negotiating his way across the intersection, she realised he was drunk.

She wheeled the bike into the garage and closed the door. Normally happy to work in the laneway and catch a bit of sun, this bike wasn't hers and she wasn't taking any risks. She took off her jacket, went inside to make a coffee, and returned to the machine to give it a final tweak and polish before the service next morning.

∽

Ottering ushered Cilla Breslin into the interview room. Birch followed her in and closed the door. Close-up and in better lighting than when she'd last seen her outside the club, Ottering still couldn't believe the girl was older than twelve. They'd picked her up after work at her retail job in Downtown Jeans. She was pale and thin. The four-inch heels that elevated her height only magnified her fragility. She looked like she might blow over in a draught.

Ottering offered her a drink.

'Diet Coke.'

Birch went to the dispenser outside in the hall, came back with a can.

'Can I get a straw? Or a glass?'

Birch disappeared again. Ottering waited until he returned with a glass.

'How long have you known Terry Scarborough?'

'Long time. Since school. Everyone knows him, the family.' Cilla shrugged, turned her glass back and forth.

'So, you knew him at school?'

'No.' Indignant. 'Not at school. He's way older. Just everyone knows who he is. The club. And his dad was some footy hero. They're like, famous.'

'Where did you meet him?'

'The club, I guess.'

'You can't remember?'

'What's he done? Am I in trouble?'

Ottering did the *good cop* smile. 'You're not in trouble. We're just asking questions of a number of people, trying to piece together events around an incident.'

'What incident? Those murders? Terry's not like that.'

Ottering took a breath, held it. 'Miss Breslin…'

'That sounds funny. Call me Cilla.'

Birch's lower jaw moved up, his lips pooched. He remained silent behind the girl.

'What do you know about his activities?'

'Activities?'

'Aside from being an owner of the club. What else does he do? Who does he hang around with? You must socialise together.' Ottering's pen balanced between her thumb and forefingers.

'Just likes me on his arm at the club. That's it.'

'You're his girlfriend. You must spend time with him.'

'Doesn't want me round any other time. Gets irritated.'

'Must be a frustrating sort of arrangement.'

'Won't like me talking to you.' She ran the base of her glass through the wet ring underneath it, back and forth.

'At the club, does Terry have business meetings with clients?'

'Sometimes. Nature of the game, I guess. Those hours.'

'So you'd be privy to those meetings?'

'Sorry?' Cilla stopped moving her glass.

'You'd be present?'

'He'd send me out to the bar or one of the private rooms.'

'Private rooms?'

Priscilla Breslin's face showed confusion, then fear, then a failed impassivity.

'Private rooms for what purpose?' Ottering asked.

'It's private. I wouldn't know.' Breslin looked triumphant.

Ottering flicked a look at Birch who came from behind the girl, stood over the desk, pulled a photograph from a file. Phillip Leuwins.

'Know this man?' Ottering watched her face, saw the flash of recognition and the cover-up.

'No.'

'Why are you lying?'

'I'm not lying.'

'Are you afraid of Terry Scarborough?'

She stared at Ottering.

'What time did you leave the club on Wednesday night?'

'Bit after midnight.'

'Where did you go?'

'Home.'

'Terry Scarborough drove you?'

'Yes.'

'Did you stop anywhere on the way?'

'He went to Macca's. Then dropped me off.'

'So you got home when?'

'About quarter to one. I had work in the morning.'

Ottering pushed the photo in front of her again. 'You've seen this man?'

Cilla Breslin set her finely-boned jaw, looked quickly at the photo, then beyond Ottering's shoulder. 'Do I have to stay here?'

'You're just helping with our inquiries. You're not obliged to stay.'

She pushed her chair back, looked at Birch. 'Can you give me a lift home?'

10

Friday morning Cal was up early to prepare for Addie's service in King's Cross. She'd laid out her gear the night before and wanted to leave plenty of time to check the bike again before she left. She'd missed a call while she was showering. She picked up a voicemail message.

It was from Di. 'We're having a memorial service for Pip. Friday week, to give people time to organise travel. Hope you can make it.'

What a week. Too much to process. As Cal closed the door and went to the garage, she felt the inside pocket of her jacket, checked for the folded cloth beside her heart. She remembered the day many years ago when she'd received it.

'Toots, I've got something for you.'

Cal, nervous. Could be a ten-ton Acme weight dropped on her head Roadrunner style; could be something squirmy they had to talk about, but framed in the offer of a gift to get her attention. She didn't dare speak lest her voice shook. A pair of raised eyebrows and fake wonder sufficed.

Addie held a crisply-folded red cloth towards her on the flat of the back of her hand. Even her gestures had their own twist.

'Addie, I never knew you ironed. What is it?' Cal reached out, hoping it was something she liked so she wouldn't be embarrassed.

Addie waited, beaming.

'Oh darl.' Cal held up the corners, unfurling a Harley Davidson bandanna. 'It's gorgeous.'

'Been saving it for you. Found it on the footpath in Surry Hills.' She must've noticed the puritan streaking through Cal's eyes. 'It's all right, I have washed it.'

'Don't want it for yourself?'

'Had your name on it, Toots.'

Cal held it to her chest, then began folding it into a triangle to tie around her forehead, but she stopped. 'Don't be offended, darl. Can't wear it til I get my bike on the road again. Just can't.'

'Of course. That won't be too long now, will it? You're living the pauper's lifestyle, stowing those pennies?'

~

Outside the Wayside Chapel in King's Cross, Cal paced backwards and forwards. She looked up and down the road, returned inside, came back outside, looked down the road. The rain had started again.

The White Ladies Funeral Service. The name was so camp that Cal thought Addie was just winding them all up when she said they were organising her funeral. Eventually it had sunken in that they weren't a product of Addie's rich fantasy life. They were, in fact, a solid business entity and who else but The White Ladies could have done Addie's service? They were perfect.

At the bottom corner of the narrow King's Cross street, the white limo spanned the entire width as it slowly approached and parked opposite the chapel steps. The diminutive driver, Helena, climbed out, immaculate right down to her ivory-toned cotton gloves.

Helena smiled and came over, taking Cal's hands in her own. Cal hoped she wouldn't soil them. In her Johnny Reb boots she towered over Helena.

'Bit nervous.' Cal clung to her warm hands.

Helena smiled again and her eyes twinkled through the sparkling glasses. 'You'll do just fine. Go nice and slowly and we'll keep together. Don't worry if you lose us, we'll catch up.'

Cal managed a small smile. 'Come and see my bike. Spent half the night polishing all the metal and paintwork.' Helena approached the machine behind her.

'Couple of white Harleys would look great as part of your permanent entourage.' Cal leaned on the seat, beaming at her.

'They really would look lovely, wouldn't they?'

'Ever ridden on a Harley, Helena? I could take you for a spin out at the crematorium.'

Helena's eyes fluttered. 'Oh, I'm much too old for that, I think. I wish I'd had your courage when I was young.'

'Never too old. There are women over sixty riding these things, so you won't get away with that.' Cal laughed.

There was movement up on the steps of the Chapel forecourt. Maur motioned for Cal to come up. It was time to put Addie's coffin in the hearse.

People poured out into the open to light up and chat. The doorways and back aisles were crowded during the service. Even though Cal knew most of the faces she was blinkered by her sense of purpose. She looked for Maur and the others who were to carry the coffin. A Bette Midler song ushered everyone from indoors. Cal realised they could've been funeral marching to one of Addie's ambient meditation tapes and somehow Bette's warbling of 'The Wind Beneath My Wings' became bearable.

Maur and the others were waiting up the front by the coffin. She put an arm out as Cal came closer. 'How you going?' Maureen had dealt with all the outsiders and authorities while coping with her own feelings about their dying friend. Cal couldn't have done it.

'I'm okay.'

'C'mon, you take the back corner.' Maur gave Cal a gentle push. The six women lined up alongside the dark, wooden panels.

The others were all dressed in black suits. *Least we all look sharp,* Cal thought. As they each grasped a handle she considered how heavy it might be. On Maur's say-so they lifted and Cal was surprised at the weight. *Lucky we're all strong.*

As they carried Addie up the aisle, she wondered what was the appropriate acknowledgement of her friends. Solemn or smiling? She fixed her face into some combination of both, a half grimace.

They emerged onto the landing as the smokers parted to let them through.

'Okay, everyone?' Maur paused before the steps. They all assented. Cal was relieved they were nearly there, shocked at how weighted the coffin was with Addie not cooperating.

She noticed there was another Harley parked in front of the hearse and a tall woman in a full-length Driza-Bone was standing beside it smoking. She wasn't familiar.

Helena held the wide rear door of the hearse and motioned for them to lift the coffin to the carpeted bed. Cal's left hand felt the brass handle welded into her flesh. Sliding the coffin in was awkward, they got in each other's way as the front ones cleared. *Not something we've had much practice at,* she thought.

'That's lovely, girls, you've done a sterling job,' Helena said.

'How are you getting out there?' Cal asked Maur.

'I'll go in the second hearse. You okay?' she asked again.

'Yeh. Just anxious about leading.' Cal tipped her head slightly towards the other Harley.

'Looks like Addie gets the full escort.'

'Do you know her?' Maur asked.

'Never seen her before.'

Cal walked over to the stranger and held out her hand. 'I'm Cal. Nice bike.'

A blue, Dyna Street Bob. Her grip was warm and strong. She was tanned and statuesque. 'Thanks. I'm Marcella.' Her accent was French.

Why have I never seen you around? Cal wondered. 'You here to lead the cortège? Did you know Addie?'

'I heard about Addie from my flatmate. She knew one of the other women you were asking to ride.'

Cal nodded, intent, hoping she didn't look gormless.

'I knew Addie from years ago, up around here.' Marcella swung her head. Her accent was so strong Cal couldn't imagine that she'd been there for years, but plenty of other ex-pats managed it so, why not.

'Great you're here. Let's do it.'

∼

They rode as slowly as they could, trying to keep the long procession together. She was proud to be leading Addie's funeral with another queer on a Harley, proud to carry her body.

Under a grey sky they rode slowly away from the city along Anzac Parade. Nearing the coast, Cal caught glimpses of the sea beyond the cliffs. The drizzle stopped. Like a dark roof breaking apart, the clouds slid away.

She rode around the tidy rosebeds where the thorny regiments were doing their last autumn bloom. She did several circuits, unsure where to park and the people clustered among the borders were looking her way in an unwelcoming manner. The noisy bike. *Where's the bloody car park?* Helena in the hearse wasn't following her at that stage. Cal guessed she'd been there enough times to know where to go. She'd also lost Marcella just beyond the entrance. Maybe she'd missed a sign. *Why does everything have to be discreet in these places? It's not like the dead are gonna be offended. A few well-placed, lairy neons wouldn't go amiss.* She found her way back to where she'd started, spotted Marcella's bike and pulled up behind it. She was still unsure if it was a parking area but they weren't going to be long.

~

'Bring her back girls, then feet first into the chapel and onto the platform.' Helena's duties with them were almost over. They pulled Addie out of the hearse. Some of the pallbearers had changed so others got a turn. Not Cal, possessive of her dead friend. She was in a trance, down along the aisles of the enormous, bright chapel. Carry the coffin feet first. *Jesus it's heavy. Feet first into the flames not head first. Why?* She thought of Joan of Arc burning at the stake, alive to her own slow death, the flames beginning at her soles. *But Addie's not alive.* The frangipani-topped coffin disappeared behind the curtain.

Afterwards, Cal went outside, stood back against a sunny wall at the chapel entrance and watched Marcella through a loose grouping of people. She had a femme aesthetic with a stroppy edge. Her hair was shortish but well cut and coloured. It would've curled if it was longer but it was just stylishly unruly. Her front teeth protruded slightly, so her lips formed a constant pout. Her walk and manner pronounced strength, self-containment rather than arrogance. Her jaw was well defined without being heavy. Cal found her physicality fascinating. She watched her standing away from the others. She seemed comfortable enough being the outsider.

Cal walked over to her. 'Are you going to the wake?' Cal asked, smiling.

'We go for coffee first?'

'Yeh, sure. Back up the Cross? I'll follow you.'

They fired up the bikes and rode sedately out along the driveway and the rural-looking road that had led them in, scrubby and sparse and devoid of houses. Cal's body felt languid, like she was drugged. It was over. She felt as though she'd been operating from the shoulders up for a long time. *Need to take my head off.*

～

Marcella pulled up at the T-intersection before the left turn towards town. The back of her Street Bob rode so low the tails of her Driza-Bone dragged on the road without the wind flying them. She opened the throttle and sped into the traffic, shooting off down the centre line, weaving as the tyre slid on the white strip marker.

Cal laughed, checked to her right and took off after her. The traffic was moving fast, three lanes deep and the pair were about fifteen kilometres from town. Cal dodged cars and changed lanes, found a gap, powered on, braked hard, snaked in, blasting between vehicles in the minimal gap. Marcella was still getting away from her. She could ride. Harleys weren't the easiest bikes to fling through traffic. Long and heavy, they felt like they were hinged in the middle. Cal could see a gap, decide the manoeuvre in her head, flick her relevant body parts in the right direction and crank open the throttle. Unfortunately, the Harley's response wasn't instantaneous so she'd have to factor that in as it was all happening. It all had to be instinctive, there was no time to think. Nothing became instinctive until you'd done it numerous times. Many didn't survive the learning curve.

She knew she shouldn't be riding like that in traffic. Marcella was in the clear up ahead. Cal slipped across two lanes, gunned the bike up 50m of space before a parked car, running out of room to pass the last two cars on the inside, pushed it harder, drove her body into the tank, yanked hard on the throttle, ground her teeth as she squeezed through the gap with her knees pulled in. She kept riding across the lanes and slowed up in the free lane beside Marcella, a huge grin on her face. Marcella was riding one-handed, looked over, big grin there too.

~

After Marcella left, Cal sat in a park in the Cross, the setting sun behind her, warmth on her back. Across the grass, nine small brown birds sat, all pointed in one direction, while a solitary one faced back at them, like a choir mistress about to tap her baton. Was she keeping watch for the others or about to lead them in a tune?

On top of a rubbish bin, an ibis pulled debris from the hole and dropped it to the other ibis, gulls and pigeons gathered below. Nice teamwork.

She had to return the bike. Get back to her mission. A warm bed was little comfort when you couldn't sleep. *One more ride. To the coast. Clear my head, refocus.*

The air was cool but not cold as she rode east towards South Head, following the high cliff road towards Dover Heights and Bondi.

She parked and locked the bike, crossed the grassland towards the cliffs. She used to visit there when she'd first come to live with Zin, desperate to find somewhere wild and unsafe, in that broiling, alien land. She found the cliffs and sat on the rocks in the middle of the night, below her the incessant, pulsing rumble of an ocean hurling itself against rock. In the face of such noise, all else was obliterated.

It wasn't until she'd met Pip she learnt it was a beat, just south of where she used to crouch and cry. Gay men thrown from the edge onto the rocks below. Queers knew it was hate crime. The police did nothing.

She thought about what Gigi had said, Terry Scarborough having sex with gay men. Presumably using beats. And Pip worked at his bar semi-regularly.

She rang Gigi. 'Being a pest, I know. Need another favour.'
'Speak, pumpkin.'
'Beats out Richmond way, especially anything off-radar.'
'Girl, you know I rarely leave King Street. Brings on anxiety. Pete'll have a better idea. Get back to you.'

11

Scobie sat in a swivel chair she'd pulled to the front of a desk. Birch had preliminaries from the techs. 'Of course, the burning of Phillip Leuwins's pick-up destroyed all the trace evidence. Forensics are trying to identify some material from the fry-up in the tray and cab. They're not hopeful.'

'That's why they torch 'em,' Cobbin grunted.

Ottering spoke. 'Got the gen on the artworks at the Toblensk property. Large pen and ink in the living room, Mike Parr. The little sardine can thing, Fiona Hall. In the bedroom, the triptych, Richard Bell. A Rosalie Gascoigne in the man-cave. Bloody who's who. Worth heaps.'

'And they're still hanging on the walls?' Scobie asked.

'Far as I know. There earlier this week.'

'So how much are they worth? Are we looking at a motive in terms of inheritance? Who would've known their value?'

'Exactly. Legals got back to me this arvo. The Toblensk property was left to Phillip Leuwins until his death, at which time it reverted to family,' Ottering said.

'So he could live there but not sell it?' Cobbin said.

'That's what I understand.'

'Did that include the artworks?' said Scobie.

'I'm assuming that formed part of his estate. I'll check it with legals.'

'So if his estate reverted to family on Phillip Leuwins's death, the sister in Vic is the beneficiary?' Cobbin said.

'Looks that way.'

'Are we sure there's no other family?' Scobie again.

'Decent motive,' Cobbin said.

Avery yawned loudly and stretched his arms above his head. 'How did Toblensk afford stuff like that?

'Bought them early in their careers,' Ottering replied. 'Definitely had an eye and a feel for upcoming artists. He wanted to support them. Bought before they went stratospheric.'

Avery pulled a face. 'How'd you know all this?'

'Spoke to the dealers who sold to him. His mother was an art historian. Always had an interest. Developed his appreciation via her. Picked up small pieces whenever he could afford it. He was never wealthy, but he was comfortable and he surrounded himself with pieces he felt passionate about.'

'Somone's done their homework.' Cobbin was smiling when Ottering looked up.

Scobie spoke. 'Thanks, Janice. How are we doing on the affair Stefan Toblensk was supposedly having?'

'That information came from his sister. How reliable can it be? Specially if she's the main beneficiary.' Birch pared a small pencil over a rubbish bin with his penknife.

'You're a cynical man, Frank.'

'Makes for a good cop.' He smiled grimly at his boss.

'She was a beneficiary until Phillip Leuwins was killed,' Avery said.

Sometimes Ottering wondered why Avery had joined the force. 'No. She was a beneficiary after he was killed. It's now reverted back to the Toblensk family. That's Sylvia. Would Di Leuwins know anything?'

Avery spoke again. 'If it was an affair, presumably it was hidden. Not going to be easy to dig things up.'

'But the sister, Sylvia, said they had an arrangement. It wasn't necessarily secret,' Ottering answered.

'Okay. Maybe just discreet then,' Cobbin added.

'Could be to throw us off,' Birch said.

'Their personal effects. We'll go back through it all. We have a new focus,' Scobie said. Groans all round. 'There must be some giveaway somewhere. We'll split teams and material. Fresh eyes.' She turned to Birch. 'How did the Breslin interview go?'

'She's scared of him. No surprise. We're all aware of his form.'

'I'm sure she recognised Phillip Leuwins,' Ottering said.

'He worked at the club sometimes.' Avery yawned.

'Why would she hide that? Doesn't make sense. It's like she recognised him in a way that wasn't good. She was definitely hiding something.'

'I agree,' Birch said. 'Pressuring her won't work. We need to find another angle.'

'Keep on it, you two. What else have we got? Tony? Glen?'

'We followed Cal Nyx, Thursday. Early afternoon, she left home on a Harley registered to Nicko da Silva.' Cobbin paused. 'Currently on remand in Silverwater. She rode to a café near Central, alone. Didn't meet anyone there. Left and walked up to Surry Hills. Got buzzed into a brothel.'

Ottering worked her keyboard. 'Little Buckingham Street?'

'Yup.'

'It's a dungeon.'

Scobie uncrossed and recrossed her ankles but didn't speak. Birch looked over to where Cobbin and Avery sat. Avery smirked.

'Not a crime,' Ottering said.

'Anything else?' Scobie asked.

Cobbin continued. 'She rode home after that. Didn't leave until Friday morning. We followed her to King's Cross. A funeral service. She hooked up with another rider. We tailed her to La Perouse, the crematorium. She left there...'

The incident room was silent but for the burr of the aircon.

Avery shook his head.

'And?' Scobie said.

'We lost them in traffic.' Cobbin dropped his head.

'Jesus, Tony.' Scobie stood.

'Bikes in traffic. We didn't have a shitshow.'

'Which way were they headed when you lost them?' Ottering.

'City. Doesn't mean much. Only two ways, city or coast.'

Scobie went to the visuals board. 'We can't afford to keep the tail on her.'

'But she has a past with Leuwins. She's riding a bike owned by a crim. She's as likely as any of them. And what's she doing in a brothel? Hello?' Avery raised his arms.

Deflecting attention from the fact they lost her, Ottering thought.

'We've got so little,' Scobie said, scanning the board.

'We've got to stay on her. And Scarborough,' Avery said. 'That's all we've got.'

'Could say the same about Dolan and Pratt,' Birch offered. 'Don't forget who was at the Toblensk property that night.'

'Drop it for now,' Scobie said.

'Scarborough was on that road...' Ottering said.

'One more day, boss. We're trying to find what she's got to do with da Silva. He's drugs. Scarborough's clubs. Leuwins has a club connection. Nyx has a link to two of those heads,' Avery whined.

Scobie stood. 'Twelve hours. No more. Make it count. Then we're focussing on Scarborough.' She stood and headed for the door. 'Chop-chop, people.'

Saturday morning, Zin swept leaves and dirt from the corners of the yard, shifted pots, whisked with her broom, left small piles. *I need a honeysuckle,* she thought. *Either trimmed into a little bush or running along that fence.* She loved the scent, so lemony and the delicate flowers, cream and gold. Like little fairies among the leaves. That's what she'd thought as a child. Winter's approach always made her think of spring flowers.

She heard the throb of the Harley's exhaust as Cal turned into the laneway and parked outside the gate. She leaned on her broom as Cal appeared, came over and hugged her. 'Stranger.'

'You'll be happy to see me when you get a gander what's in my bag.' Cal unlocked the garage door, rolled the machine inside then locked up.

'Already happy to see you. Silly.' Zin whisked an errant leaf.

Cal pulled a pair of brown paper bags, already darkened with butter-spots from her rucksack. She waved them under Zin's nose. Her eyes opened wide as she smelled the delicious aroma.

'*Black Star.*' Zin loved the tiny hole-in-the-wall patisserie.

'Tomato and onion tarts. Get the kettle on.'

~

Cal planned to return the bike to Tommy after breakfast. As she pulled on her jacket, her phone rang. Gigi. 'Pete's guy lives in the lower mountains so this is pretty up to date.'

Cal grabbed a pen and turned over an old shopping receipt, ready to take down Gigi's list of beats.

'Patterson Park at the northern walkway end, not the playground end, obviously. The Gull truck-stop on the western freeway. Lowlands River Park, between the river walk and the back of the grandstand. I need to get out more, don't I, pumpkin.'

Cal could hear paper rustling.

'Okay, on the back here, and he said there'd be others, small localised ones, but he tried to confine it to where you said. So, last two, Crockett Road North, the lay-by, loos. And Misty's Landing, the track to the old boat ramp. Lordy. Hope these make sense to you. Back to it, pumpkin.'

'So grateful, Gigi. You're a honey.' Cal thumbed the red icon and stared at the list. She needed to check them all, but the last name sent a menacing chill up her spine. *That day I saw the blond guy, Nolly, bogged on that track beside the river.* She brought up a map on her phone, zoomed in, found the turnoff, the old boat landing where the campground had been. The track below the main road. *Spot on. Jesus.*

∼

She rode to Tommy's and returned the Harley, scoring a lift back to town on the back of his own machine as he had business to attend to in the city. Not used to being a pillion, she willed a semi-relaxed mode into her limbs, acknowledging to herself that it had nothing to do with her trust in his riding ability. She managed to enjoy the ride, despite herself. By the time they reached home she felt like some kind of tourist.

She waved him off at the end of the lane, stashed her bike gear and gathered clothes and a thermos of coffee.

The boot of the car was hazed with dust and grime. She tossed her gear on the back seat and started the engine, letting it warm up as she considered the rest of her day. Where to begin? She needed to make good use of this time. Terry Scarborough. Could he lead her to anything? Misty's and that Nolly guy. She had some places to start. *Looks like I'm heading out of town to my other gaff. For now.*

She blipped the throttle. Though familiar, it felt a little confining to be surrounded again by glass and steel. She wound down both front windows and eased the Ford out into the lane.

As she headed west she called Di and put her on speakerphone. 'How've you been, girl? All set for Friday week?'

'Slow process isn't it. Good days and bad days. Police got in touch with me again. Asked about affairs, other lovers Stef and Pip might have had. Wanted to know if they ever discussed them.'

'Right.' Cal paused.

'Guess it's just another line of inquiry. I had a general knowledge of it, the concept. It's private though, isn't it? No names ever mentioned.'

'No. Agreed. They're digging everywhere, huh. Something's gotta turn up. On my way back to the mountains myself. Gonna have another sniff around. Take care, Di. See you next Friday if not before.'

∼

Liz Scobie kicked off her shoes, poured herself a pinot gris, sat in a chair beside the french doors and looked at her watch. Four more hours. At roughly ten thirty that night, the surveillance on Cal Nyx would end. For now.

As Cal headed towards the lower mountains she decided to visit Scarborough's club, Brontos, first. Get a feel for the place, the punters. Whenever she drove that route, she remembered years ago, visiting Pip one night in the psych bin. She'd been clubbing. It was late, she couldn't sleep. She borrowed a car on a whim and went on a midnight jaunt. The only other time she'd been to Richmond before then had been in daylight, a camping trip with some friends. She had remembered old apple orchards. That wasn't going to help her find a psych ward in a rehab in the middle of the night. But she had done it.

They had sneaked outside and smoked in the dark until dawn.

A dog owned by one of the staff wandered in a swampy patch of ground, rolling on its back in the soft grass beneath young paperbarks. It had made Cal think of summer. 'I was brought up by wolves,' she said.

'Did the wolves teach you how to iron?'

They had gone back inside. She had stared along the hallways to where light poured into a room at the far end, morning sun illuminating the distant space like something seen by a person coming out of coma. She had opened and closed her eyes, watching the different intensities of light playing on the walls of each room as she stared up along the corridor. Were clouds moving across the sky, bringing the light on, fading it back, each time she opened her eyes? The quality of light seemed to have altered.

It had been spring, the world was warming up. When she had walked out the door into the morning, the heat hit her like a falling wall.

A histrionic barking nearby brought her back into the present. Nightime, cool autumn air.

She walked around to the other side of the Ford. Across the car park, a small area of tarmac, bordered with temporary fence barriers, contained a chaotic assemblage of machinery, broken concrete, and pallets loaded with pavers. The council investing in some beautification works.

She followed the noise of the yapping to the far side of the car park, but there were no backyards there, no obvious signs of dog habitation. She scanned further and saw a boy with a skateboard mooching around a parked car. She stopped and watched him. Two small chihuahua type cross-breeds were leaping about inside the car, one throwing itself alternately at the passenger and driver's side windows. The other tried to get onto the rear parcel shelf, protecting the rear, but fell back onto the seat due to the cushions piled on the rear ledge.

The youth leaned on the rear spoiler of the car while balancing on his board.

'Is that your car?' Cal asked, thinking it odd the dogs would bark at him if it was and wondering why he would continue to provoke them if it wasn't.

'No, I'm waiting for someone,' he mumbled, not looking at her, pulling a phone from his pocket and looking intently at the screen.

'Why are you winding up the dogs? You're pissing them off. Why don't you move away?'

He continued fingering his phone, moved slightly from actually touching the car, but not much.

'Moron,' Cal said as she turned and walked away. She stood at the edge of the car park mess watching him, still near the car, though the dogs had calmed down. Cal pulled out her own phone and reapproached the youth, taking two pictures of him by the car, then returned to the Ford.

Five minutes later she walked into the club. She ordered a beer and sat in a booth in the back corner where she could watch both doors. The overriding smell of hops from the beer taps was a comforting one. The same couldn't be said for the lab-concocted version of what passed for perfume these days. Jesus. Everyone smelt like fly spray or toilet cleaner. What the fuck? How could people stand that under their own noses? Let alone imposing the stench on everyone around them. She took a long glug from her beer. It was early, just after eight. The DJ wouldn't arrive before 10.30. A mix of dance music from the previous ten years played at a sedate level until the place got busy. She did a search of Terry Scarborough on her phone and got a good sense of his appearance.

At a nearby table a young couple sat and talked but she could hear only the male voice, speaking loudly about dancers. 'The only pair in the country.' He went on about various fallings out in the company, his voice an annoying rasp as he gesticulated energetically. Cal could see that in her periphery, determined not to look. That might encourage him. She wondered if she needed more sleep. She was so irritable. Perhaps the woman at the table was deaf-mute? She hadn't spoken. Cal silently begged her to, hoping the volume would be reduced and she could concentrate on her other surrounds. Still, the strident pronouncements went on, as if he had just learnt some voice-throwing techniques at a workshop and was trying them out. Then, 'Enough about me, I want to hear about you, your life.'

Do people actually say that to one another? Cal took a sip of her beer. Nope. Obviously, the speaker wanted to hear about the friend's life at a later date because still he held forth, despite the disingenuous invite to his companion. Cal searched around the bar for another booth. Then noticed a movement of hands on the adjoining table, and realised the woman was actually speaking. She hadn't even heard her. The second voice was an inverse of the other, as though some cosmic force had deemed such a paired volume quotient necessary for a table of that dimension. Though momentarily relieved, Cal spotted an empty cubicle in the opposite corner of the bar. She moved there before the first speaker resumed.

She remained inside for an hour. No sight of Scarborough. Not entirely surprising. As an owner he wouldn't need to be there all the time anyway. Still, it was worth a try. Cal went outside to where the Ford was parked on the far side of the lot. As she left she noticed the gold Nissan in one of the manager parks. *So he is here. Okay. I might hang around.*

She sat in the car and watched the rear door of the bar. A guard who didn't look big or threatening enough, kept an eye on the comings and goings. *Maybe he's one of those ex-SAS assassins, small and deadly.*

Adjoining the car park, behind an irregular series of hedges and tree-plantings, a parkland and series of sports fields ran off into the distance. At the near end, a sort of play area under a group of fig trees.

She could hear something beyond the arrhythmic chaos of the fruit bats in the trees, and noticed a movement in the darkness. A girl on a swing holding her phone, arcing high, the flash of her screen visible at the high point of her trajectory. Cal watched, mesmerised by the moving light. The thrum of the Nissan broke her trance. She turned the ignition, waited for the other car to leave, then followed it from the lot.

12

Cobbin and Avery waited a few moments then tailed Cal Nyx from the Brontos car park.

'Why's she following Scarborough?' Avery drove.

'She's heading north-west, what's that? Hawkesbury?' Cobbin checked his online map.

'Scarborough lives out that way, on the flats.'

'Drop back a bit more. No traffic out here.' Cobbin brought up Scarborough's address. They followed for seven minutes heading north-west. 'Looks like he's going home. Slow up. There's a rise three hundred metres from his place. Pull off there. We can still see where they're going.'

They watched as the first car turned off left into the long driveway. Lights showed up the house and outbuildings in the distance. Cal Nyx continued past the driveway and drove north along the flats.

'Where's she going?'

'Sticks. Might just be throwing Scarborough off.'

There was only darkness on the right-hand side of the road towards the river. Rows of bare poplars ranked in angled plantings held their spiked arms high. On the other side of the road, a driveway entrance appeared every few kilometres, most unlighted.

'Why's she heading up bush? Middle of the night.' Avery slowed his speed.

'She's a crim. It's dodgy hour.'

'No one else out here. She'll know she's being tailed. Isn't this the way to Misty's?'

'Look stupid if we stop now.'

Ten clicks further on they passed a sign for Misty's Landing. Ahead of them, taillights flared in the blackness as Cal Nyx hit the brakes.

'She's turning off. Keep going. Just keep going past.' Cobbin wheezed as Cal Nyx made a right turn towards the waterway.

~

Cal turned off Juta Road into the old campground track that followed the river inland. She watched in her rear-view as the dark Falcon sedan with two men in the front seat carried on along the main route. They'd been following her since Bronto's. Coppers.

Even with her lights on full-beam the road wasn't as familiar coming from the opposite direction and in total darkness. She tried to recall where she'd seen Nolly Pratt that day when she'd returned from the bush site. She'd just crossed the bridge, coming from north to south.

When she saw the small yellow reflective sign indicating the overpass, she slowed and looked for the side track down to the river on her left. There was a break in the scrub on the verge. She wasn't in her four-wheel drive work truck. No good risking the track in the Ford, even though there'd been no rain. Too isolated. She coasted to the side of the road, parked, grabbed her torch and got out.

The roots of the casuarina trees formed a lacework of

knuckled steps down the slope to the river. She shone her torch along the banks but couldn't see any other vehicles from where she was. Picked her way along the rough access way, just to get a sense of it. It ran several kilometres in both directions, following the path of the river. She stopped and listened, hearing the occasional rustling of a nocturnal animal, nothing more. Made her way back along the track, no distant traffic noise, just the quiet of the bush and the silent river.

Maybe it's a daytime-only beat. Is there such a thing? Who'd know it's a beat? Only those looking for trade? So, if I give that bloke the benefit of the doubt, what was he doing here that day? Fishing? Just hanging out? If this is a beat what are the chances Stef and Pip used it? Was that Nolly bloke here for trade or as a basher? Think I need to pay him a visit, or check him out at least.

She got back to the car and started it, drove forwards looking for somewhere wide enough to turn around. She nosed across the bridge and saw a wider verge ahead where she could make a three-point turn. The car didn't feel quite right, even considering the rough nature of the track. Her steering was washing out on the offside. She stopped and got out with her torch, walked to the other side. Flat tyre on the left front. Dammit. Travelling long distances in the country meant flat tyres were inevitable. It had been awhile so she was probably overdue.

Least it didn't happen when I was fanging it, she thought as she lifted the jack and spare from the boot. Less than ten minutes later she had the spare bolted on, the jack lowered and the flat tyre poised to go into the boot. She shone her torch and felt across the rubber surface with her fingers, feeling for some protrusion. Eventually her fingertips ran over the roughened head of a long, metal screw, embedded deep into the tread. Could've picked that up on a road somewhere. Or maybe someone gave it a little help. Give me a slow leak. Accidental or what? She heaved the flat into the boot, closed it and dusted off her jeans.

It was 2.13am. Where to now? *I need images. I need to go to beats, talk to guys.*

She texted Di, asked her to send a recent photo of Pip. Hoped Di had her phone on silent.

~

Avery continued past Misty's Landing and powered up the hill towards Boarback Ridge.

'Now what? There's no one out here. We can't follow her. We can't get back there without her seeing or hearing us. What the hell is she doing out here?' The bush scared Avery. In daylight, it went as far as you could see. It all looked the same. It was full of snakes and you could die out there. You could die anywhere. But at least the urban environment was familiar. Concrete and roads and garbage.

'All we can do is wait. Can't sneak up on her out here. She can only come this way or back the way we came.' Cobbin fingered and scrolled the online map.

'We're in the neighbourhood. Could check on some of the others.' Avery reached behind the seat, fossicked in his sports bag, pulled out an unnaturally coloured energy drink. 'What the fuck is she doing down there at the river? Should we go back on foot?'

'We can't surprise her. We can't get within a kilometre in the car without her hearing. It's too far to walk. She'll see our torchlight and we can't do it in the dark. Let's just park up, lights out. See when she passes. If nothing else it'll give us a time fix on how long she's there.'

'Presuming she doesn't go back the other way and we miss her altogether. Fuck's sake. I'm starving.'

~

Mid-morning, Craig Dolan pulled up next to the pumps and got out, hitching his belt as he walked to the other side of the pick-up and unlocked the petrol cap. He pulled his shirt away from his back where it was already sticking in the heat, noted Pratt's silver station wagon parked beside the open door of the workshop. He couldn't see anyone through the entranceway. There were two vehicles inside, one on a hoist. Dolan put the hose nozzle into the filler-neck and clicked the autofill catch before wandering over. He peered inside, walked around a mud-spattered Nissan Patrol with the bonnet up. At the front of the truck Nolly Pratt lay on a crawler holding a work light in one hand as he ran the other hand across the bottom of the radiator. He heard someone beside him, his sight temporarily blinded by the bright LED work light. He slid out beside the heavy steel-capped work boots. Dolan stared down at him.

'Ayyy, Craigo.' Pratt got up, switched the light off.

''Cha been up to?'

'Busy here. You?' Pratt wiped his hands on a rag. 'Coffee?'

Dolan stood his ground. 'Cops been talking to ya?'

'Coupla times.' Pratt looked towards the door.

Dolan folded his arms. 'What they ask ya?'

Pratt pushed past Dolan, went to a small alcove beside the tyre machine. A fridge and bench coated uniformly in grime and fingermarks formed the kitchen. Pratt flicked on a blackened kettle and scooped instant coffee into a mug. 'Usual shit. 'Bout those guys.' He opened the fridge. It contained a litre carton of milk, and a tomato sauce squeezer.

'How many times they visit ya?'

Pratt mixed the milk and coffee first before pouring the water. He overfilled. 'Shit.' Shook his hand off. 'Couple.'

A semi-trailer pulled up beside the pumps outside. The hiss of the air brakes gave Pratt a start.

'Need a ciggy. Come outside.'

Dolan went to the pumps, clicked off the nozzle catch,

replaced the cap. When he returned, Pratt was smoking beside the air hose, flicking a loose strand of tobacco from his thumb.

'What'd they wanna know? Specifically.' The last word said with emphasis.

'Fuck me. Chill man. Just usual shit. How I knew them, when I saw them. Was I there that Friday?' He blew smoke up over his head. 'Wish I wasn't working today. Be nice on the river.'

'Let me know if they come again. Don't like all this attention. Never seen so many fuckin' coppers.' He turned to walk off.

'Mate, chill. You should be enjoying this sunshine.' Pratt stubbed out his ciggy, tossed the butt into a forty-gallon drum full of rusty water.

Dolan turned back to him. Pointed his thick, calloused index finger. 'Maybe you need to be a little less casual.' He wasn't smiling.

～

Sunday morning, Cal's phone buzzed with a text. Unknown number.

Pinks for drinks?

Cal texted back.

Who's this?

LS.

Cal smiled, felt a small jolt of excitement nudge her stomach. She looked out through the windscreen.

～

Sunday morning in the incident room, Scobie worked with Ottering and Birch. Cobbin and Avery were late.

'Do we need to go to Vic and interview Sylvia Toblensk? She's not been interviewed previously, has she?' Ottering asked.

'When her brother was murdered, she was informed as next-of-kin. Not interviewed as a suspect. So, the answer is no.'

'When it happened or after it happened?'

'Dunno if that was established. She was simply informed of his death. Next-of-kin.'

'She's now the beneficiary of the property, and the estate presumably includes the artworks. We need to look at her.'

'I agree. Now Glen and Tony are off Cal Nyx, we can focus elsewhere.' Scobie wiped some text from the display board.

'Not convinced she's clean in all this.' Birch struggled, adding another file box to the stack beside his desk.

'No one is cleared. I'm going to have a word with the super, see if we can't get some more feet on the ground. There's too much here for a team this size.'

Birch's phone rang. He answered, listened, twirled a biro. 'What name?' He pulled a pad across, wrote some notes. 'When was this again? And in Victoria?' More scribbling. 'So Vic will have the records?' He looked towards Scobie and Ottering.

Birch put his phone on the desktop. Tapped his finger on the notepad.

'That was DS Fallon. Vic Police. I filed a general query in all states on Sylvia Toblensk. She red-flagged in Victoria because her name came up in a case that never made it to court.'

Scobie and Ottering were one hundred percent focussed on Birch.

'Extortion,' he said. 'Never got to court because the plaintiff died. Ask me who the plaintiff was.' Birch held his hands wide, palms up.

Ottering obliged. 'Who?'

'Alena Toblensk. Her mother.'

'Sheeit.' Ottering slapped her thigh with a folder.

'Fallon's emailing the docs.' Birch sat down, wiggled his mouse.

'Okay. She's got form. Potentially.' Scobie stood behind Birch. 'Extortion to murder is still a big jump.'

Ottering was at Birch's other shoulder. 'Dunno, skip. Reckon your moral compass is wavering pretty much groundwards if you'd coerce your own mother for her money.'

'Keep on it. Let me know what you find.'

~

Scobie went to her office, hit a number on speed-dial. 'Hi Gwen. Short notice I know. Any chance you can squeeze me in this afternoon? Just the usual.'

In the background on the other end of the line she could hear the burr of a hairdryer, Beyonce's *Single Ladies*, a pair of voices singing along. Gwen and a friend doing cash jobs at home. She'd rescued Scobie on a Sunday once before.

'Just a tic, Liz.' The handset was put down. She heard chatter, giggling, the swish of water in a nearby sink. Gwen came back on the line. 'Must be psychic, you. Del had a cancellation. Can you be here in about forty minutes? Mani, pedi and brows. Yeh.'

'You're a saviour. See you then.'

Scobie tucked a strand of hair behind her ear, rolled her shoulders. She felt light-hearted, excited in a way she hadn't known for a long time. And she'd still have time after Gwen worked her magic to get home and change.

She hurried back to the incident room.

'Got the gen, skip. Gotta say, lookin a bit ominous for our upstanding deputy principal.' Birch waved a handful of printouts.

'Fill me in.' Scobie scooted a chair over to Birch's desk. Ottering was on the phone at her own workstation.

'Alena Toblensk went into care after a series of strokes. At that time, Sylvia Toblensk was a teacher and deputy head at Braeburn School for girls. Sylvia had homecare help for her mother after the initial strokes but later dementia was diagnosed as well. Mother couldn't be left at home on her own. Went into a care facility.' Birch looked up at Scobie. 'Nurse aide at the care home blew the whistle on Sylvia.'

Scobie nodded. 'What exactly happened?'

'Sylvia was granted power of attorney when the dementia diagnosis was made. Police began an enquiry based on the nurse aide's concerns. The mother, Alena, said Sylvia had 'taken everything'. She'd get very agitated. But with the dementia, there was some disbelief, no one taking it seriously. Except this carer. Anyway, around this time large amounts of money were also transferred to Sylvia's account. That's not necessarily dodgy as she was responsible for her mother's welfare.

'What sort of amounts are we talking?'

'Region of $400K.'

'Seems a lot for toiletries and clothing.'

Birch gave a wry smile. 'Yup. But with no written record of threats or intimidation they only had the mother's concerns as observed by a nurse's aide. Easily written off as dementia ramblings. With no evidence of duress or coercion except the opinion of this care worker who saw how upset Alena was. And then Alena died. Her testimony would have been required for a conviction. It was all too…'

'Nebulous?' Scobie offered.

Birch raised his eyebrows and gave a small shrug of resignation.

Scobie continued. 'So. We only have suspicion. We can't prove anything on that historic inquiry. Even if we fronted her with that, she's aware there's no proof. But,' she paused, 'as beneficiary of Stefan's will now Phillip Leuwins is gone she does bear some consideration. It's not as if the extortion claim and her current status as next-of-kin beneficiary are unrelated. What do you think?'

'For sure. Like to dig a little deeper. Another possibility, pay someone else to do it. What's Stefan's estate worth? And all that moolah from her mother, what did she do with all that? Fifteen grand for a hit, she still comes away with a tidy nest egg.'

'Are we drawing a bit of a long shot?' Scobie asked. Ottering had rejoined them.

'This disenchanted copper says not at all,' Birch replied. 'Always follow the money.'

'Fill Janice in.'

As Scobie walked away Ottering dropped another file box on Birch's desk.

13

Cal stopped at Misty's store to fill up with gas. She set the fuel pumping at the bowser, then opened her boot and heaved the flat tyre out.

A red Hilux pick-up was parked on the other side of the pumps, an unattended nozzle running fuel into the filler-neck. She looked around, saw a pair of familiar figures standing over by the air machine. One was that Nolly guy, with the blond hair. He was working in the garage last time she stopped there. And the heavyset bloke, he'd been there too. He was standing close, looking down, pointing his finger at the blond bloke. She lowered her head as she finished the fill up.

The big guy strolled her way. 'Nice XM.' He nodded at the car. 'Super Pursuit donk?'

Cal smiled and shook her head as he leaned in the driver's side window. 'Windsor small-block. Only way to go,' she said, returning the nozzle to the bowser.

'Console's not standard.'

'Well spotted.' She laughed.

He banged a paw on the roof. 'Nice ride.'

They both walked into the store to pay. The burly guy held out his hand to her. 'Craig Dolan.'

She grasped his hand. It was like gripping a slab of concrete, the layers of callous so thick his fingers could barely bend.

'Cal Nyx.'

'Not local.'

'Work in the parks.'

They both paid. She felt conflicted, knowing he was one of the men who visited Stef and Pip's. She wasn't prepared to identify herself just then.

'Catch ya.' He left.

Need to check him out n'all. Can't do it in the Ford now. Maybe I can swap with Dee. 'Bout time I dropped in home.

She rolled the dud wheel over to the workshop. 'Hello,' she called into the dim interior.

Nolly Pratt emerged from the front of a Toyota Troop Carrier. 'Do for ya?' he said, then saw the tyre leaning against her leg. 'Flattie?'

'Punctured. Screw. Can you pull it out and patch it?'

'Wanna wait? Do it now.'

'Great. Don't like driving out here without a spare.'

He took it from her and rolled it over to the removal machine.

Cal went out into the sunshine. Checked her phone. Read another text from Liz Scobie.

Busy tonight?

Cal texted back.

Not if DI Scobie releases me.

Pinks at 8?

10-4.

Ottering opened the file boxes on Birch's desk. He was on the phone, on hold.

'Did we get bank records?' Ottering asked.

'Think we got Stefan Toblensk's. Dunno about Phillip Leuwins's.'

'Who checked them?'

'Glen was on it, I think.'

'They in here?'

Birch clenched his phone to his cheek, riffled through the papers, lifted out a sheaf held with a bulldog clip, handed them to Ottering. She smiled her thanks, sat at the adjoining table.

'Had the airline check for bookings in Sylvia Toblensk's name. She flew to Canberra on April 10th,' Birch said.

'Two days before the shootings.' Ottering drove her pen tip into the page, marked her spot. Her eyes now on Birch.

'What's there? Nothing. Why fly there?' he said.

'Lots of galleries,' Ottering said. 'Heathen.'

'Anyway. I checked all the car rental firms at the airport. She hired a car. I asked for the mileage used and it was nearly seven hundred clicks.'

'Canberra's tiny.'

'Exactly. Nothing there.'

'Could've been touring around.'

'It's bleak as fuck.'

Ottering let that one through to the keeper. *Yes, there is nothing there if you aren't into war memorials and museums.*

Birch continued, 'That mileage would have easily got her to the Blue Mountains and back.'

'Okay. Skip know?'

'Telling her now. Think we'll be packing our bags.'

Ottering carried on with the bank statements. She never quite got used to scanning through someone's record of purchases and payments. There was something so intimate and domestic about it. She'd had to inure herself to it, like so much of their work, noseying around in someone else's business, their life. There was a level of reveal in the banality of online shopping and junk food purchases that always felt particularly intrusive. Considering she had to view bodies and go through a victim's private affairs generally, it was surprising she found this one aspect particularly invasive, but she did.

Birch returned. 'Got the go-ahead. We're off to Melbourne. Drive to Benalla tomorrow. Late flight this arvy or tonight if tickets are available.'

'We get any local help?' Ottering asked.

'Skip's teeing it up. She'll let us know who's our contact. Just protocol. But we'll be pretty much on our own. They'll be as strapped for troops as we are.'

'Okay. Gonna try and finish this.'

Ottering checked the time on her phone: 2pm. She and Birch had maybe three hours before flying out. Not even that, allowing for the airport drive. *C'mon Janice, focus.*

Avery hadn't highlighted any of the entries. She couldn't even see pen marks beside repetitive accounts, so she began for herself, scanning the previous eight months.

Most of the debits and credits were obvious and repetitive, power payments and the like. There was one semi-regular payment that caught her eye. *Gardening*, was the reference, T-Tarp the payee. The first payment began in February, the last in early April. It started. It stopped. $650.00 each time. Seemed a lot for a bit of weeding or whatever. And hadn't the sister said Phillip Leuwins looked after the gardens? Ottering did a quick search of landscaping and gardening services in the area. No T-Tarp.

She highlighted each of the entries and flicked an email to forensic accounting to see where the payments went.

∼

Some hours later, Ottering watched the snaking highway lights from the window seat. She didn't like landings. Tried to make herself relax. Birch snored, oblivious beside her. He stirred at the bump of touchdown, stretched and yawned like he was in his La-Z-Boy chair at home.

They collected their carry-on bags and left the plane, picked up the hire car. It was nearly midnight. Ottering checked her messages. One from Scobie. She turned to Birch. 'Got our contact here. Detective Albruzzi.'

'Sleep first. Drive tomorrow.'

Ottering took the wheel, thumbed the GPS and headed for the motel.

∼

Back in the NSW bush, and well beyond midnight, Avery was antsy. 'We're stuffed with her. Could sit here all night.'

'Check on our other friends while we're out here.'

'Nosey up on Boarback?' Avery started the car, headed for the ridge.

Cobbin nodded.

'Dolan?'

Cobbin nodded again. Avery turned right along Boarback Ridge Road. It was 2.15am. There was no other traffic. Outside the vehicle only the sounds of the bush or the tyres running across an occasional dry branch fallen on the tarmac. Avery drove slowly, trying to pick out the driveway in the dark on the other side of the road. When he spotted the chain barrier he turned around and parked at the side of the road behind a small copse of saplings.

They both got out, carrying torches. Cobbin led the way, climbing over the chain. Their feet made little sound on the sandy driveway. In the brush on either side of them, the occasional noise of small animals scampering through the crackly debris. A slight breeze from the north blew across the apex of the ridge, creating a sibilant hiss as it passed through the tops of the gums. They were about to round the corner to the yard when they heard a car door slamming.

Cobbin turned to Avery. 'Get off the track. Get down!' They threw themselves into the brush, crawled away as the headlights from Dolan's pick-up passed over them.

He stopped and unlocked the chain, drove through, relocked it and drove north on Boarback Ridge.

'Where the fuck's he going at this hour?' Avery dusted himself off.

'Follow him or check out here?'

'Make the most of his absence, ay?'

'Not really s'posed to be here, are we.'

'C'mon.' Avery turned and sprinted back to the car. Cobbin leapt in as Avery floored it, catching glimpses of Dolan's taillights far ahead in the darkness.

～

Craig Dolan turned his lights off and coasted into the scrub behind the Rural Fire Depot. He grabbed some gear from the back of the truck. Using the shadows alongside the road verge, he crept back along Juta Road towards the old caravan park.

～

Shortly after 9pm, Scobie arrived at Pink's and went to the upstairs bar. Cal was already there.

'Hope I didn't keep you long?' Scobie said.

'Not at all. Time for me to get primed.' Cal nodded at the empty bottle and tilted her new one on the bar. 'Gin martini?'

Scobie smiled. 'Thank you.'

Cal nodded at the bartender. 'Dry. Three olives.'

'Sydney gal?'

Scobie shook her head. 'Guess.'

'Okay.' Cal sipped from her longneck, considered Scobie's accent, her aesthetic. 'Melbourne.'

Scobie nodded.

'Why come up here. Career manoeuvring?'

'Mm hmm.'

'Miss your friends?'

'Sure. Cheap flights help. If I get time off.' Her drink arrived.

'Chin-chin.' She clinked Cal's bottle, took a sip, closed her eyes.

They chatted, had a few more drinks.

Scobie went to the powder room, touched up her make-up. She applied the matt, plum lipstick, folded a tissue, pressed her lips to it. *Not sure this is going to last through what I'm envisaging, but one can blot and hope.*

When she returned to her seat, Cal smiled. 'Feel like getting something to eat?'

Scobie gave her a long stare, not hard, a tiny lift at one corner of her mouth. She shook her head once, slowly.

'Okay. Maybe some room service later. C'mon, I'll drive.' Cal cocked her head, a partial grin.

Scobie eased off her stool. 'Let's walk.'

Cal picked up Scobie's jacket from the back of the chair, held it. Scobie turned, let her drape it across her shoulders. Cal leaned close, could feel the warmth of the other woman's body, smell the faint citrus scent of her skin. Tendrils of her hair hung close to her neck.

Cal stood aside to let Scobie walk ahead. The form-fitting pencil skirt embraced Scobie's curves to the knee. Cal saw the tiny bump of a suspender clasp as the fabric slid across Scobie's thigh when she moved.

As they strolled through the back of Chippendale, Scobie linked her arm inside Cal's and pressed close to her side. The traffic converging at Parramatta and City Roads hummed and blew in the distance. They passed a park at the end of a cul-de-sac. Beneath an old, spreading Moreton Bay fig tree, a wooden seat encircled the trunk. Cal pulled gently towards it. Before they sat down, Scobie turned to face her. Cal was only slightly taller. Scobie slipped her arms around Cal's waist, her fingers curling over the muscles at Cal's spine. She applied a small pressure through her fingers. Cal's hand closed around Scobie's neck, pulling her close. Scobie's body curved into hers.

14

Ottering woke with the birds, a noisy, rapping, cawing racket on the roof and in the trees outside the motel room. Sunlight blanched through the thin curtains. She felt hungover but she hadn't drunk the night before. It was simply lack of sleep after their late arrival. She picked up her phone. 6.17am. She texted Birch.

In the next room, Birch had already showered and been outside for his first ciggy. He leaned against the back of the rental car wearing sunglasses when Ottering emerged from her room.

'Diner back along the strip.' She indicated the dusty expanse of faded mall shops adjoining the motel. The six-lane motorway was already a river of flashing windscreens and burring engines.

'Let's walk, eh.' Though Ottering would inevitably handle the driving, Birch still wasn't keen on tackling the roads without coffee.

The traffic noise was an assault and Ottering was glad to get inside the diner and behind glass.

They ordered. Ottering checked her phone. Monday morning, unlikely forensic accounting would have anything for her yet.

Birch got up. 'Quick ciggy before my grub arrives.'

The pair finished their breakfast and walked back to the motel, packed their gear and began the drive north through the inner suburbs.

Birch's phone buzzed. Unknown number. 'DS Dan Albruzzi, Vic Police. Assigned as your liaison here. My skip spoke with yours. Wanted to let you know your interview prospect has registered firearms. An H licence for a Ruger KMK, a B licence for a Browning A-Bolt. Just thought I'd give you a heads-up.'

'Appreciate it. We're heading north now. Expect to meet her in Benalla.'

'Okay. 'Bit over two hours. Here if you need anything.'

∽

As they left the outer suburbs of Melbourne, Birch laid his seat back. 'Sing out when you need a break. I do have my full licence, y'know.'

Ottering gave him a grin. 'After lunch, eh.'

Ottering's phone rang. Jim Scanlon. Forensic accounting. She hit speakerphone. 'Got a name for you on those Toblensk account payments. One NS Pratt. It's a general account. Seems to do most of his daily banking through it. No other accounts with other banks that we could find. Pretty legit on the face of it.'

'Thanks, Jimbo. Be in touch.' Ottering turned to Birch. 'Whaddaya reckon? They seem like gardening payments to you?'

Birch's head hung back on his headrest as he watched the bleached, flat landscape skimming by. 'Hard to say. No one's hiding anything. Could be kosher.'

'Well, the payment name wasn't straightforward. Reversed letters.' She scoffed. 'Childish. Why do that?'

'Dunno. Bit odd. Can't ask him, can we. Need to have a chat with Pratt again, though.' Birch emptied the last of a litre water bottle down his neck, passed another one to Ottering.

'Would Toblensk be hiding that name from Leuwins? Why do that on his own bank statement if everything was above board. Don't get it.' She shook her head.

~

On Monday morning, Cal left Scobie's place early and drove back home to Kurrajong where she borrowed Dee's small white Hyundai hatchback. She planned to check some of the beats on the list a bit later. But she waited behind the Rural Fire Depot near the junction of Boarback and Juta roads hoping to spot Craig Dolan. Wearing a baseball cap and hoodie she felt pretty much incognito. With the seat rolled back as far as it would go, she tried to relax. At 9.15am Craig Dolan drove north along Boarback then turned left at Juta Road heading down to the river flats. Cal followed Dolan past the Misty's store as he continued south-west skirting the lower mountains.

Twenty minutes later he peeled left off the highway into the outskirts of Bently, an industrial area serving the semi-rural region with engineering, farm and building supplies. He took a road that followed the eastern side of the river. Five hundred metres further he slowed and turned into a self-storage estate.

As she passed him she saw him putting a security card into the gate machine at the entrance to the facility. *Wonder what he's got in there?* Plenty of surveillance cameras in those places. And the security cards would mean all his visits are logged on the system.

What do the cops say? *Means, motive, opportunity.* He and that Nolly guy were at Stefan's that night. They were there regularly. *And I've seen one of them at a beat.* She rapped her fingers on the edge of the steering wheel, playing a tune over and over.

Her phone pinged. Di had sent a picture of Pip. The brother and sister had the same sad eyes. Funny how someone could be born looking like they'd already lived several lives. Stef was in the photo too, standing behind Pip, holding up bunny-ear fingers.

She started the car, checked the address list Gigi had given her and drove south-east along the river, towards Lowlands River Park. It was barely five minutes away. She parked and saw the grandstand beside the main playing field.

Nearby, a guy in lycra unhooked a fancy mountain bike from the rear of his car. There were half a dozen other vehicles in the car park. Monday morning wasn't a sports day. She took a deep breath. How to approach this? Asking men at a beat if they'd seen someone in a photo, was that going to get her punched out? She couldn't think of any way to make it soft, non-threatening. Just tell the truth and hope for some compassion. Ha. She pocketed her phone and headed for the pathway behind the grandstand.

～

As Ottering drove, Birch rang Sylvia Toblensk. 'Hope to be there mid-morning.'

'I'm at the campground, north end of Gingin Road. Be here a day or so. Look for the RV with the pink stripe.'

They drove through the washed-out landscape. Birch found himself beginning to like it. His eyes filtered the stubbled forms and achromatic tones. The subtlety and softness of the faded, worn down surrounds was comforting, as long as he kept his sunglasses on.

Just before 10.30am they looped off the M31 and into Benalla.

Ottering wanted to push on to the campground.

'Just grab coffee eh. Have a quick puff.' Birch tapped the fags in his breast pocket.

Ottering couldn't get out of the car fast enough, though leaving the aircon was a shock. *So much for the pleasant May temperatures*, she thought as she stretched and bent forward, touching her toes several times. Most mornings in Sydney she'd do a run before work. Routine was kinked today.

They bought takeaways then headed north to the campground sited several kilometres out on the edge of town. It was already thirty-eight degrees outside. Ottering slowed down at the appearance of a billboard with a kangaroo in board shorts holding a beer in its paw. She drew in a noisy snort and made the turn into the entrance.

Faded plastic bunting drooped above the manager's office. Gleaming white, moulded plastic camper vans that looked to Ottering like melted Tupperware, filled grassless bays. They trailed power wires hooked into poles like umbilical cords.

Parked in a bay nearby, Sylvia Toblensk's RV was unmistakable; a Toyota school bus with a candy-pink stripe around its middle. An awning stretched out from the roofline on one side, a fold-up table and chairs beneath.

Ottering opened her door, felt like closing it again as the heat hit her. Birch got out, lit a cigarette.

Sylvia Toblensk emerged from the bus, a medium height, fit-looking woman in her mid-fifties. Her face bore the deep lines of someone who'd spent a lot of her life outdoors. Her long, greying dark hair was wound around her head with a faded scarf that held the mass off her neck. She wore a cotton blouse, Capri pants and sandals. 'How do, folks. Find it okay?' She approached with a smile and extended hand.

Ottering shook hands. 'Choice spot.'

Birch moved his ciggy to his left hand, shook with his right.

'Get you a cool drink? Herbal tea?' Toblensk stood with her hands on her hips.

'Just water for me,' Ottering said.

'Ditto. Thanks.' Birch strolled over to the edge of the parking bay, stared along the roadways and ranks of white RVs, beyond to the worn and weathered plains, wheat-coloured, shimmering and bleached.

Sylvia Toblensk disappeared inside then returned with a water jug and glasses on a tray. She put them on the small table, pulled another fold-out stool from under the RV and indicated for Ottering to sit.

'Y'know, I'm just gonna stand for a bit. Been cramped in that car too long.'

Birch ambled over after burying his ciggy butt in the sand.

'Know what you mean. I love being on the road, but when I stop, I need to do a bit of hiking. Get my blood moving.'

'So, you live on the road full-time?' Ottering said.

'Pretty much. Cashed in my super, bought the bus. Still do some teaching and marking online. Distance learning, kids in remote areas. Young artists in regional centres, I agent for them. Made a few contacts over the years.'

'Sounds like a good set-up.'

'Don't need much. Rent on the house pays my bills. Feel pretty rich with this lifestyle.' She spread her hands to the expanse in front of them.

Ottering wasn't quite convinced. It bordered on hokey.

'Not to be indelicate, Ms Toblensk, but you're now the beneficiary of Stefan's estate. Were you aware of that?'

Sylvia Toblensk's face fell somewhat and her lips drew in. 'I was made aware last week, the lawyer contacted me. I just assumed he left things to Pip. I'd never really thought about it.' She looked guarded and sad.

'I'm sorry we have to ask about these things. Just part of our investigation.' Ottering dropped her hands to her side.

Birch spoke. 'You had regular contact with your brother?'

'Well, as you can see, I'm away a lot.' A flat smile. 'Not much face-to-face. I've been based in Victoria for twenty-seven years now. We met one time in Adelaide. The Grand Prix. Stef was such a petrolhead. Left that to him. I did a few galleries.'

'You interested in art, Ms Toblensk?'

'Please call me Sylvia. I feel like I'm back in front of a class.

Our mother was an art historian. Couldn't avoid it. I'm grateful for it.'

'You were aware Stefan had a bit of a collection?'

'Of course. He liked to show off when he got something he wanted.' Her voice was without bitterness. 'He loved his pieces. He lived with them. They weren't locked away in a vault.'

'Worth a bit now.' Birch raised one eyebrow.

'He bought well. He had an eye. Like I said, he bought what he loved. He wasn't buying as an investor.' She didn't seem defensive at all.

Good actor? Ottering wondered.

'So, you didn't see a lot of him. Phone calls then?'

'We kept in touch. I'm not a big phone person, especially the places I get to. We'd email or text. We kept in touch.'

'You were close? He confided in you?' Ottering picked up again.

'As close as brother and sister are. He had a few health scares. We all do at our age.' She smiled. 'I felt I knew what was going on, if it was important.' Her brow pinched in. 'You think I should know something about… what?' She shook her head. 'If Stef was in any kind of trouble, I had no inkling. This is a total shock for me. For everyone, I'm sure.' Her voice trembled slightly. She'd been matter-of-fact until then. It was as though remembering the reality of his death, a murder, hit her again. She looked away for a moment, took a breath. Her hand squeezed her knee.

'I'm sorry. It's an awful part of our job having to ask these questions,' Ottering said.

'Out of the blue. Makes no sense.' Sylvia lifted her hands from her knees and shrugged.

'You were on the east coast recently,' Birch said. 'Didn't visit your brother?'

Sylvia Toblensk seemed to freeze frame as something shot through her. Then shook her head sadly. She didn't speak.

'Mind if I ask why you were there?'

'We've donated works in the past. To the National Gallery. Some of my mother's pieces, important artists. I was up in the Snowy Mountains. The last few pieces my mother left me. Getting them authenticated.'

Ottering's brows squeezed together. Birch gave a small shake of his head.

'Pieces from early in an artist's career. They don't have provenance. My mother had several small Isaac Heinz oils. His only daughter, Ingrid, she's unwell. Very unwell. I wanted her to see the pieces. She remembers her father painting them. She remembered my mother too, which was sweet.' Sylvia flapped her hands in a low flutter. 'I had to catch Ingrid while I could.'

Ottering scribbled a name in her notebook.

Birch cocked his head to one side, his lips compressed into a bemused grimace. 'Not cause for a get-together? You and your brother both being art lovers?'

'Stef couldn't get down there. We'd planned for me to visit him on the Sunday or Monday.'

Convenient, Birch thought.

'Obviously I cancelled my trip to the Biennale,' Sylvia said.

Birch frowned.

'Venice. I was booked to fly out that week,' she added.

'Can you give me contact details for Ingrid Heinz?' Ottering asked. 'She's still with us?'

'Far as I'm aware,' Sylvia replied. 'Let me get my address book.' She stepped inside the bus.

Ottering and Birch exchanged a look, said nothing, waited.

Sylvia returned a minute later, passed Ottering a slip of paper with an address and phone number written on it. 'That number is for Ava Trentham, Ingrid's cousin. She's living with her now. Looking after her.' She sat down with her hands under her thighs.

'It was the same weekend your brother and Phillip Leuwins were shot,' Birch said. Even Ottering was taken off guard.

Sylvia Toblensk was silent. She scanned the ground, her eyes moving quickly. A small nod.

Ottering wanted to sip her water but didn't move.

Still nothing.

'There was something else. Victoria.' Birch watched her closely as he spoke. 'Two years ago. An enquiry into a claim of extortion. Your mother. How did that go down with Stefan?' Birch's tone was brittle, crackly.

Sylvia Toblensk pulled her hands out from under her thighs, rubbed them, crossed them in her lap. Looked at Birch. 'Oh dear,' she said. 'That's going to follow me to my grave, isn't it.' She looked at them both. 'Awful, awful time. Horrible thing to have hanging over me.' She took a deep breath. 'I'm sure you've read the police reports, but I'll go over it again. My grandmother was treated rather badly by a second husband. Grasping so-and-so. They all lived together for a time, her, him and my mother. She was an addict, after the war. He got a lot of money out of her. He'd get her to sign things when she was gaga. My mother was very aware of this history. She witnessed that snake working on my grandmother when she was a teen.

'Fast forward, my mother was hospitalised with dementia. I was trying to get her to give me the background on some of her collection. I would actually bring pictures into the care home. Then take them with me when I left. My mother was apparently quite confused one time and said something to a carer. It's as though she conflated what had happened to her own mother with me trying to get her works in order.'

'A large sum of money was transferred from her account to yours. You had power of attorney.' Birch's tone was flat.

'That's right.' Sylvia Toblensk remained very still as her gaze rose to Birch's.

'Bit of an issue there?' Birch said.

Sylvia remained silent, a small sideways movement of her head.

'Extortion.' Birch's voice grated across the syllables.

Ottering almost felt sorry for the woman.

The lower part of Toblensk's face fell. Her eyebrows drew together. 'I'm sorry?'

'Your mother died before the case came to court. You could've gotten fourteen years.'

'I really don't know why you're bringing this up–'

'You tried to change your name. You couldn't because of the charge. Why would you do that unless you had something to hide?'

'My job was my life. It ruined my career.'

'Extortion is a very serious offence. I suggest you were lucky it didn't get to court.'

'As a police officer I'm sure you're familiar with the premise of innocence until proven guilty.' Sylvia Toblensk said it with some defiance.

'Still say you were lucky.'

Sylvia Toblensk looked to Ottering, back to Birch, then lowered her eyes.

'I asked you what your brother thought of it all,' Birch said.

Sylvia looked up, locked eyes with Birch. 'He was embarrassed for me. He knew it was ridiculous.' Her jaw moved from side to side in a tiny shuffle. 'We both received substantial deposits from my mother's estate. Stefan didn't have power of attorney because he was in New South Wales. I was here, with her. He was fine with that.'

'Not around to confirm that, is he,' Birch said dryly. 'We can search his account for that deposit though. You staying in this area?'

'Next three weeks. Then I'm heading for Ballarat.'

Birch nodded, started towards the car.

Ottering paused, turned back. Sylvia was still sat at the table. 'You have gun licences.'

'Absolutely. I'm a target shooter.'

'One of your licences is for a rifle.'

'Never travel the outback without one. My mother taught us both. She was a refugee. This place was like the Wild West to her after Europe.'

'You have a gun safe in that thing?' Ottering nodded at the RV.

'Absolutely.'

'Quick squizz.' Ottering followed Sylvia Toblensk inside. Stood behind her as she unlocked the purpose-built gun safe in a tight alcove beside the shower unit. Sylvia Toblensk stood back.

Ottering lifted the Browning rifle from its rack. Worked the bolt. Made sure the chamber was empty. She let the barrel drop through her hand. Sniffed the tip of the barrel. Replaced it in the rack. 'Thank you. We'll be off then.'

Birch was puffing a ciggy as he leaned on the front fender. 'Well?' he asked.

'Wasn't fired in the last few days. Murder was over a month back, though.' Ottering climbed in the driver's side.

'What'd you make of her?' Ottering turned the ignition.

'Never really know, do ya. Just gotta focus on the facts.'

'Need to follow up her alibi. The painter's daughter.'

'Yup.' Birch wound his window down. 'Gonna fill the skip in.' He thumbed his speed-dial, left a message for Scobie.

15

At the Heights Holiday Park, Dolan scuttled around the back of the first trailer and made his way past a rusting trampoline frame and overturned milk crates spilling rubbish.

Though it was close to 2.30am, the flicker of TV screens illuminated the windows of several of the trailers in the small complex. He crouched low and reached the rear of Pratt's trailer. A dim light shone feebly from one of the side windows. As Dolan paused, he heard the front screen door clatter shut. He peered around the corner of the building and watched as Nolly Pratt threw a toolbag into the passenger seat of his station wagon and drove out of the park.

'What the hell? What's that little punk up to?' Dolan hightailed it back towards the entrance, ran across the road and leapt into his car, catching sight of Pratt's taillights disappearing in the darkness, veering left onto Boarback Road.

Dolan fumed. It was okay for him to be out, doing his business at that hour, but not Pratt. He was the boss. Boarback was a long stretch following the ridge. It went nowhere, unless you were looking for bush. Dolan lived there, his work premises were there. And Stef and Phillip Leuwins's old place was there. What was Pratt up to?

∼

Cal started along the river walk. Every so often, a bench was mounted in a small lay-by off the track with a view to the river. The track was a shared cycleway and she was grateful for the gravel surface as she didn't like bikes suddenly appearing from behind her. She'd walked for five minutes or so, glad she'd worn a jacket. The air coming off the river was chilled. Ahead of her, on an open section of the walkway, a man sat on a bench seat surrounded by mown grass. He wore a black beanie and his hands were in the pockets of his jacket.

Cal took a deep breath and steadied herself. 'Hiya.' She walked over.

The man glanced at her then looked away.

'Wondering if you can help me.' Cal withdrew her phone from her pocket.

The man looked up at her, his face both stricken and angry. His shoulders rose but his hands remained in his pockets. 'Piss off,' he said.

Cal stood her ground. 'Don't want any trouble. Just want you to look at a picture for me. Brother of a friend...'

The man stood and took his hands from his pockets, balled into tight fists. 'Fuck off,' he growled through clenched teeth, and stomped off back towards the car park.

Jesus. This ain't gonna be easy.

She kept walking. Two hundred metres later there was another bench seat. Empty. She kept walking, then heard a distorted electronic voice from beyond the bare willows on the riverbank. Moments later a rowing crew appeared, the blades of their oars slicing the glassy water. Behind them, a small motorboat with one guy at the outboard engine, another in the bow, holding a megaphone, calling instructions to the rowers.

Cal carried on. *How long am I gonna give this? Another hour. That's it. Gotta try something.* She fingered the phone in her pocket, looked ahead. Another bench facing the water. Empty. Behind it a track leading through a copse of casuarina trees. The planting was on a rise that curved away from the river then back again.

Should I go in there? What if I disturb someone? What the hell.

She walked around the back of the bench and into the trees. The track was layered with fallen casuarina needles but a well-worn clearway snaked through the middle. Her attention was caught by a colour contrast off to one side: the fabric of a blue hoodie. Then she saw another figure in a plaid jacket.

Ah jeez. Now what? Don't wanna freak them out. She turned and walked back the way she'd come, sat on the bench seat and waited.

Ten minutes later, a man in a blue hoodie emerged from the track. He looked at her, looked away, kept walking towards the main track. She got up. 'Hey. I need some help. Please, just a minute.'

The guy ignored her, walked faster, kept his head down.

'Mate, I don't care what you're doing in there. I'm looking for someone. Please.' She got closer.

He turned as she got within two metres, his hands deep in his pockets. 'Fuck off. Fuck off,' he said quickly as he began to jog away.

Jesus, this is useless. No one's gonna talk to me here. They're all on high alert. Fuck this for a joke.

She turned back towards the car park and started walking. When she got to the car she sat looking through the windscreen. She pulled Gigi's list from her pocket then checked a map on her phone. Crockett Road North was fifteen minutes away max. One more try.

Cobbin and Avery gathered with Scobie Monday morning in the incident room. Cobbin began. 'Can't follow anyone in the dark out there. No other traffic. Stand out like the proverbial.'

'So we don't know where Dolan went?' Scobie folded her arms.

'Had to turn off. Same when we followed Nyx out there. We're stuffed.'

Scobie replaced an errant strand of hair behind her ear. 'Did we ever find the phones of Phillip Leuwins and Stefan Toblensk?'

Both men shook their heads.

'Data retrieval there could've been helpful. Leads aren't terribly fruitful.'

'You're aware of the payments to Pratt? Toblensk's account.' Cobbin crushed his coffee cup.

'Janice informed me on Scanlon's findings, yes.'

'Want us to question Pratt again?'

'Be good to clarify the deposits, I think.'

'Any word on more help here?'

'Still waiting. Just push on as best you can.'

As they left the incident room Avery shot a comment to Cobbin. 'Why's she decided Nyx is clean? She's as likely as anyone.'

'Don't think she has. Like she said, need more feet on the ground. Hard to put pressure on five suspects with a crew spread as thin as ours.'

Crockett Road North was a lay-by on a secondary road off the highway. Before the motorway went through it would have been heavily trafficked, but not anymore. At one end of the road a faded petrol station and peeling general store still serviced locals wanting to avoid the freeway. Cal scanned the surrounds. A trio of wooden picnic tables stood beneath tall, gangly gums which, judging by their sparse foliage, would offer little summer shade. Standing between the picnic area and the gas station was a stolid little edifice resembling a concrete bunker. Presumably this was the loos.

Two trucks were parked to the side of the throughway, nose-to-tail and parallel to the main road. One was a curtain-sider semi with dusty flanks, a long-hauler from the freeway. Promising. The other was a small, stub-nosed pantech. Probably local deliveries.

The drivers weren't in their cabs. Must be in the loos. Or maybe the sleeper on the semi. She got out of the car and leaned back on the bonnet. No point surprising anyone. Just asking for trouble. Sit and wait for one of them to appear.

Five minutes later, the passenger door of the semi opened and a balding man in chinos and a beige cotton jacket climbed down from the cab. He walked back towards the smaller truck.

Cal approached. 'S'cuse me, mate.' He gave her a quick look as he keyed the door lock. 'Looking for a friend of mine. Might've seen him round here.'

'Doubt it,' he said as he put his foot on the step-up.

'Please. Just take a look.' Behind her the semi rumbled into life, the massive Cummins engine thundering through the airspace. She held up the image on her phone that Di had sent, Pip with Stef in the background. 'You ever seen him?'

He barely flicked his eyes to the screen. 'Nah.' He pulled himself up into the cab.

'Please. It's for a friend of mine. Lost her brother. Please look again.'

'C'mon,' he said, shrugging and spreading his hands.

'He was a good man. Please help us.'

He paused, screwed his mouth up, a resigned puff. Put his hand out, took the phone, squinted. 'Yeh. He's familiar.'

An electric jolt zagged through her stomach. Cal held her breath, pointed at Pip. 'You remember him? This guy?'

'The big guy, at the back. Seen him a few times, yeh.'

Cal looked at the screen, turned it back. 'But not the other guy?'

'Nah. Just the big fella.'

~

Gayle Scarborough heard the blast of the Nissan's exhaust from the dressage ring. The mare twitched on the end of the lunge line. Scarborough soothed her with a gentle call and got her gait back on rhythm. *Need a word with that lad. His father set an example. Don't know what went wrong.*

She worked the mare a while longer then finished up and went to the studio and garage behind the house. Terry, shirtless, was on his knees beside the passenger seat, scrabbling around underneath. The stereo seemed to be rocking the car.

'Terry.' No response. She tried to move into his vision but that wasn't easy with him stuck in the doorway. A film of sweat covered his back and narrow scratches and small bruises peppered his shoulders.

'Terry!'

His head came up so sharply he whacked it into the bottom corner of the dash.

'Fuck me.'

'The noise is disturbing the horses. Can you please keep it down, darling? And what have you done to your back? I should put something on that.'

Terry Scarborough stood up. He was red-faced. His eyes seemed deeper than ever, sunken in shadowed sockets. He leaned in, lowered the volume. 'Sorry,' he mumbled.

'You don't look well, Tel. Are you getting enough sleep?'

Scarborough brushed himself off. 'I'm okay. Bit tired.'

'Dad's back tonight. Why don't you have dinner with us? Bring Cilla if you like.'

'Let you know. Got a bit on.'

~

Both the trucks had left the lay-by. Cal sat in the car trying to figure her next move. Stef was using these beats, not just Pip. *That's hardly surprising. Both gay men out here. So why am I feeling broadsided?*

What does it mean? Stef was having an affair. Was it someone he met on a beat? Do I check the other ones? Not been an easy job. Do a couple more, see if anyone else recognises him. Then what? What does that prove? If someone was having an affair with him, they're not gonna admit to it if they were the killer, are they.

She pulled out Gigi's list again. Gringly's Reserve. That was where Pip's pick-up was found. Did Pip and Stef go to the same beats? *Need to see the place for myself.* She checked a map and headed off.

~

Scobie had a muster with her reduced crew late on Monday morning.

'Need to speak with Pratt again. Those payments.' She looked at Tony Cobbin. 'You and Glen get there today?'

Cobbin nodded.

'When are Frank and Janice back? Any word?' Avery asked.

'They've spoken to Sylvia Toblensk. Not much doing yet but at least they've eyeballed her. Alibi to check out. She was in NSW when the killings occurred. They should be back tonight.'

Avery raised his eyebrows, nodded with an interested pout.

'How do you want us to approach Pratt this time?' Cobbin flicked his pen.

'Up to you. Payments could be quite innocent. But it does seem a lot for gardening. What skill does Pratt have in that area anyway?'

'Could just be for general yard clean-ups,' Avery said.

'Don't understand why he didn't name Pratt clearly. Why the subterfuge with the name?' Scobie frowned. 'Anyway, I've been thinking about the Leuwins's pick-up, the torched one. Why was it left sitting there all that time? If he'd been missing for weeks, wouldn't someone have noticed it there?' She rubbed her neck.

'You reckon it might've been stored elsewhere?' Cobbin said.

'Risky moving it if it was.' Avery threw a paper ball into a bin under Cobbin's desk, missed, left it. Picked up a mini basketball to squeeze.

'Why not torch it weeks ago? Were Parks' maintenance spoken to, re their schedule?' Scobie raised her eyebrows. 'Wouldn't they have noticed a vehicle parked there for weeks?'

'Not necessarily. Might've thought it was a hiker who came regularly,' Cobbin offered.

'Leuwins was originally a suspect for the Toblensk killing. The theory was he'd gone interstate. That was public information because we wanted help. The killer could have benefitted from that idea,' Scobie said. 'And once his body was found the vehicle was torched. Before that its presence would have pointed to his possible disappearance, yes?'

Cobbin nodded at Scobie. 'Yeh. Still risky though. His vehicle could've been found. That wouldn't confirm he hadn't scarpered. Only that he'd maybe swapped vehicles.'

'Why torch it if it didn't have forensic evidence?' Avery said.

'Exactly. We need to establish if it had sat there all that time. If it was torched by vandals, and not the killer, then it would be a startling coincidence that it only happened after Phillip's body was found. See what I mean?' Scobie looked from one to the other.

They both nodded.

Cobbin and Avery drove back to the old Holiday Park in the hills to speak with Nolly Pratt. Cobbin stood on the cracked wooden step, rapping on a screen door so ragged and torn it was unlikely to stop mosquitoes.

He could hear something scraping along a wall and a muffled call from inside. Eventually the door was partly opened, closed, opened again as the front corner of a wheelchair appeared, jammed against the wall. Myra Pratt leaned over, edged her head into the gap, peered through the screen door which she couldn't reach to open.

'Sorry to bother you, Mrs Pratt. Nolly about?' Cobbin spoke, Avery stood back, eyed the yard.

'You've missed him. Went out last night,' she wheezed, her face flushed with the effort of getting to the door.

'Any idea where he went?'

'I was asleep. Heard the screen door.'

'Expect him back today?' Cobbin grasped the door jamb.

'He comes and goes. Never far away. I need him, see.'

Cobbin opened the screen door, handed over his card. 'Mind asking him to give me a call when he gets in?'

'He's a good lad. Not mixed up in anything is he?' Her breathing was shallow, fast.

'Just routine, Mrs Pratt. Helping with our enquiries.'

When the police had left, Myra Pratt backed herself up the narrow hallway and into the slightly larger lounge area. She positioned her wheelchair beside a cluttered table and withdrew her mobile phone from a pocket in the front of her apron. She hit Nolly's number again. Eventually it went to his voicemail. 'Where are you, pet? Getting a bit worried. Give your mum a call when you can, love.' She put the phone away, stared at the walls around her, began rocking in her seat as she wept.

16

In Benalla, Ottering parked the rental car behind the main street. She and Birch walked through a shaded laneway to Palms Café. They ordered food and ate as they discussed their meeting with Sylvia Toblensk.

'So, she cancelled a trip to Europe, the Biurnal–'

'Biennale,' Ottering interrupted.

'Whatever. Anyway, that's easy enough to check.'

'Day after Phillip Leuwins went missing.' Birch picked at his teeth with a matchstick.

'So, presumably, as Stefan's next-of-kin, she would've been first call.'

'She was. They did call her. Thing is, when Phillip's body was found, it changed the whole complexion of the Toblensk murder.'

'Right. Up till then we thought Leuwins was responsible.' Ottering rolled her sleeves up. Her skin was tanned over lean forearms. 'So. What do we have? Sylvia Toblensk was in the country when the killings occurred. In fact, she was in NSW. And we've dug up something unsavoury in her past regarding money. She needs an alibi for the night of the shootings.'

'Still reckon she could've paid someone to do it. That shot on

Leuwins in the bush wasn't a fluke. Kill shot at distance. Someone knew their way around a rifle.'

'Gotta follow up this Ingrid Heinz and speak with one of the senior curators at the National Gallery in Canberra as well, see if she can cast some light. If Sylvia insists there was nothing untoward going on when her mother was in care, perhaps an independent outsider can confirm the family was aware of what she was doing.'

'And that Stefan knew the score.'

Ottering picked up her phone.

Birch wiped tomato sauce from his plate with a chip, chewed thoughtfully as he surveyed the street outside. He pushed his plate away.

Ottering thumbed her phone screen, checked the netball results. 'Swifts blasted the Vixens.' Ottering gloated. 'You like a bit of netball, doncha Birchy.'

'Like those short skirts.' He raised his eyebrows. 'C'mon. I'll drive if you wanna make those calls. Try and get a flight back tonight.' He fingered the fag packet in his pocket, pushed his chair back.

Ottering stretched. 'Let's do it.'

They walked back to the car. Ottering gazed southwest as Birch drove out of town. A bank of heavy cloud sat flat on the horizon, right across the expanse of parched fields and plains. It looked like a storm front, dark and malignant, but it sat so low, like nothing she'd seen before.

'Whaddaya make of that?' She nodded beyond.

'Bushfire haze maybe. Can't smell it though.' He looked again. 'Dust storm? Been bloody dry.'

'Yeh maybe. I'll check.' Ottering brought up a weather site. 'Shit. You're right, Birchy. Dust storm. Heading for Melbourne.'

∼

Late morning Cal was at Gringly's Reserve, several thousand hectares of forest and scrub clothing the flatlands and foothills that led up into the mountains to the northwest. A number of tributary streams ran through parts of the reserve before joining the Hawkesbury south east of the area.

The car park road ran in a loop around a central, eye-shaped grove of trees four hundred metres long and one hundred wide then back to the entrance. Parking bays were laid out between smaller groves and bordered by low log fencing. Cal parked and walked the entire loop. When she reached the furthest point, she turned and walked back. She could see the scorched area where Pip's car had been set alight and eventually towed away. The leaves of the nearby trees were burnt and the branches bare where the flames had seared skywards.

At various points, walking tracks led off from the car park through the reserve. She followed several, getting her bearings and then went back to her borrowed car. She unfolded one of her topo maps and studied it. Like much of the region, firebreaks had been cut into the bush where the hinterland neared areas of human habitation. A service track from one of the main firebreaks ran adjacent to one of the streams. It ended less than a kilometre from the car park. It was conceivable that someone could have come into the area in a 4WD on a fire-trail and walked the last of the way in on the narrow track. That way they would avoid CCTV on the highway off-ramps.

She went back to the far end of the car park. She found the track and followed it. Being on the flat ground it had a silted and muddied surface. During floods it was likely underwater. Where the track widened out approaching the fire-trail, there were distinct tyre tracks in the surface, crushed weeds on the margins. She walked on.

Eventually, she reached the firebreak. The tyre tracks continued north, they didn't follow the route south. The vehicle which had made them had probably entered the reserve from somewhere up in the hills.

Someone knows these backblocks really well, maybe someone who grew up here. A hunter or hiker, a trail-biker on the fire-tracks.

She wasn't properly kitted out to follow all the way right then, as it ran for kilometres through the bushland. She'd wait until she could study a more recent online map. She started back. The fire-trail was mostly sandstone rubble, the tyre tracks apparent but indistinct. When she got back onto the flat, she studied the ground more closely. Down on her knees, she saw the imprint clearly. Superimposed in the mud a front and rear wheel had tracked over each other. In some places, the front wheel had a curved trajectory, unsullied by the following wheel and tyre. The deep pattern showed the serrated weave of the tread, and something particular: a rough notch in the outermost tread where a chunk of the rubber had been torn away. She pulled out her phone and took a photo. Passenger side, front.

Someone had wanted to get to that car park without being seen. Whoever had torched Pip's vehicle had gone to a lot of trouble. And why had his vehicle not been torched weeks ago, when he went missing, when he was shot? Was it because torching it then would've brought more attention to his absence? It suited his killer that Pip and his vehicle were possibly interstate. Was that it?

Her phone rang. Scobie. 'How can I help, detective inspector?' She scuffed her boot through the weeds, turned her head up as a New Holland honeyeater lifted from a branch beside the track.

'Require you for a reinterview.'

'Happy to answer any questions here and now.'

'I prefer to work in my own territory. Don't want to have to post an APB. Could be embarrassing for you,' Scobie said.

'Richmond lock-up then?'

'Northern car park across Fraser Green. Less conspicuous.'

'Time, detective inspector?'

'Three thirty. Call it afternoon tea.' Scobie rang off.

Cal wore a smile back to the car park.

~

Avery pulled in beside the Misty's workshop, checking across the lot for Pratt's silver Mazda. 'Car's not here,' he said as he got out. The huge garage doors were closed. The entry-hatch hung open. He leaned down and peered in the small doorway. The dark, silent space was heavy with the smell of sump oil and metal grindings. He walked over to the store.

The russet-faced owner tossed pies into the warmer. The tongs sat unused beside the oven. 'How do,' she said, unsmiling.

'Looking for Nolly Pratt.'

'Get in the queue,' she replied, as she slammed the warmer drawer shut, jamming a wad of brown paper bags in the process. 'No show this morning. Left me in the lurch.' She wrenched the sliding door back, grabbed the bags, threw them under the counter. 'Little greaser'll be getting his marching orders when he turns up.'

'Hasn't called then?'

'Not a peep. You fellas getting petrol?'

'Nah, we're good. Any of those pies warm?'

'Only the ones I put in yesterday.' She grimaced.

'Gimme two. And four sauces. Ta.' Avery dug out his card. 'Mind if we have a quick look around the workshop?'

'Fill ya boots.' She shot the bagged pies across the counter.

Avery went outside, held a pie towards Cobbin who declined. 'You start. Be in in a tick.'

Avery lifted his head towards the workshop, started on his pie.

Cobbin took a torch from the squad car and climbed through the doorway of the workshop. Pools of light slid through a series of little windows high up under the eaves, their luminous power lost by the time they reached the floor. Cobbin looked for a light switch. Found one to the left in a roughly partitioned office area consisting of oily carpet, two filthy chairs, a chipboard counter and grimy computer terminal. Against the wall behind the counter, cardboard boxes with scrawled dates held paperwork. Brake hoses and an air filter sat on top of the pile. On the rear wall, suspended with gobs of construction adhesive, announcement of a custom rally and swap-meet in Penrith two weeks hence.

The fluorescent lights made little impression on the dim interior. Small wonder Pratt often worked near the doorway. Cobbin swept his torch across the floor as he slowly paced the workshop. He stepped cautiously around forty-gallon oil drums, tripod work lights, gearbox innards, an engine hoist. At the rear of the space, an Escort rally car shell and beside it, in pieces, the rusted body of an old Model A Ford truck. He climbed over wooden boxes spewing engine components, shone his light across stacked wheel rims, reached the opposite corner and turned back towards the front of the building.

The air smelt fungal. Shining his torch along the floor he saw moisture emanating along both walls from the corner. The wooden framework was rotting and eaten away from the floor level upwards. He swept the beam up the wall following a green slime. *Buggered spouting*, he thought as he turned back.

He could see Avery outside the doorway, his face turned up to the sun as he ate his pie. Cobbin whacked his ankle on a protruding length of steering rack. Cursed. A calico cat with a milky eye leapt from a pile of folded sacks on top of a drum where a shaft of light created a solitary patch of golden warmth. *Couldn't work in a place like this.* He shook his shoulders and head as he tried to dislodge the oppression. Returned outside with relief.

~

Cal folded herself into the hatchback. She tried to move the seat back but remembered she'd done that days ago and it was already at its limit. At least she was less recognisable in it. She tapped the steering wheel, rang Dee. No answer. Left a message: 'Okay if I hang onto your car a little longer? Just wanna stay under the radar. You know where I leave the Ford keys if you need 'em.'

She flicked off a text to Zin saying she wouldn't be there that night. She flicked another to Di. Pip's memorial was only days away. Awaiting the approaching service was probably hellish for her.

She scanned the latest topo maps. The fire-trails snaked through the lowlands and up into the mountains. She could spend days walking or riding the labyrinthine tracks. Maybe it would be quicker to eliminate possibilities from known access points up around Misty's and Boarback. She had the tyre print after all.

So, who's got a 4WD? Scarborough's Nissan is tarmac only. Pratt's bomb got bogged in a puddle by the river. Dolan has a bit of equipment and his pick-up's 4WD. Guess it's possible the other two could have borrowed vehicles.

Scarborough's folks have a Range Rover. Could be any random who knew Pip or had something going on with him that they wanted to hide. Eliminate the ones I know already? Discreetly, Cal.

Scarborough's home was closest to her current position. She put the hatchback in gear and drove north.

She parked on a rise south of the property. The main road wasn't wide but a small copse of trees had been left outside the fence on a bank carved into the sandstone. In the lee and shadow of the trees with two wheels tucked onto the verge, she couldn't be seen from the Scarborough house and outbuildings. She lifted the hatch and left it open so any passing cars would hopefully ignore the vehicle, thinking she was picnicking or fixing a tyre.

Lying on the grass with her binoculars, she scanned the main entrance. Two large pillars held the massive gates. Recessed near the top each side were tiny reflective glass screens, windows over surveillance cameras. No surprises there. She surveyed along the tree-lined drive. Twice along the stretch, hidden within the tree-line, several pole-mounted cameras were directed to the access-way. At the end of the drive, cameras under the eaves of the house and outbuildings covered all the doorways and thoroughfares.

She could go in via the adjoining paddocks in the dark. In a hoodie and cap she could be safe if her face wasn't caught on screen. But she would still have to gain access to the garage to check the tyres on the Range Rover. And she would have to be quick. Either that or try and check the vehicle off the property. At least with the club she had some idea of where Terry could be found. The mother, however, likely driver of the Range Rover, was right off her screen. Cal was stuck on that one for the time being.

Onto Mr Dolan and Mr Pratt. She drove away from the river flats and continued up into the hills and bushland. Across the grasslands bordering the river margin, she looked to the cliff face on the eastern side of the Hawkesbury. A flock of white cockatoos passed across the face of the worn sandstone.

She drove along the winding tributaries and slowed as she approached Misty's garage and store. Pratt's silver wagon wasn't in its usual spot. But a police cruiser was. She recognised the Ford and one of the detectives, kept her head down and continued up the hill. Pratt would keep.

~

Cobbin emerged from the Misty's workshop.

'No joy?' Avery wiped saucy fingers on the greasy brown paper bag.

Cobbin shook his head. 'Hard to say if he's been here. Did she open this door?' He indicated towards the store.

'Didn't ask.' Avery licked his fingers, looked up as a white hatchback slowed then passed the entrance road.

'Lookit the head,' Cobbin said. 'It's Cal Nyx. Run the plates.' He read off the number.

'What's she doing driving incognito?' Avery jumped in the car, tapped at the laptop. 'And what's she doing up here?'

'Crims change wheels like we change undies. Always check the face.' Cobbin drummed his fingers on the roof. 'Learnt that as a constable.' Cobbin gazed into the treetops, thought about payday, time off.

'Registered to a Deena Mazzanti. Kurrajong address. Not reported stolen. She's always on the spot. Find that odd?'

'Bit suss. Can't do much if the car's not flagged. Just log the sighting.'

'We could follow her.' Avery got behind the wheel.

'S'posed to be looking for Pratt, mate. Bloody goose chase following her. C'mon. Try Boarback. Might even be with his mate Dolan.'

Avery drove up to the ridge, didn't bother going to Pratt's home. There'd been no further word from the mother. He turned right into Boarback, floored the car for two clicks, slowed as they neared Dolan's home address.

'Pull in,' Cobbin grunted.

'Pick-up's not here.' Avery eased down the drive. Cobbin got out, rapped on the door. No answer. Went around the back. All quiet. Went back to the car.

'Okay. Try his depot.'

Avery reversed out. Carried on along Boarback.

Moments later Cobbin slapped his hands on the dashboard. 'Watchit!' he yelled.

Avery hit the brakes. The small rock on the road was no longer visible over the curve of the bonnet.

'Tortoise,' Cobbin said as he unclicked his seat belt and got out.

Avery watched as Cobbin lifted the creature and carried it to the other side of the road, put it down well inside the scrub margin.

'Few dams on the properties round here, eh,' Cobbin said as he got back in.

Avery carried on in silence, flicked his indicator to turn right into Dolan's depot. The chain was up. 'Waddaya reckon?'

'Let's have a nosey.'

17

Cal drove up towards Boarback Ridge, pushing the engine to the limit. *Cops might tail me again. Imagine trying to lose them in this little buzz-box.* She shook her head as she changed down another gear. She topped the rise on Juta Road, pausing at the Y-intersection where Boarback Ridge joined from the south east. A blue-liveried truck crossed in front of her, headed north: *Dolan's Earthmoves Contracting.* She stared after it, then followed.

She was on the northern end of the ridge, driving through sparse plateau bushland with glimpses through the gum trees of the endless hinterland beyond. One and a half kilometres along the ridge, the truck indicated and turned left at a sudden breach in the scrub. Cal passed the site, a freshly bulldozed subdivision. Buff-coloured sandstone exposed where the vegetation had been scraped away. Shiny fence-wire and unbleached battens beside the newly-cut entranceway and building site ran back from a gleaming three-metre galvanised gate. Someone was chopping up their farm. The nose of the Hino truck stood beside a forty-foot container inside the entrance.

She carried on along Juta Road. Two hundred metres further on the eastern side of the road, a firebreak bisected the bush. She turned the car in and drove along the sandstone rubble for fifty metres. At a curve in the track she hid the car and jogged back along Juta Road, ready to run into the scrub if necessary.

As she neared the new subdivision, she crossed the road, climbed over the five-strand wire and entered the bush. Much of the property was covered in scrub, making the cleared swathe all the more pronounced. She crept towards the container and truck at one edge of the ochre-coloured expanse, several hundred metres long. A magpie picked at the newly turned earth beyond the truck. Cal paused and listened for voices, workmen, but all she could hear was the faint rasp of a horse racing commentary from the truck cab. Across the lot a bulldozer fired up. The driver, in a blue singlet and faded red cap, edged the machine towards the face of a bank. Was that Dolan? Or was he in the container? The doors were opened away from her so she couldn't check from where she was. She crept wide and came in behind the truck to see what she could from there. The bulldozer racket was a boon as she hustled across the dry leaf debris.

Beyond the rear of the truck she could now see more parked equipment. A diesel fuel trailer and another trailer with a small aluminium punt on the back. Mud and plant debris caught in the axle clamp. Unusual leaves, dusky, pinnate. She squatted behind the punt. Drip holes dotted the ground behind the tilted craft. They were damp. Dolan a fisherman? She duck-walked around the back of the diesel trailer, then skirted along its flank. She craned low, tried to see beyond into the doorway of the container. Still didn't have enough angle without exposing her position.

She checked back towards the bulldozer. The engine was still running, but the driver wasn't in the seat. *Where's he gone?*

∼

Cobbin and Avery left Dolan's after a quick sweep of the property. The yards were mostly empty except for a small backhoe with its boom and dipper arm dismantled on a tarp at the rear. It looked like most of his digging equipment was off-site, perhaps on a big job somewhere. The red pick-up was parked in front of the office. Presumably he'd driven one of his trucks if he was off-site.

Cobbin's phone buzzed in his pocket.

'It's me, detective. Myra Pratt. Nol's not been home. Not like him. Bit worried. He's s'posed to bring my meds.'

Cobbin looked at his watch: 1.37pm. 'Could have got caught up somewhere?'

'Always rings me. He's a good lad. Does my dinner most nights.'

'Okay, Mrs Pratt. Do you have other family? Someone to help out?'

'Only Nolly. No one else here.'

'Like me to get in touch with community services for you?'

'You're a kind fella. I can ring them myself, thanks. Just want to know my boy is safe.'

'We'll keep an eye out. Got his car details here. Thanks for letting us know.'

Avery looked at Cobbin, raised his eyebrows.

'Pratt's AWOL. That was his mum,' Cobbin said.

Avery made a grim pout.

As they continued along Boarback, Avery slowed at the Toblensk property.

At the far end of the drive, partially tucked behind the house, the rear of a silver Mazda station wagon. Its driver's door stood ajar.

'Don't like the look of this.'

They both checked their sidearms and cautiously approached the vehicle. On the driver's side, twin marks scraped across the gravel then stopped. Cobbin nodded at them. Drag marks, heels perhaps. They peered into the vehicle. Junk, debris, toolbag on the passenger seat.

Cobbin dropped low, checked the ground. Blood. Not pooled. Droplets. They continued around the back of the house. A lower bathroom window was smashed. The back door was partly open.

Avery waved Cobbin on. Across the yard a window beside the workshop door, also smashed. Avery held his weapon in both hands in front of him, kept it levelled towards the shed door, nodded for Cobbin to look inside. Cobbin eased along the side of the building, kept his body flat, close to the wall.

As he neared the door he edged out to give himself a sight-angle into the room. Blood, again on the ground beside the doorway. He peered inside, following his outstretched arms and weapon. Inside the shed, the recreation end in disarray, cupboards emptied, drawers pulled, a couch slashed, its stuffing like clouds on the floor. Avery followed behind him. They cleared the room.

'Check the house,' Cobbin whispered.

This time Avery went first, nudging the unlatched door with his foot. He made his way past the bathroom wall on his left, sweeping his weapon across to the kitchen opening. A beam of light radiated across the floor. He followed it to a torch resting against the kickboard. He took a quick look over his shoulder, motioned to Cobbin that he was heading down the hallway, Cobbin to cover him. He stepped forward in a slight crouch, making his way down towards the lounge and bedrooms.

Avery swept his weapon ahead of him. Lounge on the left. A wash of light on the floor from an overhead lamp. Curtains closed. Drawers in sideboard pulled open. Glass cabinet doors open. Couch, two armchairs. Moved into the room, weapon first, stepped to rear of the couch, nothing. Behind armchair one, weapon first. Clear. Second armchair. Clear.

He turned, stepped back to the hallway. Cobbin covered from

behind. Two doorways on the right. First one, curtains closed. Set of drawers, open, contents strewn. Entered the room, waited for Cobbin. Went to the built-in wardrobe, nodded back to Cobbin. Reached for the closest door. Pulled it open. Hanging jackets, shirts. Next door, pulled it open. Coats.

Avery crossed the room to the far side of the bed, weapon steady, pointed down towards the floor beside the bed. All clear. Turned to Cobbin. Indicated he would now do the next room. Cobbin kept him covered. Avery made his way down the hall.

Entered the smaller bedroom. Curtains closed. Closet open. Approached the door with the muzzle of his weapon, reached his foot out, flicked the door fully open, swept his gun across the space. Clear. Cobbin covered the doorway. Avery approached the bed, stepped around the end, weapon to the floor. Clear. He moved back. Shook his head at Cobbin. They returned outside. Holstered their weapons.

'Call in the techs. Maybe the dog squad. He could've scarpered into the bush.'

Avery hit the comms radio. 'Might not have been alone.'

Cobbin doubted that, the toolbag was on the passenger seat. 'Or someone else turned up.' He slugged from a water bottle.

～

Scobie took a call from Cobbin who updated her on Pratt's Mazda at the Toblensk site, and the fact Nolly was still missing.

Scobie called Cal. No answer. Left a message.

'Sorry hun. Have to cancel afternoon tea. Text me to confirm you've got this message. Be in touch.'

～

Sci-fi creatures marched across the sand before Cal's eyes. Dun-coloured ground. Blurry ants. *Awake? Asleep? Dreaming?*

Gang-gang cockatoos. Not on Mars then.

Her mouth glued shut with dehydration. Throat full of sawdust. Body heavy, dull. Tried to lift her head. A deep jag of pain shot up the back of her neck beneath her skull. She lifted a hand to the spot. Sticky, brought it before her eyes. Could smell the blood before she saw the hazy clot on her fingers. Thudding ache behind her eyes. Close them. The awful light. Sleep.

No. Can't sleep. What was I doing? Need to do something.

She tried again. Drew her right arm out from under her body. Pins and needles but functional. Stopped, listened. The birds. The sun westwards. No machinery. The subdivision. The bulldozer. Couldn't hear it. The truck. *I was near the truck.*

Lifted her head. The shooting pain again. Drew both arms in front of her, pushed upwards, lifted her torso.

The bulldozer was over by the bank. Stationary. Swept her eyes around, pain lancing across her skull with the small movements. Container doors shut. Truck gone. *My car. The car. How did I get here?* Rubbed her hand across her head. Squinted her eyes against the light, the searing pain.

Oh Jesus. Dee's car. Where did I leave it? She scanned the yard again. The magpie, tapping the earth with its beak. Didn't drive in here. Dropped her head again. Went through what she remembered. Scarborough's place. Misty's. The cops. The truck. *I hid the car. Down the road.*

She stood, swaying, the movement of her body, pumping blood, sent fresh bolts of jarring pain through her skull. *Body wants me still. No. Have to move, get out of here.*

She half ran in a crouch, as though reducing her height would alleviate the pain, as well as making her a smaller target. No one was there, though. She sensed that.

Winced at the light, the bleaching, searing whiteness, agonising, through her eyes into her brain. Stopped at the entrance, hunched, looked through her squeezed eyes down the silent road. Ran north for the firebreak.

Avery reversed out of the Toblensk property, dodging the tech wagon. He drove north as Cobbin checked for updates.

'Dolan's depot first?' He looked towards Cobbin who nodded.

'Calling him now,' he said as he held his mobile to his ear.

Five clicks north he pulled into the track to Dolan's depot. This time the chain was down. He drove in. Cobbin watched through the windscreen. Avery swept around the yard and parked beside a Hino truck near the office. The door to the small building was open. Dolan appeared, stood in the doorway holding a mug.

Cobbin got out. 'Phone not working?'

Dolan reached for his pocket, pulled out a cell phone. 'Can't hear on a digger.' He pocketed it again.

Avery approached from the driver's side. They converged on the doorway.

'Few questions,' Cobbin said.

'Fire away.' Dolan raised his mug, no attempt to move from the doorway and let them in.

'Seen Nolly Pratt lately?'

'Matter of fact, no.' He sipped.

'Last time you saw him?' Avery spoke.

'Been a while.'

'Thought you were mates.' Cobbin again.

Dolan drew back.

'Where are you working at the moment?' Cobbin continued.

Dolan swung his head indicating northwest. 'Juta Road. New subdivision.'

'Address.'

'1162 Juta Road North. Can't miss it.'

'So, last time you saw Nolly Pratt?' Avery repeated.

Dolan scratched his chin with a gnarled thumb.

'Musta been last week. Yeh. At the workshop.'

'What did you see him for?'

'Eh?'

'What did you talk about?'

'Just jawin'.'

'You know he's missing?'

'No.' He raised his eyebrows. 'How would I know that?'

'Mother's worried.'

'Yeh, she would be. Might drop round. See how she's doin'.'

'We'd like to check your worksite. Problem with that?'

'Go fer broke.' Dolan swirled the dregs of his tea, tossed them on the ground in front of the cops.

~

Scobie's phone rang. Ottering.

'What's happening, Janice.'

'We're stuck here, skip. Dust storm's closed the airport. We're on standby for first flight out. Not looking good. Huge backlog now.'

'All we bloody need. Tony and Glen are stretched thinner than a wonton wrapper at the Toblensk site. Pratt's wagon abandoned on-site and he's missing. Try and make your follow-up calls on Sylvia Toblensk's alibi if you can. Getting late, I know. Just keep me appraised.'

'Will do.'

18

Cal stumbled up the road, each step sending thuds of pain up through her legs, along her spine, exploding inside her skull. She wanted to close her eyes and shut out the stabbing light. How much further?

Heard the whine of a vehicle in the distance, behind her. Threw her body sideways into the scrub. Lay on her stomach, blinked, peered back down the road, saw the police cruiser turn into the subdivision.

Pulled her body upright. Forced her way through the scrub, hands in front clearing branches until she met the breach of the fire-trail. Turned in and followed the track. Ignored the pain, the light. *Gotta get outta here.*

Reached the curve, saw the car as she rounded the bend. Felt her pockets. Where are the keys? Touched her phone. Withdrew it. Squinted. Three missed calls. Scobie.

Where are the keys? Jesus, this is all I need. Felt all her pockets again. Nothing. Her throat rasped raw with dehydration. *Dee got a spare? Please please please.* She stooped around the car, feeling along the edge of the panels. Nothing. Bumpers. Nope. Plastic. Magnetic box won't stick there.

Went to the rear, lay down, reached under the fuel tank. Ran her hand across the rough surface of the sound-deadener. Gravel and dust fell. She coughed, turned her head away. Her fingers hit the bump of a small rectangular container, pulled it away. She withdrew her hand, slid the cover open. The spare. Took it, replaced the magnetic box and got in the car. Water bottle on the floor. Half empty. Opened the glovebox, rifled for pain relief. Nothing there. She tipped the warm water down her throat and started the car.

～

Avery drove north along Boarback Ridge, came to the intersection, continued northwest on Juta Road. Just as Dolan had suggested, they couldn't miss the new subdivision. Avery pulled in, parked in the middle of the bare swathe. They got out, walked the site in different directions.

Cobbin scuffed around the bulldozer, following the ragged edge of the levelled site. On the top of a ridge, the scrapings fell away down the hillside in crumbling rivulets. He looked over the edge. Branches and root-balls of twisted brown scrub emerged in tangles from beneath the sandstone rubble.

He paced back over to where Avery inspected the other equipment and container.

'Move a lot of earth with one of those things.' He gestured back towards the heavy dozer.

Avery nodded. 'Quick hide, eh.'

'Wouldn't have taken Dolan for a fisher.' Cobbin surveyed the punt and trailer. Something caught his eye in the clearing behind it, a glint against the dull earth. He walked over, picked up a stick and used it to lift a set of keys. Held them up. Hyundai remote.

'Nyx was driving a Hyundai.'

～

Cal fanged it along the plateau road and down the southwest route towards the Scarborough estate. Desperate for water and pain relief she swerved into Misty's at the bottom of the hill, hit the brakes, spitting gravel as she came to a halt beside the store. Raced inside, wincing and bent with the pain in her head. The owner stared and Cal wondered just how disastrous she looked.

'Painkillers. Where?' she gasped at the woman, barely able to face her with the fluoro light behind the counter tormenting her troubled eyes.

The woman pointed to the second aisle. 'Top row. Halfway along.'

Cal shuffled along the aisle, grabbed a packet of ibuprofen. Went to the cooler at the back, grabbed a litre bottle of water. Returned to the counter, proffered her card.

'Looks like you need more than that,' the woman said grimly.

'No time.' Cal grabbed the gear, left. The woman watched, shaking her head at the sight of the bloodied gash and clotted hair at the back of Cal's head, her clothing dusty and stained. Looked like a hobo.

Cal sat in the car, skulled half the water and a pair of pills. Flicked her phone on, did a search of Scarborough's website. Gayle Scarborough was giving a dressage demo that afternoon at the estate. Just the distraction she needed to check that vehicle.

Glanced in the rear-view mirror, caught sight of her face. Jesus. Jumped out, ran to the tap by the bowsers, stuck her head under, swished water across her face, down her neck. Flinched as it ran over the wound. Shook off the water, new pain. Grabbed a wad of paper wipes from the dispenser, swiped her face, slicked her hair, held the wad to the back of her head.

Got back in the car, put it in gear, tore out of the driveway heading for the flatlands.

Scobie checked her phone round 4pm. Still no word from Cal.

Sure, she didn't know Cal well, but she felt certain she would have texted or called if she was held up. She didn't seem a careless type.

At 4.30pm Scobie rang comms. Asked them to ping-check Cal's phone.

Then she called Tony Cobbin for an update. 'You logged a sighting of Nyx at 12.27am. Nothing further?' She scratched at her upper arm, a fingernail catching the fabric of the fine nude crepe, despite her recent manicure.

'Ringling Circus up here. Blood at the Toblensk property. Pratt's still missing. Dog squad, techs. You want us here or looking for Nyx.' The last comment slightly bitter. And insubordinate.

'Cal Nyx is as deserving of police protection as any other citizen. If she was in the area she may have seen something. She may be in danger.' Scobie took a breath. 'I've got a ping-trace on her phone. Let me know when the techs have anything. Where's Dolan?'

'Questioned him at his depot. Reckons he hasn't seen Pratt.'

'So only you and Glen searching.' A raspy tone, Scobie clearly irritated.

'Maybe you should suit up.'

'Christ on a bike. Frank and Janice can't get back here soon enough. They're stuck in Melbourne. I'll see if any other area commands can help out.'

~

Cal passed the Scarborough property coming from the north, continued past for several hundred metres, did a U-turn and parked in the same spot as her last visit, beneath the copse of trees on the rise. Her head throbbed, like every pulse of her blood was a small punch inside her skull. So much for painkillers. Got out of the car, lay in the grass, observed.

The dressage ring was to the south of the main house, closest to Cal. The main driveway and turning zone ended at a gravelled area the size of a football field. Neatly parked prestige SUVs and sedans lined the edges. Around the dressage ring, groups of people clustered and others sat on tiered white seating which curved around one end. Potentially, Cal could be seen as she made her way along the fence-line bordering the road. Same for the adjacent driveway under the lee of the trees. She bargained on the visitors watching the horses in the ring. Pulled her hood over her head. Twigs and sand fell into the congealed mess at the nape of her neck. Nice.

Halfway along the first fence-line, she scuttled low, the heads of the ryegrass pattering across her calves. The minor exertion increased the thudding plague of spasms jarring across her skull.

She paused, squeezed her eyes, tried to calm her breathing. Nothing helped. *Move through it, Cal.*

Reached the corner, heard a polite applause from the dressage ring. Put her head down, crouch-ran along the tree-shadows. Stopped halfway. Checked her surrounds, her vision chopping her images in half. *Migraine. Great. Get this done. Top of the drive, quick sweep. Go.*

Crossed to the garage, head down. Range Rover in first bay. Do it. Passenger side front, squatted, ran her hand over the outer edge. Front to back. Nothing. Again. No joy. Flat of the tread on the concrete. Bottom of the tyre. Lay down. Switched her torch on, shone it along the floor. Put her little finger in the notch.

'You right?' Aggressive. Behind her. She turned her head, looked up, another lancing jolt of agony through her skull. Terry Scarborough.

'Dropped something. All good.' She held up her torch, smiled. Stood. Swayed. Grimaced. Ran to the rear of the vehicle. He followed. Ran down the other side and out along the drive as throngs of horsey toffs dispersed to the lawn for tea and tiny cakes.

∼

On the veranda, at home in Kurrajong, the setting sunlight hit Cal's closed eyelids. Yellow, red, green, she watched the colours slide across the dark. The sound of the Stones drifted from inside. *You Gotta Move*, Mississippi Fred McDowell track. Made her think of Robert Johnson, broken bottleneck slide guitar. The movie *Crossroads*.

That notched tyre. Means the vehicle was there near the car park where Pip's pick-up was torched. Had to have come via the firebreaks. What are the chances? Don't see Terry Scarborough's ma doing cross-country. Why the hell did he need that pick-up fried? What does he have to hide? Him and Pip? An affair? Why not? Does that mean he killed Pip? And Stef? Why? Why?

Her head hurt.

The moon rose in the east, casting a soft, silver light through the trees. No wind. Two owls flew open-winged across the field. *Ninox strenua,* the powerful owl. She stood, leaned on the rail in the shadow of the long eaves. The Stones on rotation. Something about a face in the window.

Scobie returned from down by the stream, climbed the three wooden steps. Buried her eyes in Cal's shoulder as she moved in her arms.

Just before 2am Scobie got up, dressed. Bent and kissed Cal on the temple. 'They'll want to question you. Be ready or be scarce.' She kissed her again and left.

19

Morning in the incident room, Scobie briefed the returnees, Ottering and Birch. Strands of hair hung from her hastily-pulled updo. Her eyes heavy, bloodshot, sighted languidly across the room, not resting on her colleagues.

'Things heating up, boss.' Birch snapped back the cover on his notebook.

'Bloody Desert Storm up the mountain. Glen and Tony should be relieved but I can't afford to lose any manpower. I need you two on it right away.'

'What have we got?' Ottering sat forward on her seat, fingers poised over the keyboard of her laptop.

'Nolly Pratt is missing. Not seen since early hours Monday morning. Mother expected him home that afternoon. His vehicle was found yesterday at the Toblensk property. Signs of break-in at the house and an outbuilding. Blood also found on-site. No sign of Pratt.' She looked up, returned to her notes. 'Glen and Tony are yet to speak with Craig Dolan. Techs have been on-site overnight. Cal Nyx was sighted near Misty's earlier in the day. No further sighting of her or the vehicle she was travelling in.

White Hyundai, rego BT75TA.' She looked up from her notes. 'I'd like Terry Scarborough spoken to as well.'

Birch whistled. 'Still without a reason for being out at Gringly's the night of the burn. He's linked to this in some way.'

'Where to first?' Ottering said.

'Scarborough. Keep an eye out for Nyx. Ping on her phone gives us the plateau area but the dearth of towers out there only gives us a range.'

'Why don't you put a ping on Dolan then?'

Scobie ignored Birch.

'You want us following up on Sylvia Toblensk? Her alibi?'

'If you can make calls on your way to Scarborough's, by all means. We still haven't established if we have more than one perp operating here. I want to be informed immediately on any developments.' She left the room, bypassed her office, strode down the hall to the main entrance.

Birch turned to Ottering, drew his head back, spread his hands.

Ottering raised her eyebrows. 'Losing it.'

Ottering charged into the carpool, glugging from her water bottle. 'What's with her and Nyx? Could lose her job.'

Birch sniffed. 'Wouldn't be the first time law enforcement fell for a crim.'

'Compromising the investigation. Crazy.' She started the car.

'What can we do? You wanna go over her head?'

She flicked her indicator, inched out of the driveway. 'It'll come back on us if we know about it and do nothing.'

'Could talk to Tone and Glen.'

'She's not seeing right, that's for certain.' The tyres bit into the tarmac, squealed as Ottering floored it. 'Will Scarborough be at home or the club, you reckon?'

'Home. Too early for him to be working.' Birch balanced his notebook on his lap, thumbed his phone, made a call to Dr Stephanie Powell, senior curator at the National Gallery in

Canberra. She was on another call. He left a message for her to ring him.

~

Up on Boarback Ridge at Dolan's new Juta Road worksite, Avery swept his eyes over the bland surrounds, wiped grit from his eyes as a small willy-willy funnelled dust and ran across the expanse. The miniature whirlwind disappeared off the edge of the bank.

'Think we should have a nosey down the river,' Cobbin said, coughing.

'Misty's?'

'Place to start.'

'Wanna get the dog squad to give this a once-over?'

'I'll call it through. They can come here after they finish at the Toblensk place.'

Avery drove. Cobbin made the call, gave the Juta Road address. They were down from the hills in under ten minutes. Avery slowed and made the turn left onto the river track. The area between the road and the river margin was covered in scrub and saplings.

Cobbin scanned the area beside him. 'Not easy to launch along here.'

A hundred metres along another track led off left to the lower road alongside the river.

'Park up. We'll walk it. Don't wanna drive over anything.'

Avery pulled over.

Cobbin skated down a rough incline to the lower track beside the river. Glimpsed through the trees, the quiet water reflected the sunlight. Even on the weekends, the only sounds were those produced by watercraft, creating waves that rippled and gurgled as they washed past the muddy margins. The pair parted and walked in different directions along the track. The silent waterway held its peace.

Ten minutes later they reconvened. Cobbin spoke. 'Could follow this for miles. Let's check the landing.'

'Be too obvious?'

'Crims are idiots.'

∾

Ottering waited opposite the entrance as Beemers and Audis exited the driveway. 'Christ. What's going on here?'

'Let them clear,' Birch said.

Beyond the top of the drive, fluttering white tablecloths and a cluster of small marquees were partially visible through the trees.

When the main car park appeared empty, bar a pair of caterer's vans, Ottering made a sedate entrance and parked near the main garage. She could see Gayle Scarborough speaking with a woman in a long white apron. She waited beside the car until Scarborough was done.

Birch strolled over to the garage, craned his neck around the back corner towards Terry Scarborough's cottage. All quiet. He couldn't see the Nissan GTR. He ambled back to where Ottering was in conversation with Gayle Scarborough.

'Just missed him. Probably catch him at the club.'

'Home last night, was he?' Birch had his hands in his pockets.

'Wish I could say for sure. Comes home long after I've put my head down.' She smiled politely. 'Have you had lunch?' She looked from one to the other. 'Caterers are just finishing up. Coffee there too. Please help yourselves.' She gestured towards the nearest gazebo.

Ottering was about to decline. Birch interrupted. 'Very kind. Thank you.' He smiled.

His phone rang. Dr Stephanie Powell from the National Gallery. Birch explained his reason for calling.

'We're trying to establish that the donated works were something both Sylvia and Stefan Toblensk were aware of and agreed upon.'

'I've never doubted that they were. They visited here together once or twice.' Dr Powell paused. 'After Alena died. She was a wonderful patron. We're indebted to her. To all three of them actually.'

Birch heard something being put on a glass top, a cup perhaps.

Powell continued. 'They could've contested her will, you know. Those works were worth a fair bit. I don't think either of Alena's children were exactly wealthy. If they were driven by avarice they could have fought the donation of the art works. They didn't. They honoured Alena's wishes. I think that speaks volumes as to their characters. They were very decent, the pair of them.'

'Nothing else you can add?'

'We're grateful to that family. I hold them all in high regard.'

'Thanks for your time.' Birch ended the call. Filled Ottering in.

'Okay. Still need to check Sylvia's alibi for that weekend. You wanna call or shall I?'

'Quick bite. You call.' Birch smirked, picking up a small plate and loading it. Finger food. Tiny asparagus rolls the size of a thumb joint. Mini puffed savouries with creamy filling, topped with chives. Thai fish cakes with lime and chilli dipping sauce. They weren't supposed to accept hospitality from the public. Birch's homemade cheese and chutney sandwich might become his dinner.

He returned their plates to the caterer. 'Lovely grub. Thank you.'

Ottering was leaning on the front of the squad car, shading her eyes as she spoke on the phone. Birch wandered over, lit a cigarette.

Ottering finished her call, stood up. 'Spoke to the cousin, Ava

Trentham in Jindabyne. Ingrid Heinz's main carer. She was also there when Sylvia visited. She confirmed the visit. And that Ingrid Heinz had identified her father's paintings. So, that all tallies with what Sylvia told us.' Ottering reached inside the front of the car for her water bottle.

'Sylvia's in the clear then.' Birch blew a stream of smoke over his head.

'Looks that way. Both Ingrid Heinz, or her carer cousin, and the gallery curator have confirmed her version of things.'

'I'll let skip know.'

Ottering reversed, drove out of the long driveway. Headed towards town, the club. 'So Mr Terry Scarborough. Got nothing out of him last time. What's the new angle?' She pushed herself back in her seat, straightened her neck.

'Go at it again. Same line. It's a beat. What's he doing there? He hasn't accounted for it. Have to press harder.'

'Connection with him and Phillip Leuwins at the club. Vehicle seen on road to Gringly's reserve the night the pick-up was torched. Too much coincidence for mine.' She flicked the air con down a notch. Autumn: how warm was it.

'Prod him again now Pratt is missing. No connection between those two though.' Birch thumbed the end of his pen.

'That we know of.' Ottering slowed for a T-junction.

'Cilla was nervous.'

'Yeh. She was. There's a link. Something suss with him.'

Birch shook his pen, scraped it on the back of his notepad. No joy. Dropped it in his rubbish bag on the floor, pulled another from his pocket. 'Form for assault on women, even if his money got him off.'

'Exactly. He's arrogant. And he's hiding something.'

Twenty minutes later they turned into the rear parking area. Scarborough's gold Nissan was in the manager's space.

~

Cal woke, slow and heavy, as if she was pulling her body and consciousness through molasses. Reached for painkillers on the side table. The slight movement of her head sent fresh jags of pain across her neck and skull. As she remembered Scobie and the previous night, some of the hurt diminished. She popped two painkillers from their foils and threw them back, followed by a river of water. Lay back, touched her forehead, closed her eyes.

The Range Rover was in that fire-break. Scarborough has some link to this. I was clobbered at Dolan's site. Was Scarborough there? Did he follow me? Was he there already? Or was it someone else and if so, why? Dolan? Dolan and Pratt. Where's Pratt? Why was the punt wet?

She closed her eyes, gave the drugs ten minutes to kick in. Got up, went to the other room, drawer of a small desk under the window, took out a bundle of maps. Ran her finger along several tributaries of the main rivers. Something was niggling the back of her brain. Maybe it was just general fugginess. No, an item, a thing she'd seen, important, trying to surface. Rubbed her hand across her scalp. Not firing on all cylinders yet. Coffee.

She lit the gas ring, leaned against the bench, closed her eyes.

Something bumped the front door. Her eyes flipped open, stared. She reached behind, felt for the cutlery tray, her fingers closed around a fork. Edged towards the door, a bump again. Touched the handle, whipped the door open. A thud and patter as Banjo's purple ball ran across the floor. She put her head around the edge. Looked into the eager face.

'C'mon.' She swung her head inside. 'Nothing wrong with your manners, eh.' Banjo loped in, grabbed the ball, turned to Cal, dropped it again beside his singular front paw, barked at her.

'Oo fella. Keep it down.' She winced. The coffee pot shrilled. She poured a mugful, sat at the small desk, slapped her thigh. Banjo sat against her leg as she rubbed his chest, pondered the maps again.

Misty's Landing. She followed the river in both directions. To the northeast there was no possible launch site within a forty-five minute drive. Tracks followed the river closely at numerous points, but the steep banks and scrub would make launching any watercraft virtually impossible. How far would someone go to dump something? To the south there was a junction at Cottle Flat. She could visualise the place beside the northern bank, a concrete boat ramp. Same on the opposite bank. Too obvious or doing something in plain view? She ran her finger across the map again, paused at the back of the landfill. The detail wasn't shown on the chart but she knew the layout. A series of silt collection ponds and marshes that ran down the incline before the filtered effluent joined the tributary above the main river junction. An access track looped around the settlement ponds for maintenance. It ran both sides of the ponds and down to the river.

Dolan would surely be a regular at the landfill, dumping spoil and rock from his sites.

20

Scobie strode along the hallway, juggled her coffee and notes, slipped an errant lock of hair behind her ear. She joined the team assembled in the incident room.

'The blood at the Toblensk property has been confirmed as Nolly Pratt's. We should inform his mother. At this stage we have nothing further. Obviously, it's suspicious, but until we have conclusive evidence, we're still treating this as a missing person investigation.'

'Dog squad find anything at Dolan's subdivision?' Avery asked.

Scobie shook her head.

'What about the Scarborough interview?' Cobbin said.

Scobie nodded at Ottering and Birch.

Ottering spoke first. 'Questioned him again at the club yesterday. Zero. Tight as a clam.'

Birch said, 'Definitely hiding something. He's canny. Knows we have nothing but suspicion.'

'Cilla Breslin is our only hope there unless we come up with something more incriminating. She must know something. She won't hold out like he can,' Ottering added.

Scobie nodded. 'I agree. I'd like her questioned again. I think we can apply some more pressure there.'

'What about Scarborough's mother? She lives on the same property. She must know more,' Ottering chipped in. Birch dropped his head.

'Not necessarily. His hours mean he legitimately comes and goes when the majority of people are asleep,' Scobie replied. 'I'd prefer not riling her for now. That could bring in her husband. Best avoided if not strictly necessary.'

'Is Cal Nyx being questioned?' Ottering's tone bordered on petulant. Avery watched.

Scobie held her breath and her composure, kept her eyes on the papers in her hands. 'Her keys were found at Dolan's site so we need an explanation. A face-to-face would be ideal. Try her at home first.' She looked up, her stare a challenge. 'I don't think it's necessary to bring her in unless she's obstructive. Tony and Glen, after you've spoken to Dolan.'

∞

The group dispersed. Scobie went to her office. Minutes later Cobbin knocked on the glass window beside her door, stuck his head in. 'A word, skip?'

'Come in, Tony.' She stood behind her desk, bent forward filing papers into a folder.

Cobbin had his hands in his pockets, rattled his keys, unaware of the noise. Like fingernails down a blackboard for Scobie. She raised her eyebrows, waited, leant forward, palms down on her desk supporting her body.

Cobbin was unaccountably awkward.

'Need to sit?' She gestured at the chair.

'Skip. Might be out of line.' Pulled at his earlobe, hand back in pocket. 'None of our business. Just worried about the investigation, the higher ups.' Scratched the short hair at the back of his neck, hand back in pocket. Eyes locked on Scobie. 'You and Cal Nyx. Gotta be careful.'

Scobie paused, straightened. Her eyes narrowed. The pause extended. 'No idea what you're talking about, Tony. But I'm sure I don't like your inference.' She fought the urge to cross her arms. 'Just do your job.' She touched the trackpad on her open laptop. 'And close the door on your way out.'

~

Avery pulled into the newly-scraped site. The doors of the container were open and just beyond, a large diesel generator thrummed. Beside it, an MIG welding kit and Dolan, bent over, repairing a crack in a louvred piece of engine cover. He flipped his face mask up as Avery stood in front of him. Cobbin strolled over to the pair of trailers, one a diesel tank, the other holding the aluminium punt.

'Now what? You fellas should pack a lunch.' Dolan held the handpiece in his leather mitt.

'Still looking for Nolly Pratt. You remembered anything?'

'Told you yesterday. Haven't seen 'im.'

Avery pulled out the evidence bag. 'Found these at your Juta Road site.' He handed them to Dolan who inspected them through the plastic, shook his head.

'Hyundai. Not mine. None of the fellas drive one.' He screwed up his mouth.

'Know a Cal Nyx?'

Cobbin walked back.

Avery waited.

Dolan frowned, shook his head again. 'You know who they belong to then?' he said.

'Could do.'

'What were they doing on my worksite? Trespass isn't it? You could do them.'

'Bit hard to prove when she's not actually there.'

Dolan was silent a moment. 'Unlawful entry. Isn't there a charge?' he asked.

'Like I said. Bit hard to prove. Just keys.'

Cobbin piped up. 'Do a bit of fishing?'

'When I get the time.'

'Flies or bait?'

Dolan paused. 'Depends. Too many willows for flies, lotta places.'

'Mmm. Use any yabby traps?' Just mentioning the small crayfish filled Cobbin with yearning for his next day off.

'Nah. Don't like 'em.' Dolan put his hand to his mask, ready to flip it down. 'Gotta get on. You done?'

'Drop in on Myra? How was she?' Cobbin watched him carefully.

'Might get there this arvy.' He dropped the tinted visor, struck at the metal with his handpiece, sent a blast of brilliant light arcing from the contact. Cobbin and Avery turned away.

As they drove out Avery spoke quietly. 'Notice that? Didn't balk when I said "she". Like he knew that name belonged to a woman. I expected a bit of surprise.'

'Yup.'

~

Cal watched the small plume of dust following the squad car along the drive. Sipped her coffee. Banjo took off. The car stopped at the main house. Banjo circled. One of the occupants went to the front door, familiar, the one that had been at the body site. Dee answered, stood on the porch. The detective held something up in front of her. She looked over towards Cal's place, gestured. The detective got back in the car, drove on to Cal's cabin.

Cal's phone buzzed, a text from Dee.

Coppers. Something about the car.

Both detectives got out of the vehicle, came towards the steps.

'G'day.' Cal upturned her coffee mug.

'Morning,' Cobbin replied.

Avery put a foot on the bottom step, leaned on the rail. He dangled the evidence bag containing the Hyundai keys. 'We found these at a site on Juta Road. Any idea how they might have got there?'

Cal rested both elbows on the veranda railing, dangling both arms over the edge. Her coffee mug swung from her finger. 'Must've dropped them.'

'What were you doing? What business did you have being there?' Avery stuck his chin out. Banjo nudged at Cobbin's leg, got a pat.

'Pip was my friend. I've a right to know who killed him. And Stef. You guys don't have a mortgage on that.'

'Why do you think Dolan has anything to do with it?' Cobbin spoke.

'He and Nolly Pratt were there that night. At Stef's.'

'You were trespassing,' Avery said.

She laughed, a short bark. 'Somehow I don't think Craig Dolan is going to have me charged.' She leant forward, pointed a finger at the gash on her head. 'Already whacked me. Him or someone else.'

Avery's mouth formed a grim line. 'Wants you done for unlawful entry. S'posed to ask for permission to enter.'

'Pffttt. I was trying to retrieve my keys. I was out for a run. They must've fallen out of my pocket.'

Avery stared at her.

Cal smiled, shrugged. 'I'm a fitness nut.'

Avery tossed her the plastic bag with the keys inside. Cal caught them in her right hand.

. . .

They returned to the car, drove away.

'Reckon Scobie's protecting her?' Avery spoke, tapped long fingers on the steering wheel.

'Dunno. Can't see a motive for her. Think skip's taking a big risk though. Looks corrupt even if it's not.'

'We're not getting anywhere. Money. Sex. Hate. All possible. Nothing's coming clear.'

Cobbin stretched his legs into the foot-well. 'Fear's a pretty strong motivator.'

~

After the cops left, Cal fired up the Ford. Had the landfill site to check out near Misty's. Sitting behind the wheel made her feel like she was on a quest. Anything could happen. No other vehicle had that effect on her. Transporter all right.

She idled down the long driveway, turned left, passed through the western edge of Kurrajong and headed northeast.

She drove through the flatlands, the ancient floodplains of the Hawkesbury-Nepean, began the ascent through the lowland forests, up into the sandstone escarpments. Wind-sheared and water-worn over millions of years, the crumbling rock layered in ancient brows, visible through the dusky green of the foliage. Just days til Pip's memorial. Not long since Addie's passing. What a month it had been.

She entered the familiar backroads around Misty's, passed the garage and began the climb towards Juta Road, this time turning right into the less familiar landfill access. The track led off eastwards, winding along through sparse forest before opening out to the main offload area. Like a barren moonscape, the windswept, potholed expanse was ringed by occasional mounds of broken concrete and rubble. Rusting metal hung from overflowing skips. Stacked tyres breeding mosquitoes in their lakelike water-rings. Recycling cages full of debris. A withered agave in a forty-gallon barrel leaned beside the door of a battered galv hut. Currently unmanned, the centre was too small for full-time staff. Workers came on weekly rosters to load and unload skips, swap recycling bins, scrape green waste and metal into piles.

Grit, paper and plastic bags blew across the spread. The leaves of the trees bordering the area were coated with dust, their branches adorned with tattered shreds of plastic debris. She drove slowly through the main yard and followed a track beside the green waste heaps that led down to the series of effluent ponds. Large dams lined with filter cloth, the trio of reservoirs descended the hillside. In theory, all the nasty toxins leaking from the main dump site would settle in the pools, sinking to the bottom, while a filtered overflow eventually passed over the spillways down to the river.

Tank maintenance meant the accessways were reasonably wide and drivable. At several points on the incline, side tracks went to separate dump points for rock and fill. She was certain Dolan would be familiar with these. She carried on down the slope, reaching the final pond.

Beyond it, the accessway continued half a dozen metres then terminated beside the river in a level turning bay. Saved the maintenance trucks having to reverse up the hill. She parked, got out, walked five paces to the edge of the bank. Welcome swallows dipped and flitted above the surface of the river. The muddy bank rose barely eighteen inches from the water. Right in front of her, a flat section, metre and a half across, two deep grooves at either end. A twisted indent in the middle. Looked like the base of a punt had passed over, its bow rope dragging in the mud.

∼

Ottering and Birch reinterviewed Cilla Breslin. Scobie decided to keep the familiar pair on it rather than introducing Cobbin and Avery, although this approach could be effective at times.

Ottering sat opposite the young woman, Birch at the end of the table. Ottering began by slipping out the picture of Phillip Leuwins. 'I want you to look at this again. I want you to think carefully. Have you ever seen this man?'

Cilla Breslin was silent. She looked, then moved her eyes slightly to the right of the picture, a ring on the table's surface left by a mug or can. Focussed there. Ottering didn't miss it.

'Cilla?'

The girl didn't raise her eyes.

Birch motionless, let Ottering do the talking.

'You've seen this man?' Ottering took a breath, counted, kept her voice steady. 'If Terry hasn't done anything wrong, he has nothing to fear. Two men are dead. Another is missing. This is a very serious investigation. If you know something, you need to tell us.'

Nothing. Ottering sat back.

'The truth will come out, Cilla. It always does. If you know something, it's not going to go away.' Ottering paused. 'Terry can't hurt you if he's in prison.'

Cilla shook her head.

'We can protect you, Cilla.'

She shook her head again. 'You don't know him.'

'You have to live with this one way or another. If you know anything, you're an accessory. That's a long jail stretch.' Ottering tapped the end of her pen into the notepad. 'You come clean now, they'll look on you more favourably. Especially if you've been intimidated. But the longer you withhold evidence, the worse it goes for you.'

'Not like that. He wouldn't do that.'

Birch clasped his hands under the table, squeezed, decided against cracking his knuckles.

Ottering sat back, waited.

Cilla mumbled something. Ottering sat forward again.

'Sorry?'

Cilla looked up, looked down, repeated herself. 'Club one night, near closing.'

She stopped. Ottering waited. Counted. Shut up. Let it flow.

Cilla Breslin took several small breaths. 'The upstairs room. Looking for Tez. Just looking for him.' She twitched her head towards the photo. 'He was in there. With that guy.' She sighed, shook her head slowly back and forth. Her lips parted, a frown between her brows, a look of abject sadness and bewilderment. 'An affair. Or whatever you'd call it.' She ran a finger back and forth across the circle impression on the Formica surface. 'Don't understand.' She looked up at Ottering, tears pooling in her eyes, both angry and confused, at once. 'How can he be with me and be queer?'

~

Cal's phone rang. Private number.

'Cal Nyx.'

'Royal Prince Alfred Emergency Department. You're listed as next of kin to Zinnia Nyx.'

'That's right.' Cal stopped breathing.

'Brought in after a heart attack. Stable for now. A neighbour found her under the clothesline.'

'Jesus Christ.'

'Gave her CPR until the paramedics arrived. Did a good job.'

'I'll be there as soon as I can. If she's compos, please let her know I'm on my way.'

'If she needs angioplasty they'll do it immediately. Check with the main desk when you arrive. They'll tell you which ward she's in.'

Giant claws squeezed her chest. Short gasps of air drew in but got no further than the base of her neck. Zin was her only relative. Cal suddenly felt very small, alone, vulnerable. A wobbliness shuffled in her stomach. *Fuck me.* She wanted to cry.

Not up for it eh, Nyx? The taunt from long ago.

Stared out through the windscreen, clenched her teeth.

Yeh. Then she'd pulled the trigger.

21

She arrived in Camperdown just under one and a half hours later. Parked in a lane behind King Street several hundred metres from the main entrance to the hospital. Hurried back, went to the desk, got directions to the ward. Up lifts, down corridors, got lost. Eventually found Zin, dozing in a shared ward, curtains pulled beside her bed. Cal stood over her, leaned down, kissed her on the cheek. Warm, smooth.

'What were you doing at the bloody clothesline? Climbing it?'

'Think about it.' Soft, smiling.

'You can go to the laundromat from here on.'

'Silly bugger. Wasn't hanging out my nighties that did me in. Could've been anything.'

'Well, you need to do things differently now.'

Zin closed her eyes. 'Can't do that. Can't stop living, Cal.'

Cal fidgeted, looked around the room, the laminate surfaces, the monitor machine, a small window. She couldn't remember feeling so bereft of solutions. Of course, there were none. Facing inevitability, mortality. Not comfortable for her. 'I brought you in some stuff. Anything else you need?' She held open the overnight bag. Someone in a nearby bed had a coughing spasm.

Zin rolled her head slowly on the pillow. Opened her eyes, reached her hand out for Cal's, gave it a squeeze. 'Be home soon. They won't keep me in long. Need the bed.'

'I'll take you. I'll tell them to call me.'

'Do you a dinner when I'm back.'

'Fuck's sake, Auntie. Just get yourself right.'

Cal spoke to the ward sister on her way out. Zin would remain there at least overnight and possibly one more day.

Cal left the hospital, wandered back towards King Street. She'd planned to stay in town at Zin's, save herself a trip to Kurrajong and back. Pip's memorial in a couple of days. Lotta time to kill. She changed her mind, headed back to the mountains. On her way out of town she stopped at a late vet's surgery. Bought a pair of GPS pet collars.

∼

In the incident room, Avery updated the others. 'We spoke to Dolan. Posturing about wanting Nyx trespassed. Showed no reaction when I used a female pronoun.'

Ottering pulled her chin back. *Jeez, Glen's using some fancy terminology.*

'Not outwardly. Thought I saw a tiny balk,' Cobbin added.

'If he whacked her – and that seems most likely – he would know it wasn't a bloke. Why'd he have to smack her in the head? Got something to hide.' Avery puffed up.

'You spoke to Nyx?' Scobie kept her gaze steady, slightly above Avery's buzz cut.

Cobbin picked at the callous forming around a fish-hook jag in his right middle finger, kept his eyes down for a moment, let Avery answer.

'Quick chat. Reckons she's just being loyal to her old friend. Being helpful.' Sarcastic tilt.

'Thoughts?' Scobie scanned the group. Quiet for a few moments.

Birch couldn't stand the silence. 'Of our suspects, she seems least likely. If there's a connection, bar the historic one, it's not come to light. If she had a grudge, she's nursed it for a lot of years before making a move. I don't buy it.'

Avery joined in. 'Unless it's some total random and something we've yet to unearth, our best bets are still Scarborough and Dolan. They both have a connection to both victims, and now Nolly Pratt is missing.'

Ottering spoke. 'Scarborough's firmed after the Cilla Breslin interview. Looks like he was having an affair or something sexual with Phillip Leuwins. Adds weight to the sighting of him near Gringly's that night. Why did he need that vehicle torched if there was nothing incriminating about it?'

'An affair certainly gives him a motive. Being found out, exposed. Especially after the murders. Get hold of Scarborough's phone records,' Scobie said.

'On what grounds?' Ottering asked.

'Suspicion of murder. Accessory or accomplice to murder. Destruction of evidence of a crime. See if that gets him talking.'

'We've kinda ruled out the sister.' Ottering tapped her pen against her front teeth.

'But where's she been the last day or so? Check the airlines. Couldn't have driven here since you two left Victoria,' Scobie responded.

'Still no sign of Pratt. Accounts haven't been touched. Mother's not heard from him.' Birch this time.

'Lotta forest to dump a body up there,' Avery said.

'Lotta river n'all,' Cobbin added. 'Dolan had a punt at the worksite. No clue where we could send the dive team though. Waterways everywhere. Could only hope for a sighting.'

Ottering piped up. 'Don't need a punt to dump a body.' She looked up and shrugged. 'Just sayin'.'

Scobie crossed her arms. 'Time to make a call to the public. I'll have media set it up. Cilla Breslin's information notwithstanding, we've made little progress in terms of anything concrete. We need a break and we need help.'

～

It was nearly midnight as Cal drove home, avoiding the worst of the traffic.

At the foot of the mountains she stopped at Brontos bar and parked in the far corner of the lot. Scarborough's Nissan was parked near the back door. She waited and watched. A bouncer manned the entrance. No way to sneak around the vehicle with him there. She needed a distraction. Could go and start a fight. That would only bring attention back on her. Too bad she didn't have an offsider – but she was working alone and that was that. Only needed a couple of minutes.

She pocketed one of the collars, walked over to the back entrance, smiled at the bouncer, went inside. Walked past the kitchen, two more doorways. Went to the bar, got a beer. Did a circuit of the main room, returned towards the kitchen, slipped into the alcove, smashed the fire alarm. Walked into the corridor, drank her beer. The painful squawk of the emergency bell brought kitchen staff out. The bouncer came inside.

Cal left, dropped to the ground beside the Nissan, flicked on her torch, looped the collar over the park-brake cable, fastened it. Slid out, brushed herself off, went back to her car.

Next she drove to Dolan's. It was just after 1am. Dubious as he seemed, she figured he wouldn't be at his workshop or the place where he whacked her on Juta Road. Though having decided on that, she suspected he could just as likely be anywhere at all. Still, she had to make a start. She went to the address on Boarback Ridge where she'd seen his red pick-up in the past.

It was a clear, autumn night. A slight breeze ran across the top of the ridge from the north east. She parked several hundred metres back from Dolan's property, coasting into the verge with her engine and lights off. No street lights out bush. Nothing. She quietly snicked her door shut and scurried along the edge of the road until she met his driveway. Quieter to just sneak along the tyre ruts than to navigate through the scrub on the margins. She dropped onto her stomach and crawled towards the pick-up. No lights on at the caravan or the awning opposite the container. She worked quickly, snaking under the tray, she felt for the driveshaft tunnel, went to the side, located the brake cable and looped the GPS collar over and fastened the buckle. Done.

Then the sensor light went on at the front of the awning.

She saw the lower half of his legs, backlit as he rounded the corner. She dragged herself back in under the tray, pulled her body forward. Dolan's booted feet moved slowly along the drive. He'd been inside, dressed, with the lights off. Weirdo.

Had he seen her? Night-vision glasses maybe? Or just being suss cos he's up to no good? She felt helpless under there. Nothing she could do. The feet came closer, stood near the front of the truck.

Be quiet or be proactive? *Be cool. Be cool.* She flattened her breathing, listened, watched the boots. She could hear his wheezy nasal breath. Something slithered over her collar, went down her neck. Tickled. Tiny legs down the curve of her spine. *Jesus.* Wanted to scratch, shake it out. Hoped it wasn't a scorpion. Or a funnel-web.

Fuck me, what's he doing? Move man.

And he did. Pressed down on the front of the truck, like he was checking the suspension. Then he walked back to the hut.

Don't wait for him to get his night-vision on. Go. Go!

She inched backwards out from under the tray, turned and crawled as far as she could in the blocked sightline behind the vehicle then stood and ran for the road and back to her car, pulling out her shirttail and shaking the hell out of it as she ran to dislodge whatever was there. She fired up the Ford, lights off, and turned back along Boarback Road towards home.

~

Scobie put Cobbin and Avery on the Terry Scarborough interview to mix things up. They'd both watched the filmed Cilla Breslin interview.

Terry Scarborough wore a well-cut, dark blue suit. He sat slanted back in the chair, his legs stretched out under the table. Both hands pressed at the table's edge. Every so often his fingers rapped a rhythm. His lawyer sat beside him, tall, grey-haired, rimless glasses. Desiccated-looking.

Avery kicked off. 'We've reason to believe you had a relationship with Phillip Leuwins. Care to comment?'

Scarborough took a deep breath, slowly released it. Remained silent. The lawyer impassive beside him.

'We have a witness.' Still nothing.

'We're investigating two murders and a missing person. We have a witness to your having a sexual relationship with one of the victims. So he was more than a business acquaintance. You lied about that. Combined with the fact of your vehicle being sighted in the Gringly Reserve area the night Leuwins's vehicle was torched, I'd say you need to be more forthright. You've withheld information regarding your relationship with Mr Leuwins. It doesn't look good. Juries don't look favourably on suspects who lie.'

'What are you charging me with?'

'We're not charging you with anything yet, Mr Scarborough. We'd like you to tell us why you withheld that information and why you were at Gringly's that night. Torching that vehicle could have you charged with destruction of evidence and accessory to murder. At the least, you'd be looking at fifteen years. We have

Phillip Leuwins's body. Circumstantial cases have been made on less.'

Scarborough looked up at the corner of the room. Said nothing.

'As I said, it's not looking good.' Avery folded his arms.

Scarborough leaned in to his lawyer's ear, said something. The lawyer gave a small nod. Scarborough switched the arrangement of his feet crossed at the ankles, remained silent.

Avery sat back, sighed. 'Okay, Mr Scarborough. If we do decide to charge you and this goes to court, your failure to account for yourself will be presented by the prosecution. If you have nothing more to say here now, you're free to leave. I suggest you confer with your lawyer. The next time we see you you'll be in cuffs.'

Scarborough drew himself up, pushed his chair back, left the room followed by his lawyer. As they walked together down the corridor Scarborough leaned towards the other man. 'She'll change her story.'

22

Scobie composed herself in the anteroom. Drew her breath deep, straightened her back, exhaled, walked out to the podium. She stood, flanked by brass, and spoke.

'We're asking for help from the public. Two men have been murdered. A third appears to be missing.' Images appeared on the screen above her head. 'We believe the deaths and the disappearance are linked. Our search area is a massive one.' A map of the Hawkesbury region flashed up, two red crosses at the Boarback Road address, one further west. All the surrounding region was bushland. 'We don't have the manpower to scour the countryside. We need your help. If anyone has seen anything they think may aid our inquiries, we'd like to know. Anything out of the ordinary.'

She was interrupted by a journalist from the Richmond News. 'Is there a serial killer on the loose? Should people be concerned?'

Scobie controlled her irritation, maintained the calm, authoritative tone. 'We don't believe so. We don't think the deaths are random. The missing man was known to the other victims. We are taking this matter very seriously. All information given will be treated as confidential. The number will come up on the screen. Thank you.'

∼

Terry Scarborough was canny enough not to approach Cilla Breslin at home or at work. She took an early lunch every second Thursday to get her nails done in the arcade. Scarborough parked by the back entrance to the mall, took his takeaway coffee with him. He thumbed through a Drift car mag as he sat at a table close enough to the beauty salon to see the entrance without being spotted. With one eye on the doorway of Angie's Nail Paradise, he held his mag away from the splashes of chow mein goo on the surface of the table.

At 11.45 Cilla emerged from the door of the salon. She reached into her bag using her freshly lacquered extensions like pincers. Terry was at her side by the time she'd pulled out her cigarettes. He took her arm and walked her forcefully to the rear of the arcade.

'Tez. What you doing here?' Squeaky voice, breathless.

In the car park he manoeuvred her to the other side of the vehicle. 'Had your nails done? Look nice, do they? Show me.'

As she raised her hand a tremor belied her smile.

He took her right palm, his thumb pressing against her fingernail from underneath, forcing her finger back.

'Tez!'

He kept pressing. Finally, the nail snapped, breaking her real one underneath. She screamed. He pushed her against the car with a hand to her throat, began on the next finger. She squirmed, her footing slipped on the gravel. Still he pinned her by the throat so she couldn't make a voice. Broke the next nail. She twisted and scrabbled with her free arm, clawing for his face. He hissed through his teeth. 'You saw nothing. Say it.'

She blubbered, her eyes streaming. 'Nothing.'

'Again.' He pressed at the next nail, his thumb catching the previous torn mess.

'Nothing, Tez!' Her eyes wide, terrified.

'Good girl. C'mon. Give you a lift back to work.'

As he released her neck a surge of white heat bounced across her skull, ran down her spine, through her thighs. She lifted her right leg, jamming her knee full force into his groin, plunged her instep down his shinbone, driving her stiletto heel through the top of his Nike trainer. Terry Scarborough dropped to the ground. Cilla Breslin took off.

She ran back through the arcade, out the front entrance, across the street, down a laneway beside Nillo's Electrical store, across the car park and down another laneway to a small industrial estate. Between a series of rubbish skips and stacked pallets she crouched, heaving, and lit her first ciggy. She smoked that, lit another and called work, apologised, said she needed a sick day.

Called her cousin Taleesha to meet her across the park in twenty minutes. Taleesha had brothers. Big fellas.

～

Craig Dolan flipped the half-door on the back of the pickup, threw in his bedroll and a box of food supplies. Loaded the chainsaw, pick and shovel, two ten-litre jerrycans of diesel. His rifle went on the rack behind the front seat. As an afterthought he tossed in an old fishing kreel and fractured rod. *Look convincing*, he thought.

He took the Juta Road, past the worksite, and carried on northeast into the hinterland.

～

Cal watched the public announcement on her phone. Flicked Scobie a text.

Looking good behind that podium.

Scobie texted back.

You have information?

Yeh. Can you grill me?

She checked the GPS on Dolan. He'd gone north on Juta Road then taken the eastern ridge road that carried on inland in a northeast direction. The route went deep into the wilderness. The only people who used it were off-road enthusiasts, hunters, forestry and parks staff. It really was a back of beyond trail, a lonely place to drive. Or to get stranded in. Satellite phone was in the work truck.

She couldn't trail anyone off-road in the Ford. She went back home and got Dee's old paddock-basher Mazda pickup. Though long since out of rego, it was rugged and the engine was bulletproof. She'd just have to risk it. Without her work truck she had no other option. Wasn't 4WD either. Too bad. Have to make do. She filled the tank and several smaller containers with fuel and water. Her firearms were with the work truck as well. She saw Addie's tree root club on the bench, grabbed it. Wrapped a hunting knife in her tool roll and headed off.

Cal flicked Scobie another text before she lost all signal.

Following Dolan. Juta Rd 12.7Ks. NE turnoff.

At least she'd given someone a general idea of the direction she was headed.

She drained half her water bottle, scanned the road ahead. Memorial service tomorrow. *What am I doing?* Still a couple of signal bars on the phone. Sent a text to Di.

I may not make it in the morning. Doing this for Pip. Hope you understand.

Should've rung the hospital too. Too late now. Not enough juice in the signal.

Leaving Zin, when she needs me. Should be there to support her. Can't do anything. She's in good hands. Better than mine.

She drove on. The worn sandstone ridge she followed was like the jagged back of an ancient creature at slumber. Every so often she caught a view through the trees, the endless undulating expanse of hazy green, all the way to the horizon, east, north, west.

The sun dropped towards the western horizon behind her, the rosy light reflecting off her rear-view mirror, filling the cab. *What does Terry Scarborough have to do with Pip? He nearly caught me that day in the garage. Does he know what I've seen? The notched tyre and the matching tracks at Gringly's? Hasn't come after me. Yet. Is he just cocky? Or does he not have as much to hide as someone else? He's not as desperate. His connection to Pip? It was a beat. Take it at face value, Cal. Terry Scarborough was using a beat. He could've hooked up with Pip. That's it. That's all.*

She drove on, bumping over the dusty rubble surface, searching for Dolan's dust cloud far ahead. Too many trees and bends in the road to catch sight of it.

23

The incident room was crammed with extra desks and uniformed officers taking notes on the phone-ins.

Scobie and the team conferred near the front desk. 'Court's finally allowed us access to Terry Scarborough's phone records. Using satellite locations, we know he was definitely at Gringly's that night of the burn-out.'

'Him or his phone. But we already suspected that.' Ottering was too tired to hide her irritation.

Avery drew himself up. 'That's right, we were pretty sure of it anyway. But here's the interesting bit. He was also there the night Phillip Leuwins went missing.'

'At Gringly's? So what?' Ottering raised her hands.

'We've checked Phillip Leuwins's records as well. He visited Gringly's the night he went missing. The night Stefan was shot.'

'Jesus. What are we waiting for?' Ottering again.

Cobbin picked up. 'We've put a trace on him.'

'And we never got his Nissan swabbed.' Ottering.

Sombre faces around the room.

'Didn't have enough,' Avery answered.

'Should've been done after the CCTV was found.'

'Wasn't conclusive. The GPS locators putting him there adds weight,' Scobie said.

'Car will have been valeted by now, surely. Pointless looking for trace,' Ottering said.

'We have enough now to charge him. I'll see to the warrant. Frank and Janice, go to the home. Glen and Tony, the club. And I want the car impounded. Chop-chop, guys. No time-off next twelve hours. We need to make the most of the phone-in. Pace yourselves.'

~

The pickup seemed less sure-footed. Cal was driving on gravel but the wallow was something else, the rear sliding without any feel back to her, uncontrolled. Flat tyre. Again.

She slowed, looking for somewhere to pull over. Best not to travel at night out here, anyway. Dolan would see her lights for miles. There were very few sections of road wide enough to pull in. Maintenance costs out here must be extraordinary. Road works minimal. The further she went on the flat tyre the more damage she would do. *This isn't good.* She crawled the vehicle gently around a bend and up ahead, on the verge, a fallen tree had been sawn up and disposed of. The clearance gave a small layby she could slide into, still keeping a three-metre throughway should any other vehicles pass by. Not that there were many of those. She hadn't seen a single one.

She got out, walked to the left rear. Yup, had it. Dee kept the usual spare under the tray and another chained beside the back window. Flat tyres were common on shingle roads. One wasn't always enough.

Cal pulled the jack and handle from behind the driver's seat. Loosened the lugs while the wheel was still trapped. Found a solid jacking point, began cranking. The jack wasn't original. Dee had a bottle jack and several lumps of hardwood to make up enough height to lift the wheel.

Sun was coming down fast now. Need to fix this and find a camp.

She pumped the jack to full height, could barely clear the wheel off the stub axle. Inflated spare wouldn't get on there. Need to dig out a bit of ground. Got up, went to the tray, got her folding spade, started scraping and digging under the wheel to make more space.

The vehicle creaked. Cal smelt a vaguely sulphurous odour. She looked at the jack. Hydraulic fluid was leaking from a circular machined joint. *Shit. Bloody seal's gone. Be quick.*

She got on her knees and jabbed and scraped at the ground trying to get some room for the new tyre before the fluid all leaked out and the height dropped. Panting and heaving, she grabbed the newer wheel, tried to slide it onto the stubs, angle was wrong. Laid back, balanced a foot on either side of the wheel, kicked forward, both sides, same time. *Good enough.* Five threaded stubs showing, she quickly ran the wheel nuts onto the threads.

Thought she heard something, the far-off whine of an engine. *C'mon, get this going.* The pool of fluid at the base of the jack was ominous. She spun the wrench and got the nuts seated. Stood to tighten them. Dropped the jack down before it fell of its own accord. The engine noise, closer. Diesel. Yanked on the arms of the wrench, squeaking the nuts home. Straightened her back, hand to her eyes as a vehicle rounded the corner. Red Hilux pickup.

∼

Scobie watched the live interview on computer screen. Cobbin and Avery beside her.

Scarborough arrived with his lawyer, Selwyn Borthwick.

They sat side by side, Scarborough upright, eyes focussed, hands palm down on his thighs. The bravado all but gone.

Birch sat opposite Scarborough; Ottering at the end of the table.

Borthwick arranged a stack of papers in front of him. He handed paper-clipped sheaves to both the officers and one to Terry Scarborough. 'My client would like to read a statement.' He turned and nodded to Scarborough.

Scarborough began by identifying himself and giving the date. He read.

He admitted to having met Phillip Leuwins at his Brontos club as a business associate, and that they had become sexual partners. He said they met regularly at Gringly's because he'd been sprung at the club by Cilla Breslin one night. The night of Phillip's disappearance, Scarborough had met him at Gringly's Reserve. Phillip had left his lights on and got a flat battery. Scarborough drove him home, dropped him off and left. He didn't want to be seen there. He'd never met Stefan. There were other vehicles in the driveway.

He'd thought nothing more about it until Stefan's murder hit the papers and Phillip was said to be missing. He was curious and anxious about Phillip's disappearance and the fact the police wanted to talk to Phillip, as though he was a suspect. Scarborough had been desperate to distance himself from the mess, because he had nothing to do with it. He didn't want his name dragged into the affair. At the same time, he was concerned for Phillip, but didn't think he could help.

When Phillip's body was found, Terry Scarborough knew that matters had become even worse for him. No one would believe he had nothing to do with it if the link between them was made. If he came forward he would have to explain their relationship. He was stuck. He knew there would be evidence of Phillip in his car and of him in Phillip's pickup. He had to get rid of it. He thought if he torched the truck it would simply be viewed as vandalism.

He spoke of his remorse at not coming forward earlier. He said that he was scared. That he was sorry for his mistake. There had been no proof linking him to the destruction of Phillip's pickup, only speculation. He also explained that after realising his car could have been seen on CCTV the night of the torching, he'd gone back and driven his mother's Range Rover via the firetrails to do the job. It made no sense but he'd panicked.

'I hope that my coming forward voluntarily now will be viewed favourably. I have tried to help. I hope that my name can be kept private.'

In the booth Avery scoffed. 'He barely beat us with our warrant.'

'Whaddaya reckon?' Cobbin turned to Scobie.

'Makes sense why he lit the truck. Answers one question. We've come up with nothing more to indicate he had a reason to actually kill Phillip Leuwins. He's no saint. Form for other offences. But I tend to believe his explanation. For now. Unless we come up with more.'

'We're still looking for a killer.' Cobbin sucked through his teeth.

'That's right,' Scobie sighed.

'Gotta let him go, boss?' Avery said.

'We do.'

She turned away, checked her phone. Read the last text Cal had sent, that she was following Dolan. She replied.

Current location?

Knew Cal may not get it if she was now out of range.

∼

Birch and Ottering returned to the incident room after the interview and departure of Scarborough and Borthwick.

'Back to square one, then. How's the public phone-in going?' Birch stretched. Behind him, grainy vehicles in black and white passed like toys on the endless CCTV footage.

'Thousand pieces of info to follow up. Might be one speck of gold in there. Takes time. All spare uniforms are on it,' Scobie replied.

'Anything more on Sylvia Toblensk?' Scobie peered at Ottering, who shook her head.

'No airline bookings in her name. Phone's off.'

'Does she have any other names?'

'We're onto it.'

'Should've been checked before now. Didn't we establish that when she became the beneficiary of Phillip Leuwins's death?'

'Nothing came up.'

'Check again. Why would she have her phone off? Woman travels the outback.' She shook her head.

'Where are we with Dolan?' Scobie looked across their faces.

'Nothing strong enough yet to bring him in on.' Cobbin this time. Two empty coffee cups and a ragged box of crackers beyond his keyboard.

'He's still our main bet. We have nothing else.' Birch scratched the back of his neck.

'Nolly Pratt is still missing. His bank account hasn't been accessed. If he's been dumped it's either out bush where there's no CCTV, or someone has driven on the M3 or M4 to go off their usual patch. I want all four of you on any footage we can get the night and day after he went to the Toblensk property. Dolan's vehicles, the pickup and the big truck. And I'm getting a warrant for his phone records. Got to find a crack here.'

'Could've been dumped away from Kaloola but inside M3–M4 secondary roads. Impossible to trace.' Ottering yawned into her forearm.

'Well just recheck everything. We're missing something. And when we get Dolan's records, I want all his timings and movements and alibis gone over again. Any anomalies, let me know. Meantime, maybe uniforms will give us a new lead.' She swung her head towards the busy phone desks.

'It's possible Pratt has gone to ground, moved interstate,' Avery said.

'Possible, yes. But remember we found blood at the Boarback property where his vehicle was abandoned. Not promising.'

'And he didn't drive away. Not in his own vehicle anyway,' Birch added.

24

The red pickup coasted to a stop.

Must've pulled off somewhere. Hidden. Knew I was following. Shoulda been awake to that, Cal. Now what? Knife and club are in the cab. She eyed the wrench, an awkward tool. The hardwood lumps, the bottle jack.

She stood, dusted off her jeans. Dolan was out of the Toyota quickly. Swaggered towards her, a strange, canny smile twisting his mouth. 'Fancy running into you out here. Need a hand?'

'Nah. All sorted.' Wary, certain he'd whacked her that day. Kept the point of the pickup deck between her and him. Left hand rested on the tray-side.

Dolan planted his feet about two metres from her. 'Wha'cha after out here? Lonely area. Not much doin'.'

None of your business, mate, she thought.

'My work, the bush. Not a lonely place to me.' She gently shifted her left foot, felt for the weight of the jack beside the wheel. 'Not a lot of earthworks out here. You sightseeing?'

Dolan's lips curled on one side. 'Funny lady. Bit a fishin' and huntin'. Good for the soul.'

Her right fingers drew into a tight fist. 'No lady, mate.' She swept her left arm towards the road. 'After you.'

Dolan paused, lifted his chin. His jaw slid across his clenched teeth. He turned and walked to his truck.

She waited until he got in and drove off. Her left leg trembled. *What am I doing? What the hell am I doing? Why am I following him? Because he's shifty as. You know he's got something to do with this. Probably did in Stef and Pip. He's lured you out here. You've taken the bait. What did you think was gonna happen?*

What if I'm wrong? Out here wasting time. Should be supporting Zin at the hospital. She's got no one there.

It's him. I know it. Feel it. Something clarified for the first time. Who Dolan reminded her of, like someone she'd met before. It wasn't him she'd met, literally. It was the type. Her stepfather.

Her spine stiffened. She was certain now.

~

A uniformed officer knocked and put her head round the door. 'S'cuse me all.' She looked at Cobbin. 'Have Myra Pratt on the line. Wants to speak with you, Tony.' Cobbin nodded and left the room, went to the officer's desk. Took the handset.

'Found Nol's phone. Silly sausage left it in the fridge, in a plastic bag. Battery's flat. Thought you might want it.'

'Thanks, Mrs Pratt. We'll send someone to pick it up ASAP. No word?'

'Nothing. Not looking good is it?'

'No. I'm sorry. Doing our best.'

Cobbin informed Scobie and sent a constable to pick up the phone and get it to forensics. Scobie requested an urgent on the testing.

Later that night, Nolly Pratt's mobile was fingerprinted and swabbed, then charged up. The tech officer, DS Tori Lane, quickly viewed the call log. Case detectives would later cross-check those and GPS locations. She moved onto other stored files. Several items looked to be significant. One was a sound file, a recording. The other was a video, self-shot by Nolly Pratt. She played them both. Rang Scobie immediately.

∼

Craig Dolan floored the Hilux, needed to put some distance between himself and the weirdo.

He'd fix her wagon. Knew exactly what he was looking for. He'd been driving those trails for decades. His patch. Not hers.

Scoured the margins for the right pair of trees. Twilight now. Okay for him. Best before it was fully dark though. Spotted just the thing as he rounded a curve and the track began a slow descent.

He stopped. Got out, grabbed his chainsaw. Worked quickly.

∼

She gave him ten minutes. Considered her options. Who knew what he was up to? He'd already tried to take her out, or slow her up, that day at the subdivision. What would he stop at? An angry prick. Maybe too much temper. Reacting, not planning. Threatened by her. He suspected she'd figured things out. She must be right, then.

How to protect herself? Take charge? She couldn't go at him. Could only respond to what was in front of her. He was up to something.

She went to the door of the pickup, pulled the seat forward. Undid her tool roll, put her knife down her boot.

Started the engine. She pushed her charger into the lighter socket, plugged in her phone. Fish-tailed the pickup as she powered into the twilight in pursuit.

∼

At Royal Prince Alfred Hospital the new shift came on. Staff nurse Bongiorno walked back from her locker towards reception, heard the alarm from the recovery ward. She walked briskly up the hall, called her colleague as she passed a doorway. 'Defib. Defib!'

Zinnia Nyx lay twisted on the bed, her skin bluish grey, her right hand gripping her nightie over her chest. Her eyes were closed, her body motionless.

～

Dolan's dust had settled and Cal had nothing to follow in the diminishing light, though she kept alert for anywhere he could have pulled off to get behind her again. There were no obvious breaks in the scrub. Following him was dangerous, more so as it got dark. If she wanted any kind of advantage she should camp overnight. Even Dolan couldn't sneak up on her in the dark, without her seeing his lights. Unless he had night-vision gear.

The setting sun was a thin red aura above the horizon behind her. She looked in earnest now for somewhere to pull in. Travelling on the apex of the ridge, she knew the road would have to descend at some point. The wind had come up, the way it often did when the light changed and the heat absorbed in the land was released into the cooling air. More shelter lower down the slopes. As darkness fell, she came around a bend and the nose of the truck pointed downhill. At the same moment she registered the smell of two-stroke and gum sap. She hit the brakes as the trunk of a fallen tallowwood blocked the road.

'Fuck.' No room to turn. She heard the staccato rasp of a chainsaw engine somewhere behind her.

Back up. She slammed the gearbox into reverse as she swung her neck and tried to retreat up the incline. The wheels spun, barely gaining purchase with no weight in the tray over the wheels. She followed the sound of the chainsaw. Glimpsed

Dolan's silhouette on a bank above the road, hunched beside a gumtree, working the blade. *Prick's gonna block me in.*

She eased forward. Tried again to reverse, more slowly. The wheels slewed across the loose surface. She was trapped. Got out. Gauged where she needed to run for safety. He'd probably scarfed it to drop across the road like the first one. Always need to allow for error, twisting. She calculated the arc, gave herself plenty of room, ran at a forty-five-degree angle from the trajectory into the scrub.

Scampered along the treeline on her side of the track. Keep him in sight. The chainsaw bark slowed to an idle.

She watched, her gaze rising to the lofty top against the faded sky, reading the movement of the mass against the twilit background. The wind blew into the western face of the adjacent ridge, turning upwards to release at the top.

The tree-head swayed. *It's gonna drop any second.*

Dolan straightened, watching the trunk above him.

Bet he didn't have time to clear a safety path, she thought. Waiting for the fall. Watching.

Then the strangest thing. The wind switched. It squalled up from the south side of the ridge. An impudent blast, holding the tree against its projected fall. Suspended. Then the trunk began to topple, the other way. It was dropping into Dolan's escape route.

Dolan saw it, panicked. Flailing through the scrub trying to elude the inevitable. Cal watched as the massive weight of the tree succumbed to the combination of gravity and wind. Pushed beyond the point of no return it collapsed, smashing through the lesser saplings in its path. The noise was thunderous, the air rushing through the descending mass, the creak and smash of breaking boughs. Then the trunk hit earth, bounced and crashed again.

Dolan's scream.

25

The bush resumed its hush. Leaves and dust still fluttered to the forest floor. The putter of the chainsaw where he'd dropped it.

Dolan's screams cut across the quiet. 'Help me!'

Cal scrambled down the bank to the track, crossed to the other side. She made her way along the trunk. Shards of snapped boughs and smaller casualties everywhere. Her eyes attuned to the dimness as night began to fall. His chainsaw idled beside the mess. She flicked off the ignition. Followed the cries.

'I'm coming.'

Slid down dislodged rock and debris. Close now. Dolan's screams undiminished. She found him wedged between a smaller tree and the fallen trunk. Trapped. Both his hands held the top of his caught thigh. A bad break of his femur, she guessed. Lower leg probably smashed too.

'Jeez, mate. Looks a bit sore.'

He was sweating with pain. His face a contorted, anguished grimace. He spoke through grinding teeth. 'Fuckin' help me.'

'Ohh. Nice. Some manners might be in order. Being as I'm the one standing on two good legs.'

Dolan swung his body back and forth, clutching at the mangled limb.

Cal continued. 'Could help you, couldn't I. Get your chainsaw. Cut you free.'

'Fuck me. Just do it.'

'You got any lighting in your rig?'

'Torch. Box in back.'

'Right. Thing is, I'm in no hurry.' She sat back on her haunches. 'Anything you wanna tell me about Stef's murder? And Pip's? And while we're at it, where's Nolly?'

'Fuck me. You fuckin' nutter. Help me!' he screamed at her.

She sat back. 'Mate. You're missing something. I'll just piss off now, shall I?'

Dolan groaned, swaying and falling back with the pain. He rose again, clutching, tearing at the top of his leg.

'Nolly did it. Shot them both.' He fell back again, writhing his torso against the debris underneath him. 'Taken off cos he knows they're onto him.'

'Why?'

'Jesus, help me, you fuckin' freak.'

'Why would he shoot them?' Her voice, slow, steady, firm.

'Cos he's an idiot. Who cares why?'

'Makes no sense.'

'Not the full quid, is he. Off his face. Had an argie. He shot Stef. Fruit had been muckin' round with him.' Dolan's face was so contorted with pain, trying to concentrate and speak, Cal felt a churn of guilt. But she kept on.

'What about Pip?'

He rocked towards his leg, groaned.

'Came back. Saw Stef. I tried to stop it. Nolly chased him through the bush. Nailed him.'

She shook her head. What a waste. A stupid, drunken dispute.

'Had a go at me cos he's scared I'll dob 'im. Prob'ly halfway to Timor by now.'

'Your pickup? Beyond the other roadblock?'

He nodded.

Cal scrabbled her way back to the track by following the trunk. She ran past Dee's pickup, down to the other dropped tree, climbed over it. Walked carefully down the track to where Dolan had parked his truck. Thought about what he'd said. What happened that night. All so banal. An argument. Couldn't prove anything until they spoke to Nolly. Or found his body.

It was dark now. When the moon rose there'd be some light if the clouds remained distant. But that would still be an hour or so off. She opened the rear canopy and felt around for his gearbox. Located the heavy-duty torch. On the way back she stopped at the butt of the second tree and retrieved Dolan's chainsaw. Checked the fuel and chain-oil levels. Nothing worse than running out halfway through a cut. Dangerous.

Dolan looked like he was about to pass out. Shock. Maybe he had an internal bleed in the leg. Unconsciousness might be a blessing. She primed the machine, pulled the starter. Fired first pop. Gave it a few revs, let it idle.

'What'd you use your punt for?'

He opened his eyes. Closed them again.

'Tell me. Or I'll leave you here. You won't last the night.'

'Just dumping shit. Stuff they won't take at the station.'

'Toxic shit?'

He nodded.

'Asshole.'

She aimed the torch, revved up the saw. Then moved the light.

'Why block me in? If you've nothing to hide? Why stop me following you?'

'Gotta find Nolly. Clear myself. You. The cops. All after me. Not takin' the rap for him.'

She said nothing. Positioned the torch on the log again. 'Know this is gonna hurt when the pressure comes off.'

He squeezed his eyes. Nodded.

She made the top-cut. Chips flew from the teeth. Well-maintained. Sharp chain. She pulled back, looked at Dolan again. Rolling his head. Kept her own head back from where the bough would break upwards. Began the undercut. As she severed the girth, the freed length snapped up and fell away. The weight came off Dolan's thigh. The blood began to flow again. The screaming resumed.

She adjusted the torch, saw the state of his leg. Compound fracture, bone exposed on the outside of his thigh. Serious. She undid her shirt, pulled the knife from her boot, cut the sleeves off, knotted them together. Wound the tourniquet around the top of his thigh, tied it off. She fired the chainsaw up again and cut two straight, sturdy branches from nearby saplings. Knifed off the side shoots. Laid them out beside his leg. How the hell was she gonna get him out of there? Must weigh 110kg. She dropped her jeans and cut the legs off leaving herself with shorts. Dolan moaned and wailed.

'Doing my best here.'

She cut strips from the denim fabric and tied them together. She aligned the makeshift splints to his mangled leg, trying to avoid the splintered bone. It was gonna hurt no matter what.

'Need to move you. Can't drag you up on my own. Gotta winch on your rig?'

Small nod. He was passing out.

'Keys?' She felt at his pockets. Found them. Grabbed the torch and chainsaw. Ran back up the bank.

She got to the roadblock tree, fired up the saw, sliced out sections she could move and cleared a pathway. She ran ahead to Dolan's truck, checked the front bumper. Cable and winch. Checked the back canopy, fossicked about. She'd rip his arms out of their sockets if she couldn't put him on something. Needed a sled. *Think, Cal.* Could make one from saplings. Would need lashings to tie them together. Had nothing. Bark strips? Be there forever. Fuck. And she needed a bed that would slide over the debris on the incline. She was staring at his truck in a daze.

The fibreglass canopy. She crawled inside, unbolted the internal latches. Too heavy for her to lift or carry. She lay back on the floor, braced her feet on the roof, kicked until she tipped it over the side. Fired up the chainsaw, set the torchlight, cut the windows and most of the depth of the sides off, left a small lip. Got rid of the weight. Left an upturn at one end to keep him on board the thing. Left the rear hatch so she could wrap and tie the cable, get some purchase. She hefted the roof-sled back on the deck with the saw. Got in the cab, fired up his truck and put it in 4WD.

Then she reversed up the incline, squeezing past the dropped tree and climbing the nearside wheels up the bank to clear Dee's pickup, back up to the second tree. She kept going until she could manoeuvre the front end and the winch above the incline. Climbed out, unhooked the cable, got the sled on the ground, attached the cable and slid down to where Dolan lay.

He seemed unconscious. She couldn't move him alone. Nudged him. 'Gotta roll you. Need your help.'

Nothing.

She adjusted the makeshift sled beside him. Dragged him into alignment as best she could. Dolan howled at the movement of his shattered limb. She got beside him, put her back against the tree and pushed with her feet. The screaming began again as she rolled him into the base.

She checked the cable attachment.

'Going up to winch you now. Hang on tight.' She put his hands on the cut sides. At least he could brace there and with his one good leg against the bottom curve. If he didn't pass out again.

She scrambled up to the truck, the engine still idling. Standing well away from the cable, she flicked the switch on the winch. It whined into life, slowly taking up the slack, then the twined wire sprang and vibrated into a taut line. Hopefully the curved roof of the canopy would skim over any snags. There was little she could do now. She peered over the edge watching for the appearance of the upturned shell carrying Dolan. The headlights shone through the trees above the incline, casting no light below.

The electric motor driving the winch, the muffled clatter of the diesel engine and the whoosh of the dragging canopy bed combined into a grotesque cacophony in the otherwise quiet surrounds. She flicked the beam of the torch across the mess of debris, the light glinting on the stainless-steel cable and the rocking boat of the fibreglass canopy. Dolan's hands gripping the sides like gunwales as the thing inched closer.

Finally, the machine pulled the battered canopy over the lip of the bank where it thumped down onto the road. Cal flipped off the winch.

Now what? Gotta get him to a hospital. Can't leave him in that thing. Can't fit him in the cab with his leg splinted like that. He'll have to go on the truck bed. Can't lift him on my own.

She unhooked the cable. Got in the truck, did a ten-point turn until she had the thing backed around to the makeshift sled. She ran the winch cable over the roof of the cab to the rear and hooked it up again. She had to retrieve the chainsaw from down the bank. The torchlight was losing its strength. *Hurry up, Cal.* Got the saw, got up the bank, cut four three-metre boughs and laid them from the ground to the truck bed. It was a rough skid but would have to do.

Dolan was quiet. Unconscious or near dead. *Could he die from that wound? Loss of blood maybe. Just keep going.* Nearly there. She hit the winch button at the front and the cable pulled tight. This was going to ruin his bonnet, windshield and roof. Too bad. The cable bit into the paintwork and steel panels as it strained to wrench the fibreglass sled up the poles. Cal scurried to the back and steadied the thing as it ascended so Dolan wasn't tipped off. As soon as it topped the edge she ran back to the front to shut it off before it rammed him into the rear of the cab. She winched in the cable and locked the hook.

At the back of the ute she trimmed off two of the ramp saplings and jammed them across the deck inside the tailgate to hold the skiff in place.

'Getting you to hospital. Hang in there.'

No response. She jumped in the cab and took off. As soon as she had a signal she could ring for help. She drove back the long way she'd come, heading for Kaloola and Misty's and Boarback Ridge.

26

It was after 11pm. The crew were overtired. Scobie stood beside the desk, watched Nolly Pratt's video with the rest of the team. Then listened to the recording made the night of Stefan Toblensk's murder.

'Jesus H Christ. Get a team on Dolan. Now!'

Again she checked her phone. Still nothing from Cal. Flicked off a text.

I'm worried. Call me.

If Dolan had gone bush and Cal had followed, she'd be totally out of range.

'Get a satellite ping on Dolan's phone. And Cal Nyx's as well. They're both out in the sticks.'

∼

Cal gazed at the shrubs coated in yellow dust by the roadside, illuminated in the headlights. Something else was nagging at her brain.

Too tired. Hungry. Fossicked in her knapsack. Pulled out a small packet of nuts. Ate a handful. Washed them down with water.

The thought, an irritant. Trying to clarify. She wasn't getting it. A plant, the flower. A tiny, tufted head. Insignificant. Cottony. Rare.

She stared at the roadside. Then she slammed on the brakes.

Through the rear of the cab she heard Dolan's scream as his moving body rammed forward into the back of the stationary deck.

Fuck me. I know where he's dumped Nolly.
Can't get a message to Scobie. Will have to wait till I've got signal.

∼

While her squad went into action, Scobie ran the video again. Nolly Pratt, dimly lit from the side by a lamp clamped on his bedhead. A tatty Panthers team poster behind his head. The night he went to Stefan Toblensk's property. The last time he was seen or heard of.

'Need to be quick. Craig wants to kill me. Never meant Stef or Pip any harm. Stef was good to me, they both were. Stef looked after me. Helped me with money.'

Pratt keeps looking to the side, the closed door, the window. He does it repeatedly during the recording as though expecting an ambush.

'Craig was envious. Especially of Stef. We had Friday nights, it was all good, friendly. But Craig was hard towards Stef, like jealous. Wanted to rob him. Thought he had money there, somewhere.

'When I told him I'd played around with Stef a couple of times, he got weird. Freaked him out. Think it gave him an excuse. Just got outta hand that night. Craig was in a mood. All night, he had a bee in his bonnet. Pip wasn't there. Just the three of us. Stef went to get more beers. When he came back, Craig confronted him. About money. Stef tried to calm things. Couldn't figure him.'

Pratt blinked several times, shook his head. He compressed his mouth, sniffed, carried on.

'Craig got more wound up, went out to his truck. That's when I put my recorder on. I knew something was going down. Just kept it in my pocket. Craig came back with a rifle. Called me a fag. Told me to shoot Stef. He was crazy. Freaked Stef out. I tried to calm him down. Craig just took the rifle back, smacked me in the head. He shot Stef. Blew him away. Just like that.'

Pratt's voice is wobbly, his breathing high and fast, like he's panting.

'I was on the floor. He said we had to get rid of the body. Starts dragging Stef towards the door. Then he hears a car door slam outside and someone driving away. It was Pip. Someone dropped him off. Craig went outside, to waylay him. Pip got away. Ran into the scrub. Craig chased him. I took off. I was packin' it.' Pratt's voice is thin, brittle as he relates the story.

'I'm fuckin' scared of him. Stef's dead. Pip too. I'm a liability. Craig wants me gone. Gotta do a runner.'

He looked towards the door again. His voice dropped further. 'Don't wanna leave her. Can't look after herself. Dunno what else to do. Going to Stef's. See if I can find something to sell. Think he'd understand. Gotta get away. This is my insurance. Anything happens to me.'

A pause.

'Sorry, Mum.'

~

Cal kept checking her phone for a signal as she got closer to Juta Road. She was travelling along the ridge but still surrounded by forest. As soon as she had a couple of bars she thumbed 111.

Asked for an ambo to meet her at Misty's. Then she called Scobie. 'Coming in. I've got Dolan.'

'Cal, you're in danger.'

'He's on the deck, he's fucked. I've called an ambo.'

'He did it, Cal. We've got Nolly Pratt's phone. You must be careful.'

Cal looked through the rear-view mirror, could see the darkness of the pickup tray. There was little moonlight. She could barely make out the hump of the sled on the back.

'Should be at Misty's in forty-five minutes.'

'Two squad cars are on their way. They'll escort you when they intercept. I'll inform them now.'

'You need to check Settler's Inlet. The north end. You need to send divers, into the deep channel.'

'On what grounds?'

'I think that's where he's dumped Nolly.'

She swerved as a rock wallaby bounced across the track in front of the truck.

'He told me Nolly had gone north, caught a boat offshore beyond Katherine. But I reckon he's dumped stuff in two places. One below the refuse station above Misty's. Think this is the other. I saw Brydon's dew-wort on the trailer frame, at his worksite. Probably backed into it. Plant's a protected species. There's a patch near Settler's Inlet. We get cuttings and seed from it, propagation at work. Misty's dumpsite is too close to home for him. I reckon he hoped the channel would drag the body downriver. But he would've weighted it too if he didn't want gases bringing it to the surface again. Why else would he be there? Fishing's no good. It's a speedboat ramp.'

Scobie called the diving unit then updated the squad cars heading for Cal. She waited. Replayed Nolly Pratt's recording from the night Stefan was shot. Made while his phone was in his pocket, a haze of ambient noise overlaid the recording, but the events were clear.

'Where's ya fuckin' money?' A thwack as something hard connected with flesh.

Dolan's voice like a guttural animal. 'Shoot 'im. Shoot 'im ya gutless cunt.'

'I can't. He's done nothing. Lay off, Craig.'

'Fuckin' man up.'

'Let's go. Just leave it.'

'You're a fag. Just proved it.'

A scuffle. Dolan's voice. 'Gimme the thing.'

'Let's go. Don't make things worse.'

The metallic click of a rifle hammer being cocked. 'Fuckin' do it myself.'

'Noooo!'

The recording distorted with the massive retort from the rifle.

'You fuckin' done! He never hurt you.'

'Be something here, somewhere. Help me look.'

'Calling an ambulance.'

The thump and slap of a heavy object hitting flesh, again. Then another sound in the background, outside. Muffled footsteps, running, growing faint. Footfalls close, then going outside, diminishing.

Then closer, presumably Pratt, groaning, coming around, then running, panting. A car door slamming, vehicle starting, driving. Pratt leaving.

∽

Forty minutes later Cal was nearing the intersection of Juta Road and Boarback Ridge. She turned down the incline towards Misty's. Eerie red and blue lights strobed through the trees as she neared the store. Two squad cars and an ambulance waited in the car park.

She got out, thumbed behind her cab. 'He's on the back.'

The paramedics wheeled their gear over.

Cobbin spoke to Cal. 'DI Scobie would like you to come back with us.'

She nodded. Grabbed her rucksack from the cab, sat in the back of the squad car. Rang RPA hospital in Camperdown.

～

It was 12.45am when Scobie entered the incident room at Richmond Police Station.

'Okay everyone, debrief in five.'

A group formed around the coffee table, grabbed snacks, dispersed to desks. With her full team present Scobie outlined the next moves.

'I'm deferring Dolan's interrogation until the diving unit have had a go at Settler's Inlet. We're hopeful of finding Nolly Pratt's body. Tony, I want you to hold the fort here. Work with the phone-in team, tech and legals. You've got help.' She nodded towards the rear of the room. 'Frank and Janice to interview Cal Nyx. Glen and I are off to Settler's. As officer-in-charge they need me to supervise. Any developments, call me.' Scobie left the room while Avery got the squad car.

Scobie stepped into the small interview room down the hallway. Cal held the edge of her chair, her body swaying with fatigue, a tepid cup of coffee on the table. Scobie crouched beside her.

Cal's head dropped forward, her voice quiet, rough with exhaustion. 'Zin had a second attack. Fatal. The nursing staff couldn't revive her.'

Scobie put a hand on her knee. 'She had the best care available, Cal. Don't be hard on yourself.'

Cal shook her head. 'Shoulda been there. She was alone.' She curled her body forward, rocked in the chair.

'You want me to come stay? After I'm done here?' Scobie said softly.

Cal covered her face with her hands, shook her head. 'Just need to sleep,' she mumbled.

Scobie nodded, silent.

A quiet tap on the door and a constable appeared, raised her eyebrows in acknowledgement of Scobie.

Scobie stood. 'Your driver's here, Cal.' She rubbed her hand across Cal's shoulders. 'I'm needed with the diving unit. I'll be in touch.' She gave the constable a small smile as she left the room.

27

At 2am Scobie dropped her seat back, stretched her legs into the foot-well and closed her eyes. 'Wake me when they get here.'

'Mm hmm.' Avery ran his hands over the steering wheel then rested his head against the side window.

The diving unit trucks arrived forty minutes later. Scobie got out, stretched, ran on the spot to get her blood moving.

A burly fellow approached Scobie, shook her hand. 'DS Coughlin.'

'Thanks for getting here so quickly.'

'Time's of the essence. These currents. Lucky it's been dry.' Behind him three other divers unloaded equipment from the truck.

'Well, if he weighted the body, we're hoping it's not gone far,' Scobie said. 'We think it was dumped at night from a punt, directly out in the channel. Not far from shore, hopefully.'

'You're right. Deep channel here due to the curve.' Coughlin indicated north. 'Water gathers speed off the bend, gouges the floor this side. We've looked over the charts. Better get started.'

He shrugged off his jacket, went to the truck where the others were changing. Two guys, one woman.

Fifteen minutes later the control boat was launched. Work lights on huge tripods lit the area and cast knobbled patterns across the black rippled surface of the river. Fluorescent floats bobbed at the margins of the initial survey area behind them. As the investigating officer, Scobie oversaw the onboard video feed and comms. Coughlin stood beside her at the screen as the first pair entered the water. Another team member controlled the airline feeds and cables from the stern of the boat.

Inside the cabin Scobie watched the screen as high-powered underwater lights illuminated the gloom, a greenish black murk. She rubbed her eyes, peered closer, realised that wasn't helping. How did these guys ever find anything? Maybe they had some kind of inbuilt sonar. Scobie stared as the diver's gloved hand explored ahead of his mask. Of course. That was how they searched, not with their eyes but with their fingers.

Forty-five minutes later, the first pair of chilled divers emerged from the water and sat on the edge of the boat-ramp among the ropes and gear. The second pair of divers took their place. Avery was in the squad car on the phone to the Richmond Station for an update.

Scobie watched the screen, squinted, drew back. There was a change in the intensity, less light reflecting back through the suspended silt in the cloudy black water.

'Who's the diver?' Scobie asked Coughlin.

'Sonny Gallo,' he replied.

Scobie spoke into her mic. 'Sonny, sweep left again. One metre. Your ten o'clock.' The closer he got, the less sure she was. Whatever density she believed she'd seen disappeared. She squeezed her eyes shut. A headache brewed as she rubbed the back of her hand across her forehead, dropped her head. She'd have to justify the expense of pulling this crew in.

Gallo's metallic voice scratched across the sound feed. 'Got something, skip.'

Gallo ran his hands across the surface, palpated the mass. Cloth and something stiffer, canvas perhaps. Interruptions around the mass. Chain, looped. Up and down the length he ran his hands. Felt like it could be a body.

~

Late Thursday afternoon Cal showered, packed gear in an army tote-bag. She rang her boss and extended her leave. Couldn't face Zin's apartment. Not yet. It would keep. She pinned a note on her door for Dee. Couldn't front her either. Inside the garage she emptied a carry-all and gathered together a small assortment of hand tools, stashed them in the boot beside her other gear. Hopefully she wouldn't need them but better to have them than not. She stowed an empty twenty-litre jerrycan as well. She closed the boot-lid, sat in the driver's seat, turned the key, grateful Banjo was off in the far paddocks with Dee.

She headed for the city on autopilot, her body heavy with a dull lethargy despite her long sleep. Addie and Zin in the space of two weeks. Pip's death coming to light in the same mix. Insane. She really was an orphan now.

She drove to Scobie's apartment in town, parked in the Alexandria laneway. Wound down her window, dozed awhile. As dusk fell she got out, walked up the lane. A dog nutted off from behind a fence, stuck its nose under a corro flap, puffs of dust shifting on the ground as the nostrils worked the air. Cal returned to the Ford, got her tote from the boot. Walked up the stairs and sat outside Scobie's back door, watched the orange haze intensifying over the northwest as the sun dropped.

Scobie's Holden turned into the lane. Her headlights illuminated the stretch of battered fencing and wheelie bins. The vehicle paused beside Cal's car and Scobie looked up, saw Cal on the stairs. Then her car disappeared into the underground car park.

Minutes later Scobie gently cracked the back door from inside, caught Cal's shoulders with her hands as she sat behind her. She pressed her body against Cal's back, slipped her arms around her waist and squeezed, her cheek against Cal's shoulder.

'You still got a job?' Cal asked

'We found him.' Scobie's voice almost a whisper, tired.

Cal leaned back into her embrace. 'What now?'

'I want a drink.' She kissed Cal's neck. 'A long one.' She pulled back the collar of Cal's denim jacket. 'I want dinner.' She ran her teeth down the back of Cal's neck. 'And I want you.'

'That an order of priority?' Cal reached back, ran her hands down Scobie's thighs.

'Dinner can wait,' Scobie breathed.

Cal pushed backwards, put Scobie flat to the floor, rolled so she faced her. She pinned Scobie's arms above her head, used one hand to hold Scobie's wrists, began unbuttoning her blouse.

'You're not even pretending to struggle.' She kissed her. 'No bevvy till I'm done.'

∼

Birch and Ottering were still at Richmond Command. 'They've taken the body for ID.' Birch thumbed his keypad.

'Glen and Tony have prepped for Dolan's interview. Boss'll wanna be here.' Ottering reached up, pulled her short ponytail free, rubbed her neck with her fingers, retied her hair. 'We should get some shut-eye while we can.'

Birch nodded.

∼

Next morning Cal sat on a barstool beside an island bench while Scobie made coffee, pushed the plunger.

'Would've taken you for a Nespresso type. Melbourne n'all.'

Scobie flicked her a glance. 'Overrated. Burn the grounds. Plunger is quicker.' She gave Cal a stare. 'Mine'd be a La Pavoni anyway. And no bloody plastic pods to infest our beaches.'

Scobie's phone skidded across the benchtop. She glanced at the screen as she poured coffee into the two mugs. 'What have you got for me, Glen?'

'Positive ID. Nolly Pratt, skip.'

Scobie closed her eyes a moment, felt a heaviness in her stomach.

'Good man. Thanks for letting me know. You get home. Janice and Frank can take over for now. Get back for the Dolan interview later.'

'Cheers, skip.'

Scobie came around the bench. She stood behind Cal, draped her arms down Cal's front as she pressed into her back.

'You were right,' she whispered into Cal's ear.

'Well, I guess I have mixed feelings about that.' Cal puffed a sigh from her nose.

She leaned into the warmth of Scobie's body. 'So, you probably want to show your appreciation.'

Scobie's teeth bit into her shoulder.

'Plans?' Scobie leaned over to the bench, topped up their coffees.

'Gonna make arrangements for Zin. Drop in on Di. Missed the memorial, obviously.'

'You must feel shell-shocked.'

'Taken more leave. Get away for a bit.' Cal sipped her drink, looked back up at Scobie. 'Seriously. You in trouble? Demotion?' She slipped an arm around Scobie's waist.

Scobie shrugged. 'Great tip-off from you. Might go in my favour.'

Cal nodded, a small movement. 'Protected species. Only a couple patches left. Took me a while.'

Scobie leaned down, rubbed the side of her cheek gently against Cal's. 'You leaving town?' she asked.

Cal put her mug on the table. 'Dunno what I'm up to.' She stood, one arm around Scobie, then both. Scobie's lips pressed to her neck, her jaw.

A moment passed.

'Gotta go.'

Scobie squeezed her. 'Keep in touch,' she whispered.

Cal nodded. Couldn't look at her.

She walked downstairs. A veil of rain softened the view across the corrugated rooftops and tiles of the old terraces, the city to the northeast. Cal tossed her tote in the boot. She opened the driver's door, resisted looking up the stairs, fired up the Futura. Her tyres threw small fans of muddy water as she drove down the puddled laneway.

ACKNOWLEDGEMENTS

My immense gratitude to publishers Betsy Reavley and Fred Freeman at Bloodhound Books for saying yes. Huge thanks to my editor Clare Law for her clarity and wit. Thank you Tara Lyons, production manager dynamo, for ensuring the wheels turn smoothly. Thanks also to my proofreader and to the designer for making such a standout cover.

I'm indebted to my friend, fellow rose enthusiast and writing mentor Renee, for reading every word, month after month and for pointing a way through the thorns. I'm grateful also to my early mentors in Australia, David Brooks and the late Glenda Adams for their precious, unswerving encouragement.

Thanks to my early readers, Tanya, Kathleen and Olga for their time and feedback and to Cait for proofreading my submission.

And finally, thank you for always telling it how it is, Biz, my greatest champion.